Volume VI

Carry on, Jack

Frank English

2QT Limited (Publishing)

First Edition published 2020

2QT Limited (Publishing)
Settle
North Yorkshire
BD24 9BZ

Cover design: Charlotte Mouncey
Cover images: main photographs supplied by ©Frank English
Additional images from iStockhoto.com and wikimedia

Printed in Great Britain by IngramSparks UK Ltd

A CIP catalogue record for this book is available
from the British Library
ISBN 978-1-913071-48-6

This is for my wife, Denise's Mam, Annie.
Never far from our hearts and minds.

Chapter 1

"So, this is it, then?" Jack asked, half expecting but not wanting her answer.

"This is what, Jack?" Jenny replied, not quite sure what he meant, or why he was raising 'it'.

"The end of it all," he added, mystery still surrounding what he was saying.

"What?" she continued. "The end of it all? The end of the day? The end—?"

"Don't be so bloomin' obtuse and evasive," he said sharply. "The end of us … you and me."

"I have no idea what you are on about," she replied, a nervous smile betraying her indecision. It wasn't like Jack to be unsure of what he was saying, so she assumed that whatever he had to say was important and needed her explanation. "Spit it out, Jack. Let's be hearing why you *think* you and I, despite all we've been through together, have no future. I assume that's what you mean?"

"Several things happened today that, to my knowledge, haven't happened before," he insisted, trying hard to control his jangling emotions. "Not while we've been together, at any rate. This morning, because you weren't at breakfast, I decided—"

"To go for a walk in Roundhay Park," she interrupted, guessing where this was leading.

"I went—" he continued but stopped in surprise. "How did you know that?"

"Because I wasn't at breakfast," she started to explain, "and you saw me in the park – with another man."

"Tha's brazen abaht it," he harrumphed, dropping into his native dialect. "I'll gi' thee that."

She smiled ruefully, feeling significantly remorseful that she had caused him so much pain, to see the suspicion, the hurt and betrayal in his eyes. How could she have put him through it all, on the insistence of her mother – this man whom she adored and had endured so much to secure? Never again would she sacrifice their happiness on another's whim!

"Have you stopped trusting me, then, Our Jack?" she asked quietly, feeling his arm stiffen as she reached for his hand. "Does it take so little?"

"Little?" he gasped, surprised at her brass neck. "Might I remind you about Simon? Was that the man I saw you cosying up to, or was he another 'boyfriend'?"

She put her arm around his waist and drew him forcibly to her. "Simon was someone I talked to – innocently, I might add," she said, "and is now not even a memory."

"What do you expect from me?" Jack protested, feeling aggrieved at what she had put him through. "You've been off-hand and evasive for some time. The business with your mother, for example. We've *never* done things separately before."

"There was a reason for that," she tried to explain. "I—"

"Not good enough!" he interrupted, his anger rising. "Then why didn't you include me in your subterfuge?"

She remained silent for a few moments, still gripping him so he couldn't escape. "I had to go to Mum's without you because she asked me not to tell you," she started again.

"Tell me what?" he answered, boredom with the whole

sorry charade starting to grow.

"The man you saw me with was … my brother," she replied almost in a whisper.

"Yeah! Right!" he scoffed. "You don't *have* a brother. So how can you expect me to believe *that*?"

"I didn't know I had a brother until a week ago," she said, trying to make him believe her. Without the trust they had always shared, underpinning the basis of everything they had and were, their relationship meant nothing. They couldn't even *have* a meaningful relationship without that special trust. Jack hadn't ever been a possessive or a jealous or mistrustful person – that is, until now. Jenny had never seen him like this before and, if she wasn't very careful, she wouldn't see him like this for much longer. *This* she had brought about because she had put her mother's feelings first without doing Jack the courtesy of telling him why. *He* would have understood. She *knew* he would.

"If we sit down," she asked urgently, "will you stay long enough to hear my explanation of what's been going on? A few minutes is all I ask and then, if you still can't believe all I say, I won't stand in your way."

"You see," he replied, sitting next to her, "*my* Jenny would never have said that. *She* wouldn't have let me go anywhere without a fight."

Tears were streaming down her flushed cheeks now as she began her sorry tale. His face softened markedly as the story unfurled. Not one of modern-day intrigue and subterfuge, but an all-too-common story of a young lass falling pregnant and not being able to keep her bairn.

That was Flora Mae's story that she had needed to hide from all save her close family.

Jack was saddened that he hadn't been thought close enough to have been considered one of those.

"If you had told me this sooner," Jack said, his doubts evaporating rapidly, "there would have been no need for suspicion and mistrust. You know how much I hate all that uncertainty and untruth."

"I couldn't, Jack," she replied, drawing him closer. "Mum made me promise."

"But I'm family," he insisted, "or so I thought. Now I'm not so sure."

"I don't imagine for a minute that she thinks any the less of you," Jenny tried to explain the inexplicable. "It's just that I suppose she thought you might have tried to protect us and put right what was wrong."

"Why would anything need to be put right?" he asked, not understanding that strange logic. "He's *your* brother and *her* son, no matter in what circumstances he was conceived or born."

"He's my dad's son," she said, looking into his deep green eyes, "and so he's my full-blood brother. A bit late, but now he's here. Jim accepted him straight away."

"And William?" Jack queried. "I assume he knows. How did he react?"

"Doesn't know yet, I don't think, but I'm sure he won't understand – or care," she said, shrugging her shoulders.

"Nothing new there, then," he harrumphed. "You can't expect him to understand, because he doesn't even understand his own family.

"Anyway," he went on after a brief pause, "nuff said. When do I get to meet him?"

"Then, you and I are … OK?" she whispered tentatively.

"Daft bugger," he said with a frown. "How else could we be? You're my life, Jenny. Wi'out thee, there in't one."

She flung her arms around his neck in relief, tears mixed

wi' snot as they trickled down her now smiling face.

"What's up, Our Jen?" he said with a guffaw. "As tha caught a cold?"

They hugged and laughed as they had always done.

"So, how did she get to know?" Jack asked again.

"*He* approached *her*," Jenny replied with a shrug. "Simple as that. She started the day normally, having arranged a day out with Jim, and by the end of that day the son she had brought into the world when she was sixteen had walked back into her life."

"Does this explain her reasonably conciliatory attitude towards your unmarried pregnancy, do you think?" Jack said, his king-sized hammer hitting the nail squarely on the head.

"To a certain extent, yes, I suppose," Jenny agreed. "But it wasn't *all* plain sailing. She often let me know – in no uncertain terms – what a bad decision I'd made. With a certain degree of hypocrisy, I suppose."

A hefty banging on the door interrupted them as Jack's second pot of Yorkshire Tea marched towards its perfect mashing.

"Who on earth…?" he muttered as he headed for the front door.

"Val," he greeted his sister-in-law, as she marched past him without a glance as if he wasn't there. "Do come in. Don't just stand … there."

"And this … *brother* we are supposed to have?" she snarled, unable to accept he was real. "What do you know about him? Jenny? Jack?"

"I should imagine that I found out a bit after you, it seems," Jack replied quickly. "So, it seems as if you and I share a similar dark space."

"Jenny?" Val asked, turning on her sister for a straight answer. "I assume you've known for some time?"

"Round about a week or so," her sister explained. "No

more, really. Mum swore me to secrecy."

Jenny told her all she knew about the circumstances surrounding their brother, Michael, and how he had now come to share their world. Unsure of the wisdom of their mother's action in allowing him in and accepting him into their family without consultation with her significant others, they could only accept him for what he was. They didn't really need this sort of a distraction in their lives right now – but that was the feeling that seemed to matter least in Flora Mae's eyes.

-o-

"You're never going to believe this," Jack said, bringing his usual tray of goodies into the lounge to dish out to David and Irene.

"What have they done to you now, Jacky-boy?" David replied, his hands wrapped around his second mug of Columbian, and his eyes assessing the relative sizes of butter and jam-topped scones on the plate before him.

"Another addition to t'family is what," Jack sighed. "Getting more like t'Yorkshire Mafia every day. Michael Kurlionny, he's called."

"Not another *brother*?" Irene asked tentatively when she joined them after helping Jenny with the after-meal tidying up. "Strange name?"

"In a manner of speaking," Jack replied with a shrug and a wry smile.

"Mine, I'm afraid," Jenny admitted with little enthusiasm.

"But I thought…?" Irene replied, a seriously confused look beginning to shroud her face.

"Mum didn't tell us that she had him when she was sixteen," Jenny explained with a sigh. "To my dad. She didn't tell us until a couple of weeks ago, setting the cat among the family pigeons."

"So, why now?" David ventured. "How old must he be? Mid-forties?"

"Spot on," Jenny replied. "She says it was out of a sense of duty and it was the right thing to do."

"The ridiculously funny thing is," Jack said with a light guffaw, "that, unbeknown to her, he lived in the next street in Normanton, a matter of two hundred crow-flying yards away. Caused a good deal of consternation with Sister-in-law and Brother, I can tell you."

"Val?" Irene asked.

"Furious," Jack said.

"William?" David added.

"His usual churlish self," Jack replied, with a resigned shrug. "We've been summoned to a family get-together next weekend, which I don't think I will attend.

"Anyway, enough of all that. We wanted you to come because we haven't seen you socially for ever such a long time. I was beginning to think Irene had emigrated and left David to muddle along on his own. Another cup of Yorkshire, anyone? Or maybe something a little … stronger?"

-o-

"Not going?" Jenny queried, once their friends had set off home. "As in staying at home, boycotting, ignoring?"

"Indeed," Jack replied categorically. "Your mum thought so little about the effect her decision would have on me, she won't miss me – I am so obviously not an important part of this family."

"Don't be like that, Jack," she pleaded urgently. "She wants you there as one of the most important members of our clan, and—"

"Then why did she behave like that?" he interrupted her sharply. "Bit of a contradiction, don't you think?"

"The last thing she would have wanted was to have alienated *you*," Jenny tried to reassure him. "She values your opinion over everybody else's, save Jim's."

"Then she needs to *think* twice before she acts once," Jack harrumphed. "I certainly didn't expect *this* from *her*, of all people. Anyway, I suppose I'd better come because no-one knows anything about this person. As far as you are concerned, he could be a mass murderer, and…"

"Jack!" she gasped. "How could you think such things?"

"Because I am sensible and pragmatic and I trust nobody on *his* word alone," he replied quickly, emphasising his point forcefully. "You need me as your protector, your impartial intermediary, who will see through any subterfuge, and ultimately corroborate his story one way or another. *That's* why I am important to you. Then, of course, there are my extreme good looks, charm and charisma."

She burst out laughing at his attempted George Sanders' voice and suave move and she threw her arms about his neck, pushing him backwards on to the settee. "I love you, Jack," she said softly, between kisses.

"I know," he replied, words muffled because his lips were otherwise engaged. "I'm more than a bit keen on you as well."

"Mother," Jessie said sternly, marching purposefully into the room, "I need to talk to you – about boys."

Jack and Jenny looked at each other, not really knowing what to say, as Jessie fixed her gaze on Jack with raised eyebrows and that steely stare that said, 'You need not be here, Daddy Jack. This is going to be women's talk and you wouldn't understand.'

"I'll just pop out to see what Florence and George are up to then," he threw over his shoulder as he made a beeline for the door. "Later. Bloomin' 'eck!" he muttered with a huge 'phew!' "Kids, eh?"

Chapter 2

Ellen's nervousness and excitement became opposing factions as she closed in on her late September start at Bretton Hall Teacher Training College. She couldn't imagine how this had happened to her, and how she was to be the first in her family to enter such a hallowed establishment. She had felt all along that she was destined to do something out of the ordinary, and Jack had opened the door to her ambitions.

She loved her Eric dearly, and he was clever in his own engineering way, but Jack had shown her the road she wanted to travel so she could develop her talents and make life better for her little family.

"Look," her Eric pointed out, "I know there's a – what do they call it? – a cresh at yon college, but tha's got to 'ave thi mind on t'job from t'start."

"It'll be rayt, Our Eric," she replied swiftly, without too much thought.

"Nar, 'ere's t'thing," he responded deliberately. "I've got two days when I'll be laykin' from tomorrer, an' so I've decided as I want to look after Our James missen for a while. Us two blokes together – just 'im an' me. All rayt?"

"Aye, all rayt," she agreed, with a smile, imagining father and son having quality time together. Not as 'ard as he looked on t'outside, her Eric. Not by a long chalk – and she loved what she heard and saw. "It'll gi' me time to get missen sorted and settled, but I shall be tekin' 'im wi' me soon after that, mind."

"Aye, all rayt, lass," Eric replied, a satisfied look on his face as he stood with his back to the fireless hearth, his thumbs through his trouser braces like the lord of the household he wasn't. "So, I'll run thee ower tomorrer like, tha knows, wi' t'motor."

"That won't do me a world o' good, Our Eric," she replied in mock horror, a cheeky smile lurking behind her gaze.

His puzzled eyes searched for the reason for her response, not sure what was going on after their tacit agreement. "'Ow does tha mean?" he faltered, with a lowering brow of indecision.

"Come on, Our Eric," she started to explain, on the back of a giggle, "if tha ran me ower, I'd be … dead."

"Ee, thee and thy sense of yoomer'll be t'death o' me one o' these days," he replied, a light dawning in him finally, as a great rumbling guffaw burst from his lungs like a rolling dam burst. "So, tha's gor all thi stuff ready for t'day after tomorrer, then?"

"Eric," she sighed, "stop fussing. I'm all right. Nervous but ready. Now where's that cup of Yorkshire Tea tha promised me a while ago?"

"Promised…?" he replied, letting one of his braces go in surprise quickly enough to cause him to 'ouch' as it rattled across his chest. "Oh, aye. All rayt. Coming up in a jiffy."

She laughed heartily, watching his muscular body shuffle through to the kitchen, still rubbing his smarting chest from its encounter with his elastic trouser braces. She loved his gruff exterior that hid a soft interior, at the centre of which beat a warm and loving heart. He was the man with whom she would share the rest of her life.

"I'm proud o' thee, does tha know, Ellen Ingles?" he said

seriously, setting down the tray. "For ivry thing tha's going to do to make our lives better and, more than anything else, for thissen."

"Are you getting emotional, my lovely man?" Ellen said, a warm loving smile greeting his remarks. "Only, in all the years I've known thee, tha's never reacted like this."

"Yon Jack's shown me 'ow a gentleman can and should behave towards his wife in all respects," he replied. "That's summat as I never saw nor learned as a growing nipper, si thi, and Our Jack, mi new-found brother, 'as shown me t'rayt road to treat my lovely wife. Now I'm not afraid to say as 'ow much I love thee, Ellen Ingles."

She shuffled over to him and, slipping an arm around his broad shoulders, she pulled him towards her. Their kiss was long and passionate, where he gave back as much as he received. Never in all their time together had their love been a two-way street … before now. He was starting to enjoy the give and take of married life with all its foibles and excitements.

–o–

"Oh my God!" Jenny gasped as she put down the phone.

"What's up?" Jack asked as he finished off his cup of tea. "You look like someone's stamped on your grave."

"Mum thinks Jim has had a heart attack," she gasped, picking up the phone again to call Val. "She's panicking, saying she's afraid it's déjà vu."

"Where've they taken him?" he asked, a rack of concern disfiguring his face. "Pinderfields? Pontefract General?"

"Don't know. She didn't say, but I can find out easily," she replied, concern driving her actions automatically.

"Probably Pinderfields, I should think," he added. "You probably need to get off with your Val, and I'll look after the brood and come later. I'll ask Joyce if she could take 'em."

"Pinderfields it is, then," she said, once she had checked with Val. "Joey's taking us in his Rover 95. William's not in."

"Ha ha!" Jack laughed. "Outstanding. Jim would appreciate that – if he's still with us, that is."

"Jack!" she gasped. "You can't say that! If anything happens, Mum will be devastated. Anyway, I'm off."

"Have you forgotten anything?" he asked as she turned to go. "Anything important?"

"I don't think so," she replied, opening the lounge door into the hall.

"Jenny!" he called when she reached the front door.

She tutted and turned to answer his call, a little irritated that she had to go back. Walking into the lounge, she saw Jack sitting in his favourite chair, pointing at his pursed lips.

"Sorry, I forgot," she said with a grin, kissing him. "You only had to say."

"I thought I just did," he replied, a sanctimonious smile playing havoc with Jenny's plans.

"Get on with you," she laughed, closing the door behind her.

She knew that he was trying to bolster her against the difficulties ahead – particularly with the state her mother would be in.

"William not in yet?" Jenny asked, as she clunked the Rover 95's rear door.

"Been in and gone out again," Val replied, her non-committal, couldn't-care-less attitude about her husband surfacing sharply. "Don't ask. When did you get to know about Jim?"

"Literally five minutes before I rang you," Jenny replied.

"Did she give any indication as to how he is?" Val asked.

"She sounded very upset, so I didn't expect anything much," Jenny added. "I telephoned the hospital, and they gave me the usual non-committal standard stuff about his being comfortable, and that they are doing everything they can for him, blah-di-blah."

-o-

The hospital was cool and had that singular hospital smell of disinfectant and carbolic throughout. The intensive care ward was only a short hop and skip away from reception to allow ease and speed of admission for initial medical care and subsequent family access.

Jim cut a forlorn figure in his single room, hooked up to a paraphernalia of monitors and tubes and masks that, supposedly, were keeping him in this world. Flo was at his bedside, suitably masked and gowned to prevent outside infections from sneaking under the hospital's forbidding defences. She too looked forlornly upset, watching as the man she loved teetered on the edge of oblivion before her eyes, willing him to balance on that final tightrope.

"You two go in," Jack urged Val and Jenny as he arrived, once the ward sister had kitted them out ready. "Joey and I will wait here and watch. Or we might even nip off for a quick coffee."

Not one for waiting aimlessly around in hospitals, Joey nodded eagerly. Jenny agreed and muttered something almost inaudible that sounded suspiciously like 'I love you, Jack' before being ushered into the ward by the sister. When *she* emerged, she advised them where the café was.

"Mum," Jenny murmured as they hugged, "how is he and how are you bearing up?"

"I'm all right," Flo answered stoically, "but it was touch and go for him. So sudden – one minute he was all right, cracking jokes like he does, and the next on the floor barely able to breathe. The ambulance was at the bungalow within five minutes, and then it was bells and blue lights all the way. I've never seen so many people move so quickly to sort Jim out. The medical staff has been wonderful."

"How long before he's out of danger?" Val asked, concerned that they were about to lose another father figure from their lives.

"Next twenty-four hours are crucial, apparently," Flo replied quietly, resigned to the inevitable.

"And after that?" Jenny said, knowing that her Jack would have added 'should he survive'. Fortunately for them, he had chosen to take his forthright Yorkshireness off to the canteen.

"Probably another week or so in here," Flo went on, "and then a period of stress-free recuperation somewhere warm. I'll probably take him to the Canaries for a month or two's total rest. But we've got to keep our fingers crossed for the next twenty-four hours at least."

"Have you let Michael know?" Jenny asked, careful not to tread on toes.

"Yes, briefly," Flo answered, "but I've only given him the basics. I've let him know that I won't be seeing him for a while at least."

-o-

"How do you think things are going with what you've seen so far?" Joey asked Jack. "You don't think he's going to…?"

"I shouldn't have thought so," Jack replied with a shrug. "He seems to be hanging in there, but you never know."

"Wait and see, I suppose," Joey offered.

"Hang on a bit," Jack said, looking around the canteen. "I think I see somebody I know over there. Hang on here and I'll be back shortly."

"Please stop calling me Shortly," Joey said, laughing at

his own funny.

Jack smiled, striding across the canteen towards a man sitting in an alcove next to the exit, a plastic cup of coffee to hand.

"Pierre?" Jack said as he approached the man. "John Pierre Gwillow?"

"You've got to be joking me!" the man gasped as he looked up. "Jack Ingles! It's got to be – how many years? Fifteen? – since we last saw each other. You were at teacher training college, if my memory serves."

"And you showed me around your research on congenital heart conditions at Leeds Medical School, I believe," Jack replied, recalling those heady days when both were intent on changing the world in their chosen fields. "Weren't you going out with a young lady from Normanton High School at the time? Joan Rush, or some similar name?"

"Not really," John Pierre replied. "We broke up when she got to uni. Found somebody else."

"Sorry," Jack apologised. "Bummer. But hey, stuff happens, sometimes for the better."

"Indeed, it does," John Pierre agreed. "I'm now courting a mature research student in another department, and I'm hoping this one will last the course – with me, that is."

"What are you doing now?" Jack asked. "Something very important, I have no doubt?"

"I've just been offered a professorship in Surgery at Jimmy's Hospital," he said as he stood up. "Starts in January. Look, Jack, here's my number. I'm due back in theatre in fifteen minutes. Call me, please? We must get together for a proper chinwag."

"You're on," Jack agreed. "Soon?"

"Too right!" his friend said. "Got to go."

They shook hands in the particular way that was peculiar to them, laughed, and took their leave.

"Amazing," Jack sighed as he went back to sit with his nephew.

"Obviously someone you knew from way back?" Joey asked, a grin on his face.

"Steady," Jack laughed. "Not so much of the 'way back' if you don't mind, youngster."

They ordered another coffee and sat back as Jack explained the association and its context.

"Jack! Joey!" Jenny's voice accosted them excitedly from the canteen door. "Jim's awake and asking to see you both. Come on."

-o-

"Don't do things in half measures, eh, Jim?" Jack said with a shrug.

"Well, you know *me*, Jack," Jim replied, a strained smile creeping across his lips. "Always one to demand attention."

"I don't think we ought to tax you too much," Val said, a look of serious concern flicking across her face, recalling distressing memories of her father's last moments not long after *his* heart attack. Of course, there wasn't the same degree of expert care available when he passed away, but she wanted to be extra careful with Jim.

"I'll be all right, love," Jim assured her. "Sorry I'm a bit distant and quiet, but I find it difficult to even fart with all this paraphernalia stuffed in every available orifice."

They laughed at the image he conjured, feeling sure he would recover in the near future, although they weren't sure to what degree or when this might happen.

"Just remember, please," Jim continued, trying to hutch his backside further up the bed so he could see them better, "that *you* are all my family now. So, I don't want anyone getting in touch with my son. He has proved to me over the years that he doesn't care two tosses whether I live or die. Consequently, Jack, I should like you to be the executor of my will, which is lodged with my solicitor. We've had it done recently, and all it needs is the necessary formalities to be attended to. I'll give you all the details when I get out of this place. The solicitor will be waiting for you to get in touch as and when. I know I can trust you, and I know you'll look after Flo in the event of … well, you know what I mean."

"I'd be honoured, Our Jim," Jack replied, his serious look flooding the room. "But tha'll be rayt as rain soon, I'll be bound."

"Flo gets everything, but I want thee to tek charge. All rayt?" Jim went on, to be reinforced by Jack's serious nod. "Now then, young feller, how's yon Rover 95 bearing up under a younger boot?"

"It's belting, Grandpa Jim," Joey replied, a huge grin splitting his face. "Goes a dream, and I *am* looking after her, I'll have you know."

"Shining as a new pin," Flo butted in. "The lad is doing her proud. Tell him your news, Joey."

"News?" Jim replied, a little puzzled. "What news?"

"Well," Joey started, "I've decided to take your advice, and I've been offered an apprenticeship wi' Grace and Cahill, the mining engineers in Aberford. Start in two weeks."

"Good man!" Jim enthused, smiling at the good news. "That's where I worked before I set up mi own business."

"Aye," Joey added, "and they still speak about you in hushed, respectful tones, although Joe Cahill insists you still owe him a pint of Tetley's."

"He always was a cheapskate," Jim laughed, as an air of tiredness ambushed him.

"Time to go then," Jenny insisted. "Everybody out! Mum?"

"I'll stay a bit longer, lass," Flo replied, much more cheerfully. "Car's in t'car park, so I won't be wanting."

-o-

"Ee, lad!" Flo sighed, once the rabble had departed. "Tha gev me a rayt fright then. Tha'd better not do *that* again."

"Nay, lass!" Jim replied. "It'd tek more than a flutter to see me off. I've got too much goin' on to jack it in now. Tha should know that. So, please don't fret. This'n has been a bit on a wake-up call that I won't – can't – ignore. So, I'll be taking it a bit easier when I'm out."

"The doctor told me it wasn't a serious attack," she replied, squeezing his hand, "but how you can say *any* heart attack isn't serious is beyond me. You *will* take it easy; I'll make sure of that."

His head relaxed back onto his standard hospital pillow, a smile playing around his still slightly blue lips.

"Don't look so concerned, Flora," Jim said, trying to dispel the seriously gloomy face she wore. "I'm going to be fine, especially when I can wrap mi lips around one of those meat-and-taty pies tha'll no doubt be forcing me to eat."

They both laughed, a little more relaxed than several hours before.

Ee men! The trouble they cause you, eh!

Chapter 3

Jim's heart problem was a short-lived but serious wake-up call for all the family. True to her word, Flora Mae had booked a relaxing break under the clear blue skies and warm-all-over sunshine of Tenerife in the Canary Islands, where they stayed for the best part of two months. Consequently, the much-anticipated family get-together with Jenny and Val's newfound brother had to be put on hold. The sisters could have arranged to see him but this was Mum's show, and the show wouldn't have been much good without Punch.

"I know what it's like, this hospital lark," Jack observed through a mighty grimace, Saturday morning at breakfast. "I had to endure it three times in all."

"And me, Our Jack?" Jenny replied, a disbelieving grin on her face to remind him of what *she* had had to endure.

"I know," he said with an accepting shrug, "but I still feel the terror of that muslin and gauze mask on mi face and the overwhelming stench of yon ether in mi nostrils when I had mi tonsils out as a seven year old."

"Do they still do that butchery for something so simple?" Jenny asked, marvelling at the extremes of modern medicine; on the one hand heart transplantation and, on the other, hacking out a small but troublesome organ.

"Don't think so," Jack replied with a non-committal

shrug and a recalled-pain grimace. "I think in this instance some of these newfangled drugs have consigned the surgeon's knife to the history books.

"Still no drugs to cure a broken arm, though," he added, causing Jenny to chuckle at his funny. "It was touch and go as to whether I would lose mi right arm with its second break in eighteen months."

"You never told me that," she gasped in shock. "Was that the 'sliding down the icy hill' accident?"

"Aye, it was that!" he replied, as he narrowed his eyes with retrospective concern. "December, just before mi ninth birthday, we'd med a slide about thirty yards long down our road. Course, there weren't any cars to bother us, and so it wor a belter. Onny problem was, once you were on it, you couldn't stop or get off until you ran out of slide. That is, unless somebody fell – and then everybody piled onto the heap. That's what happened to me. Sumb'dy had to rush down to t'telephone box on Dalefield Road to phone for t'ambulance.

"Mi mam and dad had to set up mi bed in t'front room to watch ower me at night. As I had broken the tail end of the growing bone on mi elbow, they had to watch that the arm didn't discolour. *That* would have meant that I could have lost mi arm."

"Jack!" Jenny gasped. "Not sure I want to hear any more of your gory past. Jack Ingles – a one-armed bandit! For goodness' sake!"

"I remember when mi mam sent me – at seven years old – to t'Co-op to get some butter," he went on.

"Hang on a bit," she laughed, "shall I get mi pad and pencil?"

"Well," he harrumphed, "if'n you don't want to hear about it…"

"No," she insisted, "I do. It's just that I thought you

might want me to write it down for your memoirs when you're seventy."

He laughed that easy laugh they had always shared, as he slipped his arm around her shoulders. "That was funny," he said as he continued to grin. "You've always been able to make me laugh, Our Jen."

"Yep," she added. "Co-op? Butter?"

"Oh aye," he started again. "You know the loose-pat butter they used to sell?"

"Erm," she replied slowly, "no, I don't. We always used to have packet butter."

"'Ark at you! Posh," he laughed. "Anyway, I asked her not to give me a note to hand to the grocer. Wanted to appear grown up, you see. The problem was, she had either not told me how much to get, or I had forgotten."

"And?" she asked, eager to know. "What did you ask for?"

"Er, two ounces," he chortled. "Well, at seven years old, *I* didn't know."

Jenny laughed at the image that jumped into her mind. A little scrawny, spiky-haired seven-year-old in short pants, with one long stocking to his knee and the other concertinaed by his ankle, standing at the counter with a seriously puzzled look on his face.

"What?" he smiled. "I watched him cut the butter from the tub and weigh this little sliver carefully to give me the right amount – not a smearing more, not a scrap less. He wrapped it and handed it to me – very carefully – for me to take home in the brown-paper carrier bag mi mam had given me."

"What did she say when she saw your offering?" Jenny asked, barely able to hold in her chuckles.

"She laughed and said 'Has tha brought none for me, Our Jack?'" he replied with a guffaw. "She laughed and reminded me several times over the few years she … was

… alive."

He fell silent suddenly, his eyes glazing over and tears threatening to gather in their corners. Jenny could see that, even getting on for fifteen years later, her death was still raw for him. His grieving process was close to the surface even now, because he had tried to put off the inevitable for such a long time.

Jenny had learned not to labour the obvious at times like this because it only made matters worse for Jack, and he didn't like to be reminded of his shortcomings.

-o-

"Well, our lass," young Eric urged, "time to be on your way, dun't tha know? I've put thi stuff in yon boot, t'young un's seat is fastened in t'back, and t'car's filled wi' juice. Time to be off?"

"OK, lovely. Do you like my outfit?" she said, parading her new college clothes and giving him a show-off twirl. "Will I do?"

"You look rayt grand," he replied with a grin of satisfaction. "I wish I wor coming wi' thee."

"You've done all you can to make my life easier, my lovely man," Ellen said, kissing his craggy, bearded face, "and now it's up to me to find mi way. We've bin ower the route so many times, I feel I could drive it wi' mi eyes shut."

"Don't thee do that, Our Ellen!" he replied quickly. "What would me and our James do wi'out thee, eh?"

They both laughed that easy laugh they had come to enjoy since their extended family had enriched their lives, both personally and socially. From a classically introverted coal miner, her Eric had become open, positive and forward-looking since spending time with his half-brother, Jack. *He* had introduced her husband to the excitement and wonder of vibrant and sometimes unexpected extended family life. She had never seen her husband happier or more alive.

"Tell me agen," Eric said, as he walked her out to her new Mini with James in his arms. "How many days will tha be doin' this week, then?"

She grinned as she wound down her window and settled behind the steering wheel, knowing full well how excited he was for her and that he knew her timetable not only this, her first week, but also for the rest of the academic year.

"Today's Tuesday," she started. "Just a registration and settling-in day. So, I should be back no later than three. Then I've Thursday and Friday. I should imagine that the work starts in earnest next week."

"Is tha allus off to be free on Wednesdays, then, like?" he asked, quite excited that he might have her to himself on those days.

"Aye," she replied, as her engine spat into life, "I reckon so, unless a 'special' project or event jumps out at me. See you at three, then."

Her Mini inched away from the road edge slowly as she aimed for Dalefield Road, Garth Avenue and Wakefield Road beyond. He turned back to the house, looking forward to spending some 'man' time with his son. Happence, too, he would traipse up to yon new houses at Ash Gap Lane as his wife had suggested.

There were two or three she said she liked and perhaps it was time to put some money down to secure one of 'em. He had better make sure that the one he chose was the one she wanted. Now, what were the three things she needed more than anything? Big garden, spacious and well-laid out inside. Now, what was the third thing? He had no idea! Bloomin' 'ummer! It'd have to be a good guess on his part, because what did he know abaht the workings of a woman's mind? What did any man know…?

The roads were quiet at that time of day on her way to becoming a teacher. A slight frisson of excitement travelled Ellen's body as a smile attacked her face, remembering the many times Eric had driven her from their home to her new chalkface. She could now travel the byways with eyes closed. That was his way – preparation, he called it – and she loved him for it. Attention to detail was like life blood to him, and that was one of the things that linked him closely with his half-brother, Jack. No wonder they got on so well.

It hadn't seemed worth it, spending all that time on that particular road, but that's how he was. According to Jenny, that was a mirror image of what her Jack would have done.

She wasn't sure just how useful this particular day was going to be – registration, a tour of the campus, timetable gathering and then home. Jack had explained all this to her, because first days in most colleges seemed to follow a set pattern – a bit of a bind but no doubt a necessary one.

"Don't forget to bring thi 'omework 'ome, an' I'll watch thee doin' it," Eric had said, grinning at what he thought was funny, which was greeted by a grimace and a tongue pulling as the car moved away slowly.

"If'n tha wants a whack around t'lugoyl, Our Eric," she had shouted back. "Don't thee forget to feed, water and change mi little bairn."

"Change 'im for what?" he had shouted back. "A monkey?" God! He loved that woman. Centre of his universe. Nobody like her.

"Nar then, Ar James," Eric said to his son as he carried him back into the house. "'Ow's abaht a nice cup o' tea and a bun? I'm sure tha'll come to love 'em when tha's owd enough, but not just yet, eh? A rusk, sir? Would tha like a rusk and a drop o' milk, eh?"

Although he was looking forward to spending his day with his son, he couldn't wait for Ellen to walk back through yon kitchen door.

–o–

"I think I've gone and bowt us a 'ouse, Our Ellen," Eric said as they sat down for tea that Friday. "Down Castleford Road."

"Castleford Road?" she gasped, almost spluttering her mouthful of food back onto the plate. "Castleford Road? Then tha can just unbuy it and give … back … word. You bugger! You're having me on, aren't you?"

He burst into a peal of great guffaws as he settled back in his chair. "Ee, lass!" he said, when he had stopped laughing. "Your face wor a picture.

"Them there detached 'ouses on Ash Gap Lane," he went on, when they had settled down in the front room. "Are you sure that's what you want? Onny, I've put a deposit down on one o' them four-bedroomed 'uns."

"You've…?" she gasped, almost stopping breathing.

"I 'ad to," he explained quickly. "There were onny two left. Selling like 'ot cakes, t'salesman said. I knocked 'im down a good few 'undred into t'bargain."

"How did you know which to get?" she said, catching her breath.

"No choice," he replied quietly. "Fower bedrooms plus dressing room and a on sweet, a lounge big enough to hangar a Jumbo Jet, kitchen tha needed a telescope to see t'other end on, yooj gardens back and front, double garage, and a view ower t'fields to Altofts."

"On yer bike, Eric Ingles!" she scoffed nervously. "We couldn't possibly afford yon."

"Oh yes we can," he assured her. "As I said, last two. I got a bargain by barterin'. They were keen to sell because they're wanting to move to a site in Glasshoughton, and – nob'dy else wanted it. Too big for 'em, so t'salesman said. *I* loved it. We're off to see it tomorrer, to see if'n tha likes it or not."

"I'm sure I'll love it, my wonderful man," she replied, getting quite excited at the prospect of moving into her new palace. "But we'll need furniture and…"

"We'll mek do," he said firmly, "and buy stuff as we go on. Don't forget, Our Ellen, as I've a couple o' bob put by just for this. Whereas mi fatha spends all on 'is spare cash on beer and lives to drink, I put all of mine in t'bank and only drink to live. So, whatever tha wants in t'new 'ouse thy shall 'ave – if'n tha likes it, that is.

"'Ello," he continued, as the telephone's modern warble leapt into their discussion. "I wonder 'oo yon is at this time o' day? Do we know anybody?"

"Is thy growing a sense of humour, my lad?" she laughed. "Tha'll nay find out unless thy asks yon telephone."

"Well," he said as he sat beside her once again, "it wor Our Jack. Wants to come ower and 'ave a look at 'ouses wi' us. Says also 'e 'as a proposition to run by *you*."

"Did he say what?" she puzzled.

"Nay," he replied. "You know Our Jack. Talks in riddles sometimes, mekin' you try to puzzle it aht. 'E's deep, is that one."

"Then it must be important," Ellen said. "What time?"

"About eleven-ish tomorrow, all rayt?" Eric replied, a quizzical look hovering, hoping he'd done t'rayt thing.

-o-

"And I thought our house was big, Our Eric," Jack gasped as they walked through the door. "Thinking on taking in lodgers?"

"No fear!" Eric said with feeling. "I lived wi' mi fatha and mother for umpteen years, and it dint suit me at all. Niver agen."

"Snap!" Jack agreed. "I know how *that* feels, though not wi' *your* mam."

"Don't you ever feel sorry for them?" Stick asked, not too sure about the sentiment.

"Did your father spend most of his time and money drinking beer in a working men's club wi' other men?" Eric explained keeping his emotions severely in check. "Wi' your mam 'avin' eyes only for 'im, and the violent quarrels and arguments wi' cussin' and swearin' after each drinking session?"

"I can relate to that, Our Eric," Jack agreed, as *his* memories flooded back, dragging his still raw emotions to the surface. Some would have said that *that* was unnecessary, with a need to forgive and forget being important. Jack would do neither because he hated his father for what he had done to his mother. This hatred was one of the many traits that he and his half-brother shared. Yet neither of them shared anything with Brother William, pushing Jack to wonder about any shared genetic traits at all.

End of argument.

"Wrong tack, Husband," Joyce whispered with a wry smile. "You've been lucky with your parents. We haven't. There's a lot of hurt still for the three of us that's been brought about by two selfish people, and Eric's caught the brunt from both."

"Any road up," Eric said, "enough o' them buggers. Come on. We're off to t'Majestic Caff for us tea. Anybody 'ungry?"

"I have a proposition for you, Ellen," Jack said, once tea at the Majestic had become a memory and they were sitting in the front room in Favell Avenue with a pot of tea and a piece of spice cake with a chunk of Stilton cheese. Joyce and Stick had left already to collect their youngsters from his mam's.

"Go on then," she said with a smile. "Surprise me."

"I've been having a word with Mrs Silvester, the head of the Common School," he started, while munching his favourite cake.

"Never heard of her," she replied, "though my cousin, Alice, went there when Mr Teasedale was the head. Nice school."

"It was built around the same time as Woodhouse Junior but a bit earlier than Queen Street, where you would likely have gone," he said. "Anyway, she said she'd be more than happy to have someone with your credentials to go in occasionally – particularly on a Wednesday – to do work with groups of youngsters in the upper part of the school. If you're up for it, that is?"

"Wow! Jack Ingles!" she gasped. "What can I say? Is there no end to your contacts?"

"Between you and me, Ellen," he went on, "if you stick with it until the end of your course, I'm convinced there'll be a paid post in it for you."

"I don't know what to say, Our Jack," Eric chipped in. "I knew we did t'rayt thing shacking up wi' thee, despite what others might a said abaht thee."

They all laughed at Eric's joke. He was getting to be more like his brother the longer they spent in each other's company.

"There is a price to pay, of course," Jack said, to Jenny's frown.

"Aye, go on then," Eric added.

"Another piece of that lovely cake wi' another cup of tea would just about cover the debt," Jack said, as a great grin split his face.

All right, Jack.

Chapter 4

Ellen's first year at teacher training college was exciting, if a little mundane at times, particularly when travelling throughout the winter. Fortunately, the terms weren't overly long, and she was able to spend time at home during her 'short' weeks.

She didn't have to worry about how James would travel, because her mum and her sister had insisted he stay with them. Her mum loved him to bits. Since she had lost her husband to a pit accident in 1956, she had been longing for grandchildren to ease her loss. Now she had two – a girl from Ellen's elder sister and now James, who she looked after Mondays and Tuesdays. This allowed Ellen's sister to do a part-time job on those days and to look after the children the other two days in the week.

Consequently, James and his cousin Emily were brought up more like siblings, spending a lot of time learning about life and growing up together.

Ellen's three weeks' teaching practice in the first term of that year was spent at a junior school close to the new 'mansion' they had moved into during the autumn. Jack and Jenny and Stick and Joyce had been on hand to help, along with Barry, Ellen's sister Joan's husband.

What a wonderful and exciting day that was! Ellen had thought that the house would be sparsely furnished from their old home after Eric had declared they could 'mek do' for the time being. However, unbeknown to her he had ordered the furniture she had liked on one of their 'window shopping' sorties a month or two before removal day, and had it delivered once the removal men had gone. She was so moved by his thoughtfulness she had burst into tears when she saw it being put into place.

"How did tha know what to buy?" she had said, once everyone had gone. "It's … beautiful."

"Well," Eric replied as he stood by the fireplace, thumbs lodged under imaginary trouser braces, "thy chose it all."

"How do you make that one out?" she said, a puzzled frown drawing down her brow.

"Does tha remember when we went for a sortie around Leeds t'other month wi' our James?" he replied. "When we looked in all them furniture shops, Lewis's and Schofield's on yon Headrow, t'Co-op in Albion Street, and all them others as I can't draw to mind? Tha pointed out a lot of stuff that tha said we wouldn't be able to afford and that tha loved."

"Aye?" she said, a smile gathering. "And…?"

"Well," he went on, "I chose the best o' what tha liked and 'ere it is."

"I love you, Eric Ingles," she cooed, drawing him towards her. "It's all exactly what I would have chosen. So not only is thy a good man, tha's a connoisseur of good furniture too."

"A conwazzer o' good furniture, eh?" he said, puffing out his chest in pride. "Nowt's too much for thee, Our Lass."

"But you *do* like it?" she asked, a simple question that would have flummoxed most males in his position. "Don't you?"

"Aye lass," he replied slowly, a grin heralding his agreement. "Whatever *thy* likes, *I* like."

"You do realise," she said, a cheeky smile betraying her

thoughts, "that wi' all this furniture and all this space, the house needs … filling up a bit?"

"If tha means what I *think* tha means," he answered, a great grin breaking out, "I'll start mi countdown now. Now where's yon calendar?"

-o-

"You've got to take it easy, Jim," Jack advised. "Doing what you're doing is not good for your heart."

"Can't do it, Jack," Jim replied, a definite shrug of the shoulders heralding his resignation. "I've always been active, and I don't intend having my arse measured for a wheelchair just yet."

"Then let me do the hard stuff," Jack offered. "There's no heroism in pushing thissen *too* hard."

"All right, Jack," Jim agreed. "Tha's a good man and I *will* ask if I need you to gi' me a hand."

The early evening get-together that Flo had arranged to celebrate Jim's return to health and to introduce son Michael to the family went down a treat, and even William was reasonably affable. Val's three children had other plans, as had Jessie, so it was an adult affair with Florence May and George William doing their own thing after dinner.

"I was told from an early age that I was adopted," Michael replied in answer to Val's question. "So, with due deference to my adoptive parents, I put off searching for my natural mother until *they* were no longer with us.

"And in answer to your next question," he went on, after a slight pause for a coffee and Victoria sponge replenishment, "no, it wasn't hard to wait because they had given me everything I could have needed as a growing child – love, affection, care, opportunity."

"But didn't you *want* or *need* to find your biological

parents?" William's voice entered the discussion.

"Of course I did," Michael replied, "but it wasn't urgent."

"Enough of this," Jenny butted in. "It's getting to sound a bit like an inquisition. Your wife's lovely, but the underlying accent hints that she's not Yorkshire born."

"I met Inga ten years ago on a trip to Amsterdam," Michael said. "A mutual friend introduced us and the rest, as they say, is history."

"I was born in the Hague," Inga joined in, pleased to be part of this family discussion, "but spent a good many years here in Britain. My mother is from Yorkshire, but my father was German. He was a pilot in the war. He was shot down in his Messerschmitt and was interned for the duration. He died as a result of his injuries three years after I was born."

Jack's eyebrows raised instinctively at the mention of the words 'German' and 'pilot'. Noticing the signs and understanding the history, Flo stiffened, expecting the worst.

"Then we are alike, Inga," Jack stated slowly, "because you lost a father whom you barely knew, and I lost an uncle who I never met. We are both losers because of a conflict we had no part in starting."

To everyone's surprise, they hugged each other spontaneously in a significant show of understanding and togetherness.

"We have a surprise for you, Mother," Michael announced, a huge smile decorating his face. "Inga and I are soon to be three."

"Wonderful," Flo exclaimed, a very satisfied smile warming her face. Not only had she found a long-lost son but there were soon to be *three* more members to her family. "That'll make seven grandchildren, then."

"Maybe even eight," Inga added.

"How come?" Jack said, more than a little confusion

invading his precision-dominated mind.

"She thinks she might be having twins?" Val's voice entered the conversation.

"It's a while to go yet," Inga replied, "but I have this overwhelming feeling at times that there's more than one in there. It takes a woman to know, Sister."

"Wow!" Michael gasped, stunned and ecstatic at the news. "So, one and one *do* make three. Bloomin''ummer!"

"Is your mother still with us, Inga?" Jenny ventured.

"Yes, she is," Inga replied happily. "She lives in Skipton. Although Dad was the love of her life, she remarried and now has twin daughters who are lovely."

"Wonders will never cease," Flo gushed, a secretly happy smile breaking out.

"They *are* lovely," Inga reiterated slowly, "but beware – they *are* sixteen."

They all laughed at the unexpected revelations from this gathering that some of them had welcomed with trepidation and caution. Now, this *was* something to celebrate.

-o-

"And why wouldn't tha meet thi cousin?" Eric asked his mate Jack Holmes as he propped up the bar in the White Swan. He had made it in his way to have it out with his 'pal' to find out why he had snubbed his brother, Jack Ingles. Eric was a loyal friend but anyone that snubbed *his* family snubbed *him*.

"I can please missen 'oo I decide to see and talk to, can't I?" Jack Holmes replied as he wiped the froth from his stubbly top lip.

"Tha can please thissen what tha does," Eric agreed, "but tha'd better mek sure tha dunt slight anybody as belongs to *me*. I put missen out to bring you two together, and tha can't be bothered to be civil to a brother who wanted to meet thee."

"Bugger off, Eric Ingles," Jack Holmes replied sharply. "It's none o' thy business *what* I do wi' mi time or who I meet. 'E's nowt to me and never will be."

"Thi mother thinks different from thee," Eric interrupted. "*She* rates him higher than she rates thee, if truth be known. Reading between t'lines, tha's allus been a disappointment to her and would have been to thi father, rest his soul, if he'd iver met thee."

"What does *she* know abaht what's good for me?" Jack Holmes shouted. "She's allus been a bit soft, living in t'past as long as I've bin able to understand."

"Tha's *never* bin old enough to understand anything, Jack Holmes – ever," Eric replied, keeping his anger and frustration under control – just. "And I can't be doing with arseholes like thee, particularly when tha's talking about good people – and family to boot – like thi mother and my brother. So as far as I'm concerned, I want nowt further to do wi' thee. Tha's become a arsehole o' t'worst sort, as I've no doubt most folk who sup in this shit hole already know."

The room had fallen silent during this altercation, with drinkers taking mental sides and placing mental bets as to whether the exchange might turn physical. Eric, however, turned on his heels and headed for the door as Jack shuffled on his stool, a glass of beer attached to his face.

"I knew his father," an elderly voice crept up on Eric, shaking him out of his anger. "And a nicer chap you couldn't have hoped to meet. He would have been horrified to see how his son has turned out."

"Thanks for that, Horace," Eric said as he turned to face his new companion. "Did thy know him well?"

"We were inseparable as nippers," Horace replied, "rayt from junior school up to t'day bloody Jerry knocked 'im out o' t'sky."

"A blow for thee, then," Eric said. "Why is it good 'uns allus seem to get teken, and t'bad buggers allus get left to stew and survive, eh?"

"Did I 'ear thi say summat about thi … brother?" Horace queried. "Would that be Eric Ingles' son by his first wife, Florence May Morley?"

"Aye," Eric Junior replied. "Did tha know any on 'em?"

"I knew 'er real dad, 'Erbert," Horace agreed. "Now 'e would have knocked thi father's block off rayt enough. Sorry, but it's true, but 'e wor killed when she wor three."

"It's nowt to me, Horace," Eric replied. "Mi fatha proved *his* worth during most of my life, and that I wasn't what 'e wanted. I pity Jack and his mother's existence wi"im in their lives, si thi."

Eric turned and headed for Ash Gap Lane and home, sad that things had turned out as they had with his now former pal, Jack Holmes. It wasn't what he had expected or wanted, but better to find out what sort of a man he was *now* rather than later.

"Hello, lovely man," his wife greeted him as he snecked the front door quietly. "I didn't expect you this early. Beer not up to it?"

"Nay lass," he answered as he pulled her to him. "Heart worn't in it and neither wor t'company."

They sat together with a cup of tea as he explained his feelings about the chap that used to be his pal.

"Never bother, love," she advised, gently stroking his hair. "Family's a sight more important. Just think on what we have and let stuff we don't need slide away from thee. Oh, by the way, t'manager at St Peter's pit down Hopetown phoned. He wanted to know if you could go in tomorrow early. Summat up wi' t'ripper on t'A seam – whatever *that* is."

"Aye," he replied. "Course I can. It's a coal-cutting machine that t'face workers can't really do wi'out. One of my specialities. It'll be extra money so I can keep thee in t'manner tha's grown accustomed."

His deep throaty chuckle made her smile. He was growing a defined sense of humour that she hadn't noticed much before. Must be the result of his association with his brother, Jack, whose humour infected everyone he came into contact with.

-o-

"Take it steadily, Ellen," Jack said, trying to calm her near-hysterical voice. "Yes, I know it … of course. Does your mum know? OK, I'll come straight away. I'll be there in an hour."

"What is it, Jack?" Jenny asked, a concerned frown invading her brow as he replaced the phone.

"It's our Eric," he replied, dragging on his coat and collecting his keys from the hall table. "He's had an accident."

"Oh no!" she gasped. "What's he been doing? Car?"

"He was called in to St Peter's pit this morning to mend some coal-cutting machinery or other," he stated, "and there was an explosion."

"Oh my God!" Jenny said, concern for Eric's well-being bubbling to the surface. "Is he…?"

"I don't know," Jack replied, "and I won't until I get there. I couldn't get anything else out of Ellen because she was distraught, as you would expect. I'll phone you when I get there. It won't take me long. Traffic shouldn't be too bad this late on a Saturday afternoon."

Jack was a very pragmatic and thoughtful man and, although he needed to get there as quickly as he could, he would never break laws or speed limits no matter what the emergency.

The Castleford and Airedale Hospital seemed to be busy, although he had no yardstick by which to judge as he had never been there before. That distinctive hospital smell brought back uncomfortably painful memories of his mam and granddad's stay; he held uneasy and resentful thoughts in his mind that took little encouragement to resurface. The corridors and wards could all have been shaped from the same blueprint.

"Thank God you're here!" Ellen sighed as Jack strode though the swing doors of Ward 4. He drew her to him in an embrace that told her to not worry because he was there and would take care of her.

"How is he?" Jack asked in that hushed whisper used in *all* hospital wards.

"They've sedated him," she replied. "Chipped right elbow, two broken ribs and a bang to the head. Otherwise he's OK."

Jack laughed at the grimace she pulled, even though she was still somewhat shocked.

"He was in shock, you know, Jack," she said after a while, still holding Eric's hand. "You hear all these stories about the injuries down the pit, but you never take *too* much notice until it hits one of your own."

"He *will* be all right, won't he?" Jack asked, a hint of concern edging his words. "Only…"

"He'll survive," she replied, brushing aside his concerns. "He *has* to. He's got a son to—"

"Is that you, Our Jack?" a slow, weak, quiet voice crawled up from the bed. "I dint expect to see *thee* 'ere."

"Aye, Our Eric," Jack replied, a ready smile always available to greet, "I am that. Just thowt I'd drop in, like, to see that tha's be'avin' thissen."

"But tha lives in Leeds," Eric said, puzzled. "An' that's over an 'our off."

"I wor just passin' by, so I thowt I'd nip in, si thi," Jack replied. No answer to that one. "And 'appence 'ave a cup o' Yorkshire Tea wi' thi. All rayt?"

"Appreciate it, Jack," Eric said, a grimace growing. "Could tha just 'utch me up a bit? These bloody ribs are killing."

"Aye," Jack replied with a smile. "An' I'll push thee round in thi bathchair as well when tha's ready."

"Cheeky bugger," Eric said, trying not to laugh. "For God's sake don't make me laugh, else these brocken ribs'll be t'death o' me."

"Thank you for coming, Jack," Ellen said, hugging her brother-in-law once they were in the corridor at the end of visiting time. "It's made all the difference to him. Good to see him smiling instead of frowning and cursing his bad luck. You really are good for us all."

"And I don't cost anything," he replied, a half-smile beginning to dance around the corners of his mouth.

"Don't cost…?" she said, not understanding.

"Yes, I'm good for nothing," he laughed.

"Daft bugger," she said, giving him a playful push. "You're so sharp, one day you'll cut yourself."

Chapter 5

"He'll be all rayt," Jack said, as he sat down with his family to dinner shortly after his return from Castleford.

"What happened to him, Daddy Jack?" Jessie asked, as she poked and picked at her roast dinner as usual.

"If you don't want *that*, young lady," Jack interrupted very quickly, "you can just spoon it onto my plate. What do *you* say, George William?"

"Me too, Daddy," the boy shouted through a mouthful of gravy-soaked Yorkshire Pudding. "My favourite."

"Just like his daddy," Jenny said through a giggle. "Always his favourite."

"It's all right," Jessie added. "I'll eat it in my own way and in my own good time. You were saying? Uncle Eric? His injury?"

"He was called in to the pit to mend a machine that cuts coal quickly and efficiently," Jack explained. "Without a properly working piece of kit, coal production would have been stopped. As he closed down the machine, the engine sparked – and a spark underground could mean curtains. There must have been a small pocket of firedamp. Spark? Firedamp? Boom!"

"Firedamp?" Jessie asked. "Damp fire? How can that work?"

"It's a miner's name for methane gas," Jack went on. "Add a spark to methane gas and it *will* explode – the cause of many a fatal accident in the mines."

"Will he die, Daddy?" George William asked naively.

"No, George, he won't," Jack started to explain. "Fortunately, the gas explosion was only a small one, but big enough to throw him backwards a matter of ten feet against a wall of rock, breaking his right elbow and two ribs, along with giving him a nasty bang to his head. He was unconscious for a minute or two, but he *will* recover."

"We're doing a project on coal and coal mining in school," Jessie said. "It's like a newspaper report with things to illustrate the talk we have to do. Do you think Uncle Eric would agree to help with the talk and perhaps come in to school to do an interview?"

"I'm sure he'd be delighted," Jack replied, a huge grin showing his delight. "He'll be out of hospital in a couple of days so you can ask him yourself.

"Brings back memories of when I was a nipper at Woodhouse," he went on after a moment or two, "when we did a similar project and mi granddad agreed to come in to support and talk about stuff. It was brilliant. He told 'em things nobody else could have known, brought things in to show that nobody else could have brought, and gave us all, teacher included, a great time."

He fell silent, a faraway look in his eyes as he slid quietly into the days he had spent with his granddad – the things they'd done and the places they'd been.

"Are you all right, Daddy Jack?" Jessie asked gently, realising he was somewhere else. "I never knew Granddad Jud, and I wish I had."

"Yes, Jessie," he replied quietly, "I am. Just thinking. He'd have loved you. The only female child in his life that was never to be."

"Ee, Jessie, lass," Eric said, a great smile of satisfaction splitting his face. "Nobody 'as iver asked me for owt like that before, so I'd be delighted to help thee wi' thi project. Coal mining, eh? Nar, what does tha want mi to do?"

"Well, Uncle Eric," Jessie started, shuffling her bottom onto the tuffet next to his armchair, taking care not to knock his potted limb that lay next to useless along the chair arm. The murmur of her voice tailed away as she explained carefully what she wanted him to do.

Jack thought back to the time he broke *his* elbow – first time straight pot, second time bent pot. The two different approaches for the same sort of injury still intrigued him. Was there some sort of printed list of rules that had to be followed that gave a different outcome each time? How many rules were there? How...?

"Have *you*, Daddy Jack?" Jessie's voice crashed into his memory vault, dragging his conscious mind back to the here and now.

"Have I what?" he replied, with no idea what she was asking or for how long she had been asking it. "Sorry, I was centuries away."

"Got anything to add to what Uncle Eric has been saying for the last four hours?" Jessie replied, her pert answer taking Jack by surprise.

"Four—?" he said, a puzzled look taking over.

Eric could contain his mirth no longer as his huge guffaw – followed by gasps of pain – burst from his lips.

"She's got thee thiyer, Ar Jack," he growled, holding his ribs. "My, she's a quick 'un, all rayt."

"Keep up, Daddy Jack. Keep up," Jessie continued, mildly chastising him. "We've been talking for about twenty-two minutes and wondered if you needed to add anything, but apparently … not."

"I'm sorry," he apologised, "but seeing your Uncle Eric's potted arm dragged back memories from the sands of time of *my* potted arm when I was a nipper. Now then, *is* there anything you need me to add?"

"Not really," Jessie replied. "I think we've got it all covered, eh, Uncle Eric?"

"We 'ave that, Our Lass," he grinned. "And I'm rayt looking forward to tekin' part."

"I'll just write down a few notes for you," she went on, as if she was about to put on a production of a Shakespeare masterpiece. "Then we'll be good to go."

Jenny had been sitting by listening with awe and pride to the interchange between these two grown men and her little girl. Jessie had come such a long way since Jack had walked into their lives, and *he* had been largely responsible for holding her hand throughout the journey. Although at times she wouldn't like to admit in her cool teenage way that she loved him, Jessie *knew* she couldn't have managed without his guiding hand. Nothing had ever been too much trouble for him with Jessie and she had really become *his* daughter.

"Cup of Yorkshire Tea time then, I think," Jack offered, "and one of yon home-baked scones."

"She's a smart one, yon daughter o' thine, Our Jack," Eric said, hobbling carefully into the kitchen with his brother. "Clever, just like her father."

"More like her mam, I think, Eric," Jack replied with a nod and a grin. "Jessie likes to think she's her own woman, and why shouldn't she? She rationalises and thinks like a woman twice her age. All I do is help her along when needs must."

"Tha knows as well as I do that we've both had to mek it under our own steam," Eric said, as he inched his backside carefully into his favourite chair by the chimney breast. "Tha shouldn't minimise t'effect tha's 'ad on 'er life. Even I can see *that* in the short time I've known thee."

"Tha'll do t'same wi' yon James, si thi," Jack replied, "and…"

"Ah but, t'difference there'll be that I'll 'ave 'ad 'im since 'e wor born," Eric said slowly.

"Same difference to me," Jack explained intensely. "As far as I'm concerned, she's mine, no matter t'circumstances o' conception or birth. There's niver been any question."

-o-

"No Stick, is it today?" Jane Alison Bradley fondly asked, as she linked Jack's arm across Boar Lane onto Bishopgate Street and the Dark Arches to their Broughton bus stop.

"Hello, Jane," Jack greeted her with a cheery smile and drew her arm close to him. "My lucky day today. No, he's poorly – a touch of the dreaded lurgy, I believe."

"Lucky day?" she puzzled.

"Got you to myself, at least for ten minutes," he grinned.

"We could always 'miss' the bus," she suggested, quietly mischievous, a twinkle in her eye, "and go in … late?"

"Oo, you are wicked," he said, drawing her arm even closer, a smile betraying his thoughts, "but I like you."

"I did actually rather like you at college, you know," she said candidly, when they had found seats together on the lower deck. "It's just that I had to concentrate on my work. If I'd let other things and thoughts intrude, I wouldn't have qualified. But now…"

A rush of excitement made the hairs on the back of Jack's neck stand up and take note. Could she be letting him know her intent? No, surely not. She was taken. Wasn't she? Ian?

"How's Ian?" he asked simply.

Straight away, she knew that it wasn't a genuine question, so she made her intentions as obvious as possible.

"Ian and I split up some time ago," she started to explain. "He decided that a blonde floozie with bigger boobs was more appealing than me, so I left him to it."

"Unbelievable," Jack gasped. "Turning down a lifetime of eternal bliss with you! He must be ga-ga."

"That's one of the things I've always found attractive about you, Jack," Jane replied. "You always know what to say. My stop, I think."

The bus slowed and, as Jack turned to her to bid his *au revoir*, her lips brushed his.

"Should have done that a long time ago, eh Jack?" she whispered, a warmingly waspish smile dancing around her full red lips. Then she was gone.

"Woulda, coulda, shoulda," he murmured, watching her shapely body cross the road.

She reached the other side and turned to wave. Their eyes locked for an instant, sending his mind into convulsions of confusion and uncertainty. She was lovely was Jane, and he had always carried a fluttering candle for her until she had met Ian and he had met Jenny again after all those years. *Jenny* had all but extinguished the flame and it had guttered for a time. He was shocked now to experience the stirrings of its rebirth. That wasn't what he either expected or, indeed, was looking for. He would have loved to have taken Jane out at college, but she wasn't interested in relationships and he, on the whole, had had too much else on *his* mind.

As the bus reached the terminus and Jack made to move, thoughts of Jenny shouldered their way into his mind reminding him why *they* were together, and why thoughts of someone else had no place is *his* head.

"Penny?" David's voice swept away all other voices in

Jack's head as he pored over paperwork for his forthcoming visit to a junior school in Alwoodley, North Leeds, to support them in their attempt to squeeze a foreign language into their already struggling curriculum.

"Stop calling me Penny, David," Jack chuckled as he tidied away his papers and explained what he was about to do.

"Things all right with your son?" David asked, knowing that nothing had ever been plain sailing in Jack's dealings with his former wife Lee.

Jack knew that he couldn't have maintained a long-distance relationship with his son, Sam, if the boy had remained in Canada. However, Sam and Lee seemed to have decided that *here* should be their home, and it puzzled David why his pal hadn't made any sort of a move to spend more time with his son – or even to apply for joint custody.

"Shan't be seeing him much longer, David," Jack replied, a resigned look intruding.

"How come?" his friend asked quietly, puzzled at the reference. "I didn't realise there had been a change."

"They'll be off back to Canada within the next few weeks," Jack explained. "Permanently. That's why Lee's suggested I might want to see more of him now. I don't think we'll be getting an invite to stay in Canada any time soon, so…"

"So, what will you do?" David went on, wondering how *he* would feel if he was in Jack's shoes.

"Maintain the status quo, my friend," Jack said, shrugging his shoulders, resigned to the inevitable. "Can't do any more. As like as not, I won't be seeing him again, so I won't become further involved. If I did, it would make it all the more difficult for the lad, having to leave when we were just getting to know each other."

'Compassionately hard' was how David described his

close friend. He didn't think he would be able to do that, should *he* be forced into a similar situation. He understood Jack's position perfectly, though. *His* best avenue was the one he had chosen to follow to make things easier for them all, particularly his boy Sam.

Chapter 6

"Hello, Mary," Jack greeted his niece, as he strode through the lounge doors to be welcomed by a steaming pot of mashing Yorkshire Tea after a busy day at school. "Social or advice?"

"You know me so well, Uncle Jack," Mary replied, a little giggle giving away her motive. "A bit of both really. But please, get your cup of tea and a digestive. My problem can wait."

"Fire away, lovely," Jack said, pouring his tea. "I can multitask – eat, drink and talk at the same time. But tell me," he added after taking his initial drink, "why are you not having this conversation with—?"

"Dad?" she interrupted. "To put it bluntly, he is not interested in my social life. Doesn't think I should have a boyfriend, and he reckons he's too busy to help. I'm almost sixteen, for goodness' sake. *Everybody* has a boyfriend at my age."

"Even the boys?" Jack said, a giggle erupting.

"Uncle Jack!" Mary gasped, joining in the mirth.

"OK, spill," Jack said, once his tea and digestive had become a cherished memory. "What's the problem?"

"My new boyfriend's a bit older than me," she started, "but he's – well, cool."

"So, he's your sugar daddy, then?" Jack smiled, pulling

her leg in a way that she didn't understand.

"Sugar—?" she puzzled. "I don't—?"

"Pulling your leg, my dear niece," Jack laughed. "A sugar daddy is a much older man with a younger woman."

"Oh, right," Mary replied, *still* not understanding. "Well, Terence has only just come into our Upper Sixth for the last few months to top up his chances in the exams."

"Terence, you say?" Jack asked, a slightly puzzled frown drawing down his brow. "What's his surname? Not Ingles by any chance?"

"I don't … know," she said, unsure why it was so important. "Why?"

"Probably nothing, really," he said slowly. "It's just that I once taught an eleven-year-old boy at one of my previous schools and he was called—"

"Terence Ingles?" she replied almost in a whisper. "What was he like?"

"An eleven-year-old boy, actually," Jack smiled. "A thoroughly nice young man from lovely parents."

"So, what do you think, Uncle Jack?" Mary asked tentatively.

"Do you like him, Mary?" he answered simply.

"Of course I do," she replied, unsure why he should ask such an obvious question.

"Then," he said finally, "go for it, but be … careful. Ask him a few surreptitious questions – about his name and his parents, particularly about his uncles."

"His uncles?" she asked, dumbfounded by this suggestion.

"Just do as I ask," he said, eyebrows raised in encouragement, "and I'll explain when I see you again. OK, one further thing. Is your mum on board with your new man?"

"Haven't told her yet," she said, hesitating. "Why?"

"Get her on board," he explained, "by telling her what

I've said. Your mum is an amazing ally who can temper your dad's sometimes quite extreme opinions. You *need* her in your corner."

"Got to go," Mary said, as she made for the lounge door. "Thank you, Uncle Jack. As ever."

"Listen to him, Mary," Jenny advised as soon as her niece reached the door. "He has lots of irons in lots of fires, and he talks sense."

"I know," Mary replied, "and I love him for it. Why can't my dad be more like him? Uncle Jack thinks he's funny sometimes, but he's one of the few people I can trust to be honest in his opinions and who will *always* help without question. Joey thinks he's great, too."

-o-

"Talk to her Jack … please!" Val pleaded. "You're the only person she'll listen to."

"Give me one good reason why I should talk her out of the path she desperately wants to tread?" Jack replied, his logic very difficult to break. "Two simple questions really, Val: will this chosen way make her happy, and how far is she prepared to go to make it happen? Mary?"

"I've always been interested in health and beauty, as you know, Uncle Jack," Mary replied earnestly. "And I'm prepared to do whatever it takes to be successful. Honestly."

"Then what can I say?" he said, turning to Val with his hands open and fingers spread in confusion. "University isn't the answer for everybody, you know Val – never has been, never will be. I've come across many university graduates who have had no idea what they wanted to do or to be. I've got to say also that many had become unemployable because university was their only goal."

"But—" Val tried to protest.

"Hear me out, please," Jack interrupted. "The difference between them and Mary? *She knows* what she wants and is prepared to do what it takes to achieve it. I feel we owe it to her to let her run with her plan and support it one hundred per cent. She has my vote, and – here's the killer, for what it's worth – I'm prepared to support her, even if no-one else is."

"And I thought—" Val harrumphed.

"You could count on me to toe the party and family line?" Jack replied, a triumphant grin on his face. "And I thought you knew me better, Valerie Ingles."

"One final thing, Val," Jack said, after Mary had hugged and kissed her most fave uncle and was heading for the front door. "Support her in *all* her endeavours. I have a deep feeling in my innards that she will be successful, despite her dad's opposition – if he shows any interest at all. If either of you needs my input or help, *please* don't hesitate to ask."

"Should you have done that, Jack?" Jenny asked, a hint of concern tingeing her words. "I mean, she is *their* daughter."

"What?" he replied firmly. "Allow a youngster to be browbeaten into following a path she passionately does *not* want to follow? Hell, no. I had too much of that when I was her age from mi fatha. *She* needs help from someone who is not prepared to see her dragooned and that person is … me. She is my only niece, when all's said and done. If they want to do right by her, they should listen to her and explore her options and wishes."

He could be irritating at times, could her lovely man, but one admirable trait Jack had had for as long as Jenny had known him was the ability to shut down dissenters when he was convinced he was right. Mary – and Joey and Ed, and all their own children – couldn't have had a better and more supportive advocate than Jack Ingles, the only real committed family man in its widest sense that she had ever met.

The doorbell summoned someone urgently to account. As Jack opened the door, a delighted young lady flung her arms about his neck and kissed him on the cheeks.

"Mary!" he exclaimed. "Didn't I see your twin sister only a short while ago?"

"Just wanted to say thank you – for the second time in as many days," she replied. "Mum has said that if Uncle Jack thinks it's OK, then it's all right by her."

"And your dad?" Jack asked, with a raised eyebrow and a slight inclination of the head.

"He doesn't seem to care these days," she replied with a disdainful grimace, "if he ever did. Can I ask another favour whilst I'm here?"

"Whatever you need," he replied with a grin, "the answer's yes. If you want to borrow money, the answer's ten per cent."

They laughed easily together as family should. Mary had come to realise that her closest ally was her Uncle Jack, the man to whom all her siblings could turn in their hour of need, who would give them honest counsel and the sort of support they might need at any time.

"Fire away," he added, as they had sat down at the dining room table, a cup of Columbian coffee to hand and a Danish pastry.

"Bit of a departure for you?" she said, nodding at the strange mugful of steaming liquid and nibble to hand. "Gone off Yorkshire Tea, Uncle Jack?"

"Just thought I'd give this a bit of a try by means of a change, don't you know," he replied with a chuckle. "Getting used to it gradually. It won't take the place of Yorkshire Tea, though. Anyway, do I see you've got some paperwork you'd like me to peruse?"

"You know that I'm into make-up and health and such like," Mary stated, spreading the documents in front of him. "Well, I've been thinking I'd like to start my own little business – in a small way, you understand – to see how I might get on."

"Excellent," Jack said with a grin, rubbing his hands together in anticipation. "Now, I know nothing about beauty and make-up, as you might guess to look at me, but I'm quite good with ideas. What was on your mind…?"

Their discussion faded into the background as Jenny decided to make a lunch snack, a smile on her face as she saw how involved niece and uncle had become over Mary's ideas. It had always been a wonder how easy her Jack found it to enthuse and become engaged with youngsters – he was one of life's real teachers. How lucky they all were to have him and to be able to tap into his boundless energy, enthusiasm and skill. Lucky for William's children they had an Uncle Jack they could rely on.

"Is this really a possibility for her?" Jenny asked, when their niece had departed. "I mean—"

"I have to say she has some wonderful ideas, Our Jen," Jack said, once there was a proper mug of hot liquid to hand. "She wants, ultimately, to source and make some of her own products using Hello Vera…"

"I think you'll find it's *Aloe* Vera," Jenny corrected, smiling at his funny pronunciation.

"Whatever," he replied with a shrug. "She could have a goer there if she sets out her stall properly."

–o–

"Final exams yesterday, eh, Ellen?" Jack asked his sister-in-law as they sat together for coffee in their conservatory. James was in the corner near to the outside door so he could keep an eye on the local bird population while he played with his Lego bricks. He loved watching 'his' birds and building wonderful structures at the same time. Eric was convinced his son would be an engineer, while Ellen believed he would be an ornithologist. James wanted to do both.

"Last lap, Our Jack," Ellen replied. "It's been an eye-opener and no mistake, but an experience I wouldn't have missed for the world."

"It's a matter of achieving a lifetime ambition, really," Eric butted in, "and one we've all bin party to. Me an' our James 'ave enjoyed t'process as well."

"Watch out for the postman ower t'next few days," Jack advised.

"And why should we do that, Jack Ingles?" Ellen said, a smile betraying her thoughts.

"For that, Our Ellen, you'll have to wait and see," Jack said, touching the side of his nose with his forefinger while trying to hide a sly smile.

"It's difficult to think that in one week it'll all be over," Ellen sighed. "Three years of laughter, excitement, and a few tears of frustration. It's not been an easy, straightforward path because sometimes it's been a real slog when I wasn't able to see any way forward – or way out, as *you* know yourself only too well."

"What'll you do now all your exams are done with?" Jack asked, knowing what her answer would be.

"You know as well as I do, Our Jack," she said with a grimaced grin. "And it doesn't involve 'work'. I'm going to rest my weary bones – and brain – for a week or two and devote all my spare time to my son and husband."

"Being waited on hand and foot then, eh?" Jack added with a mischievous wink, nodding in Eric's direction.

"I'll go an' get mi pinny on now then, shall ah?' Eric replied, a belly-rumbling guffaw surfacing slowly. "It's on its way to bein' aired, as we speak. But in t'meantime, t'postman's just dropped this letter through t'door. It's for you, Our Lass."

A look of surprise and uncertainty flitted across Ellen's face as a smile stole into Jack's. She examined the envelope for a few moments to see if she might glean its origin.

"Is tha off to try to read its contents through t'envelope?" Eric said, a mite impatiently. "Tha knows, like Superman?"

"Oh … my … God!" she exclaimed through clenched teeth.

"Well," Eric asked, intrigued by what sort of a Pandora's Box she had opened, "what is it?"

"I've got an interview," she said almost in a hoarse whisper, "at Castleford Road Junior School. A permanent job interview."

"They must have liked what you've been doing on Wednesdays, then, Ellen," Jack said. "Congratulations. I had words with the head before you started your voluntary Wednesdays there, as I told you," he explained, "but I had nothing to do with this, although I knew. All this is down to you, Ellen Ingles. They recognise quality when they see it and would have been stupid to let it pass them by because if they hadn't snapped you up, someone else would have."

"What chance does tha think she 'as, Jack?" Eric asked, almost thinking that his opinion would count for something in the final analysis.

"Significantly better than average, Old Chap," Jack replied, putting on the best spin he could realistically muster. There were no guarantees in this game. "And when is it for, Ellen?"

"A week on Wednesday," she replied, almost too overcome to speak.

"The only thing you have to focus on is … you," Jack advised. "You know what the score is with the school because you've been there for the last year or two. You know the children and the school in general and, more importantly, they know you. Just be yourself."

"Ee, bloody 'ell!" Eric exclaimed to the world. "Mi wife's a fully-qualified teacher!"

"Steady, Trigger," Ellen said quietly. "Two stages to get over yet. I need mi paper to say I've passed, and a letter to say the school wants me. Let's not get too in front on us sens just yet."

All this was said with her barely able to contain the suppressed excitement that she had managed to keep in check over the last three years or so. Now her goal was within touching distance. Only one more *real* hurdle to handle, and Jack knew that would prove to be no barrier at all.

Chapter 7

"Well, here we are again," David said, as they enjoyed their customary Friday evening celebration for reaching the end of another week's grind in school. "Staring over the precipice at another adventure. Brandy, Old Chap?"

"You know me so well," Jack replied as their wives turned out the light in the kitchen. "Precipice?"

"As you know, our Jessies are just about to stamp their mark on adult life now they've come to the end of university," David answered, a brandy bowl warming its contents in his hands. "Florence May and Imogen Rose are about to follow in their footsteps, and George William has reached the crisis time of mid-teenage. What's he going to do, do you think?"

"He wants to be an engineer," Jack replied, a smile on his face, "like his uncle Eric, who is sorting him out with an apprenticeship."

"How's your brother William's family getting on?" David asked, not really knowing much about them, although Irene was technically William's cousin.

"Mary's business is going from strength to strength," Jack replied. "She's a right little businesswoman. Under Jim's tutelage, her brother Joey has become an engineer and now works for the company where he did his apprenticeship. Her other brother, Ed, is a bit like his dad – struggles with knowing how he fits in."

"And I know Jenny's sister has her own headship," David said, "because I've seen her at meetings."

"You mentioned a precipice earlier on," Jack reminded him, once he had recharged his brandy glass. "Sounds ominous."

"How long have we worked together, Jacky-boy?" David asked, his usual rhetorical question. "It's a long time in educational circles. The office has 'offered' me a larger school that needs some 'work' – and you understand what I mean by 'offered'."

"Indeed I do," Jack replied, the raising of both eyebrows showing how seriously he took it. "And despite how incredibly successful my French project has been across the authority, a little dickie-bird tells me the project is to be shelved. The new supremo for modern foreign languages, a Mr Woodage, has decided there are other more pressing things in the junior curriculum than MFL."

"A euphemism for 'too costly', methinks," David added. "Too long in the tooth to believe *that* claptrap. So, what'll you do, Old Man?"

"Do, Old Chap?" Jack replied with a sardonic smile.

"Come on!" David said, knowing full well there would be something afoot. "I've known you too long to be kidded you're about to let somebody like Woodage trample over you. What's next in the Jack Ingles' saga?"

"I've always harboured a hankering for working with youngsters with behavioural issues, don't you know," Jack began slowly. "So, I was wondering whether to apply for the headship of Royd Castle Residential School – and you just gave me my answer."

"You sure about that, Jack?" David replied, trying to be careful what he said and be diplomatic at the same time. "I mean – behaviour? Don't you think that's a bit over the top?"

"I've seen too many youngsters pilloried and pitched out

of school for issues not of their choice or making," Jack said. "There's more to it than there's a new race being born."

"Even so…?" David added with a cautionary raising of his brow.

"Last week I received a letter from admin at Leeds Uni to say they are offering me a place on the MEd course for the next academic year," Jack started to explain. "All I have to do now is to accept and apply for a twelve-month sabbatical from my job here to do the course. Simple."

"Never thought of that," David replied, gobsmacked by his friend's ingenuity. "That could work. Go for it, Old Chap. I won't be here, and it'll give you time to think about your future as well. If I remember right – though don't quote me – Royd Castle School might be independent."

"And what does that mean?" Jenny asked as she and Irene came back into the lounge.

"It means that the school isn't run or – more importantly – *funded* by the local authority," David replied. "As far as I'm aware, it charges local education departments for taking and educating their children who usually can't function in ordinary schools."

"Wage-wise?" she asked again.

"Again, don't quote me," he said, "but I think the salary is substantially more, to reflect the extra responsibilities and duties. That's about as much as I know, I'm afraid. It would have been better, of course, if we could have kept the old team together but that's not possible, I'm afraid."

"Still," Jack added, "there's a few weeks left until we have to face the trump of doom, so I propose not to let it get me down."

-o-

"Goodness gracious me," Jack gasped. "You can't be *that* age already. It only seems five minutes since you were knee high to a grasshopper and here you are knee high to a giraffe, and a giant one at that."

"You'd better believe it, Uncle Jack," James replied, aged nine going on nineteen, with a guffaw he had tried to copy from his uncle.

Ellen smiled at their little wonder's antics at trying to be so old and cool. He was a lovely boy who took after his dad Eric in so many ways, what with looking after his two sisters, Victoria aged seven and Julie who was five – a regular little troupe he had to keep in order and be responsible for, which pleased his dad no end. Ellen would attach that knowing smile to her face in her motherly way, usually saying, "Just wait until…"

"Do you realise how long it is since you were a newbie at college," Jack pointed out, "practising how to be a student?"

"A lifetime it seems, Our Jack," she replied with a hefty sigh and a satisfied smile decorating her already happy face. "Without you, Jack Ingles, it wouldn't have happened, and I wouldn't have reached my lifelong dream. Do you know how much I owe you?"

"Reciprocated, my lovely," Jack said, equally satisfied with the family he never thought he would have to enjoy. He loved his sister-in-law, Val, along with her grown-up children; his brother William, however, he could take or leave. But his half-brother Eric, and *his* lovely family, took things to an entirely different level. Having them in his life also drew him closer to his lifelong friend, Joyce, and her crew by association.

An entirely happy and fulfilled exercise – and then Jane swam back into his mind. They had travelled together almost daily for several years, becoming as close as his situation would comfortably allow, always wondering 'what if'. Then suddenly, she was gone without a word. He had thought at first that she'd be back from sick leave after a few days but after two weeks her absence began to worry him. Had something happened to her?

Unable to contain himself any longer, one free lunchtime at school he phoned her at work. She had left for another job, apparently somewhere close to where she had lived in South Yorkshire.

No forwarding details. No by your leave. No kiss mi arse. No goodbye.

They had become cosily close – but obviously not close enough for her to confide her innermost thoughts and feelings. She was lovely, was Jane. She reminded Jack of his relatively carefree younger days as a student, when Jenny had made her decision to tread her own path that didn't include him. There had been times in his quieter moments when he'd pondered on Jenny's reasons but had felt it would serve no useful purpose to explore these thoughts and feelings with her.

The year before, Jack's good pal Stick had moved on to a bigger, newer school to the north of the city. Same status, more money. He didn't feel like he needed to be a head teacher – just yet. They still spent regular social time together – how could they not? Joyce had been Jack's best friend for most of his life and she and Stick still lived just around the corner.

"But in truth, Ellen," Jack replied, "I am the one in your debt. Without you and Our Eric and James and Victoria and Julie, our lives would be been all the poorer."

"Ah'd recognise that there voice anywhere," Eric's boom bounced into the room before anyone had seen his face. "Now then, Our Jack. Long time no see. What's tha bin doin'?"

"Aye, Our Eric," Jack replied, "a week's a long time in the life of a flea."

They all laughed that easy laugh that comes with a close-knit clan where all values are shared, and memories are forged together.

"Any thoughts of moving onwards and upwards perhaps, Ellen?" Jack said as Jenny sat next to him on the settee.

"I'm not a career teacher," Ellen replied, a satisfied smile emphasising her words. "I'm ecstatically happy to be living my forever dream."

"Can't believe it's over ten years since tha pointed her in t'rayt direction, Our Jack," Eric added. "When we first 'eard on each other's existence, I'd niver a' thaut we'd be sittin' 'ere 'aving this conversation, Ellen the teacher she'd allus wanted to be and me t'boss o' mi own little engineering works."

"Any regrets tha din't mek it up wi' father, Eric?" Jack asked pointedly. "Tha knows, before he died, like?"

"There are allus regrets, no matter what tha does," Eric replied. "But in that respect, no. 'E tried to meddle in mi life too much ower t'last few years, and I 'ad to decide enough was enough. It's Mother I feel sorry for, to some extent, because really 'e controlled 'er life, and it shouldn't 'ave bin like that. Now she's a sorry and sad person, living on her own."

"Is there ever any chance you might want to make things right with her?" Jack asked. "Too late?"

"Nothing's iver too late, Jack," Eric said. "We've nothing in common anymore, but I don't know."

"Joyce thought about it for all o' ten seconds when I asked her t'same t'other day," Jack went on, a slight smile flicking across his mouth. "And then her answer was predictable, if unprintable."

"Mother med her feelings known when she left her first family," Eric replied. "Mebbe in similar circumstances I'd a' reacted t'same as Our Joyce. You can't do t'dirty on folks like that an' 'ope to keep t'oss fastened to t'cart."

"What about you then, Jack?" Ellen ventured, once another mug of Yorkshire Tea was nestling in his grasp. "What plans for you? Looking for that junior school headship?"

"Not quite sure where it'll tek me," he replied slowly, looking into the fire, "but I've been granted leave of absence for twelve months on full pay to study for a Masters degree in Education, and that starts next September."

"Why that, and why now?" Ellen asked, not sure that she understood his reasoning.

"That qualification will give me a head start in an increasingly competitive educational world," he began to explain. "It will also allow me to study student behavioural issues – an area of expertise I've thought a lot about over the last year or two."

"But why?" she insisted, still no clearer about his motive.

"I've applied for the headship of a residential school for youngsters with social, emotional and behavioural difficulties," Jack said, not expecting them to understand, "at The Royd Castle School."

A stunned silence enveloped them like a heavy blanket, effectively smothering the life out of their conversation. Ellen looked at Jenny, who simply shrugged, raised her eyebrows and inclined her head in resigned capitulation.

-o-

"I think you're going to have a dose of snow, Our Jack," Jenny warned, as she scanned the black clouds crowding in from the north. "Sky's full of it, by the looks."

"None forecast," he said, "so I'll believe it when I see it."

"Remember the weather forecaster who famously said, 'Snow? What snow?'" she went on. "Well it looks like one of those times, I think."

"Michael Whale, wasn't it?" he replied with a laugh. "Or Ian Katskill or McTavish or something? Or was he the one that assured us there was going to be no hurricane when soon afterwards Sevenoaks in Kent became One Oak?"

"Are you sure this is really what you want to do?" Jenny asked, straightening his tie and kissing him.

"No, I'm not," he sighed, "but I'm sure I'll soon find out. Ostensibly it's got a lot going for it, with a salary at least fifty per cent more than I'm getting now. With the closure of the French programme, they've taken mi money back to what it was before it started."

"But I thought they couldn't do that?" she replied, puzzled at all this misinformation.

"According to David, they couldn't," he said with a grimace. "But you tend to find that local education authorities can do what they damn well want, with little redress."

They stood together in the lounge, arm in arm at the large picture window, watching a smattering of tiny white flakes falling lazily to ground. The house was eerily quiet, its ghostly whoops and screeches of exiled childish glee still reverberating in their minds.

"Do you remember when Florence May and George William saw snow for the first time?" Jack asked quietly, remembering their happy yet awe-struck faces as they hopped from foot to foot in front of this very window.

"And you, like the loving dad you are, to their delight let them build strange-looking snowmen with stick noses and pebble eyes," Jenny replied, a glistening of reminiscence in her eye corners.

"And when there wasn't enough snow," Jack said quickly, "Jessie suggested a snow boy?"

"Isn't it time you were off," Jenny warned, "if you're set on going for this interview? Oh, by the way, did I tell you that I have an interview as well?"

"No, you didn't," Jack replied, a little sharply because of her timing. "A bit of a strange time to tell me, don't you think?"

"They've advertised for someone to help with classes where children are struggling with their learning," she said, ignoring his remark. "I think I know about children as well as anyone else, having had three of my own."

"I agree completely," he said guardedly. "And whatever you want to do, I'm completely behind you – but can we talk about it when I get back? I need to be off in ten minutes."

Jack always had that uncanny ability to inject you with an enormous dose of confidence for whatever you wanted to do, and now Jenny felt a bit guilty for doubting his decision to step into the frighteningly dark unknown. She *knew* he would succeed, but the uncertainty of an untried venture was a little unsettling for her. She supposed she was concerned that their standard of living might be about to change for the worse after the few years of plenty. Hence the reason for her taking *her* daunting steps into the world of paid labour.

Chapter 8

As with any new mission, doubts lingered in Jack's mind. They weren't serious enough for him to abort his decision but concerning enough to make him revisit it. His extreme enthusiasm at times blotted out his legendary pragmatism – that is until he was able to rationalise and re-evaluate. This day was no different. The telephone call he had received just after breakfast concerning his interview for the headship of Royd Castle Residential School had done nothing to dispel those qualms.

"Problems, my lovely?" Jenny commented, seeing the serious look growing on his face.

"Nothing I can't handle," he replied, a rueful smile forcing its way to his face. "It's just that my half day has turned into a full one. Morning in Boston Spa. Afternoon in Todmorden."

"But I thought …?" she puzzled, not entirely sure how things had changed so radically in such a short time.

"Apparently, the Boston Spa school will be moving to premises on Shadwell Lane in the near future," Jack explained, "but if I got the job, it would be in Todmorden. I'll know more after today."

"More?" Jenny puzzled

"Whether I want it or not," he replied, winding his scarf round his neck and then burying it under his padded winter coat. "If you're doing nothing better, I'll call in to have a bite with you at about half twelve?"

"Corned-beef sandwich, tea and a mince pie?" she offered with a smile, knowing the question was unnecessary. "But if you've other plans?"

"Try and keep me away!" he insisted, snecking the front door behind him.

A seriously cold blast slapped him across the face, as he fumbled with the car door. My God! Who would keep permanent winter out of choice? He always pitied folks who wasted good money on holidays in the snow.

The sullen sky scowled back at him, threatening dire consequences for anyone foolish enough to venture any distance from hearth and home. Yet this was an adventure Jack *had* to undertake to decide the path his remaining career might take so he could provide long-term for his family. He wasn't too sure about the motives for Jenny's decision to step into paid work, but if that was genuinely the way she wanted to go, who was he to gainsay? No doubt they would talk it through later.

Backing the car away from the house, he waved at her solitary, lonely-looking silhouette in the lounge window, urging the car into forward gear for the tedious trek to Boston Spa. Realising that this might be the first leg of his new-found career, he began to run over in his head his reasons for pursuing what most right-minded folk would consider to be a fool's errand.

-o-

"That was a waste of a morning," Jack said, striking his 'alas-poor-Yorick' pose and drooling over the contents of the corned-beef sandwich in his hand. "If this afternoon is no better…"

"No better than…?" Jenny asked, nonplussed by his disappointedly concerned frown as he studied his sandwich.

Seeing her reaction, he added hurriedly, "What I found at Boston Spa, *not* my sandwich, of course."

"Phew!" she gasped good-humouredly. "I thought tha'd gone off thi vittels, Ar Jack."

They laughed at the thought and at her pathetic attempt at dialect. She never improved *those* skills, even though she'd known and lived with him almost … forever. Too posh an upbringing.

"There was nothing much there of any note, really," he continued, chomping his favourite dinnertime repast. "At least, nothing I would want to get my teeth into. Second best to mi corned-beef sandwich, really."

"Most everything's second best to your corned-beef sandwich, my lovely man," she countered, starting to giggle as she recognised his good-humoured grin.

"Good job you said 'almost everything'," he replied, sliding his arm around her waist – after he had finished his sandwich. They snuggled together on the settee, watching the clouds gathering and darkening, ready, no doubt, to paint their neck of the woods a colder shade of white.

"Hello, Dad," a rumbly voice attacked Jack's ears from behind. "Didn't expect to see you here at this time of day. Any chance of a sandwich or three, Mam?"

"Need I ask what sort?" she sighed with a knowing smile.

"Corned beef!" father and son chorused loudly, both falling into fits of laughter.

"I should have known," Jenny said, making her way to the food room quickly. "You need to be making your way, Jack. Time's moving on and you've a way to go. Where is Todmorden, by the way?"

-o-

"Where's Todmorden?" Jack muttered to himself as he exited the M62 onto the road through Hipperholm to Halifax. He knew perfectly well where he was heading. Several days of preparation and the use of detailed maps of the West Riding had seen to that – but what he would find when he got there, heaven only knew.

He had never come across such strange village and town names before – Hipperholm, Luddendenfoot, Mytholmroyd, Hebden Bridge and Todmorden itself. To a large extent, the names in the area relied on Old English or Anglo-Saxon for their origins – origins that Jack had researched and committed to memory. How did Jenny know that that's what he would do? She knew him so well.

The A646 between Luddendenfoot and Todmorden urged travellers to hurry along as it jostled with river, canal and railway to claim its fair share of the limited space offered by this ice-age valley. Over the years, each had claimed its rightful place as the most important – and in some cases the only – route from Halifax to Todmorden.

For the most part, the road squeezed between dry stone walls, ditches, hedges and houses as it tiptoed its way over bridges and around discarded conical bollards along its eight-and-a-half-mile stretch from town to town.

"Well, this isn't so bad," he muttered, noticing the twenty-two-minute journey time with glee. The eastern edge of Todmorden almost caught him napping when the speed restriction sign jumped out at him, ordering him to slow down.

By this time large white flakes had started to drop increasingly quickly from the leaden sky that had been threatening since he had left Halifax in his wake.

"Bugger!" he hissed while approaching a simple T-junction in the centre of town. Simple left turn to Rochdale, or less simple right towards Burnley at the mini roundabout?

"Excuse me," Jack said, stopping by the Duke of York pub to ask a passing local. "Could you tell me which way to Pexwood Road, please?"

"Aye lad," a dour flat-capped older chap in greasy overalls answered. "Tha needs to tek t'left, Rochdale Road, and carry on for a mile or so. Then it's rayt and sharp rayt up t'hill. Tha'll not be able ter miss t'railway viadoc next to t'road tha wants. Is it t'school tha's after?"

"Yes, it is," Jack replied.

"Then tha needs to go on up to Stones Road," Flat Cap carried on, "and then tha can't miss it. Gates and stone gate posts'll be starin' thee in t'face. It's a narrer windy road, mind."

Not giving Jack the chance to express his gratitude, the man turned sharply into the pub.

-o-

The ride up Pexwood Road towards the school was a nightmare Jack hoped he wouldn't need to replicate. Narrow in the extreme, it had tiny ancient houses crouching to the left where the occupants took extreme chances by stepping out of their front doors directly on to the road. Opposite, a two-foot-high wall prevented the narrow pavement from falling into the steep valley below.

When he'd reached the junction with Stones Road and Dobroyd Road, the snowfall had thickened considerably, blocking the entrance to the school's grounds as if to warn him to enter at his peril. He stopped, perplexed as to his whereabouts.

"Over here," a muffled voice caught his attention. "Park your car in the space at the corner and follow me."

Jack looked around, once he had squeezed his car into

the tiny space the voice had indicated, confused as to where it had had its origin.

"Over here," it repeated, a little less muffled. "See the little path we've dug in the wall of snow? Well, that's me with the red pom-pom on mi 'ead."

"Got you!" Jack shouted back with relief. "Did you shift this lot yourself?"

"I suppose I could impress you by saying yes," the deep throaty voice replied, "but I had help from these good-looking lads over here."

Sniggers and guffaws escaped from the group, the majority of whom was standing behind the snow barrier in time-honoured workman fashion, leaning on their shovels.

The whole of a wide, long, winding driveway had been cleared by the lads, leaving a random six-foot-high wall of grey, stone-pitted snow to line the tarmac on both sides as they trudged towards a dour, forbidding-looking line of crenellations that peeped over a large island of evergreen shrubs.

Then there it was! An old folly of a castle building erected in the late-nineteenth century, in much need of repair and refurbishment. It rocked Jack back on his pragmatic heels.

"Here we are," Jack's companion said in a deep, resonant Paul Robeson-esque voice that seemed to ooze out of his huge operatic chest. "My name's Dave, by the way, Dave Towler."

"Pleased to meet you, Dave," Jack said, shaking the man's enormous ham of a hand. "I'm…"

"Pleased to meet you, Jack Ingles," Dave replied, a wicked grin crawling through his goatee beard and 'tash. "I know who you are. The owner's been talking about you for long enough."

"Notoriety at last!" Jack hooted, much to Dave's amusement.

"Be careful," he said quietly, stopping Jack before he crossed the building's threshold. "*This* chap is a sly devious owd fox, so be sure any offer he meks thee he can and will substantiate. Because, if tha doesn't, he'll take thee for a ride."

"But what…?" Jack started to ask.

"I've said enough," Dave whispered, as he looked around to check there were no eavesdroppers close by. "I like what I see, Jack. Being forewarned is being forearmed. Si thi later?" He touched the side of his nose with his forefinger and turned to go.

"How do I get hold of you?" Jack called, as Dave rounded the building.

"I live on site," he called back. "Just ask for me next time you're here." And then he was gone.

"Well, Mr Ingles," a big, bluff man sporting a grey comb-over said as Jack opened the door. "Bring thissen in lad. Cup of tea?"

-o-

Unsure whether he could work with this new employer, Jack's return journey to Leeds caused him a good deal of confused thought. On the face of it, an ordinary chap who knew precious little about education; beneath it, Dave's brief words pointed to a devious and manipulative charlatan who wasn't afraid to use the folks under his roof for his own nefarious ends.

What was he to believe? Who was he to trust? The words of a man he did not know or his instincts? His instincts had rarely been wrong before—

What would his granddad have said? He would have told him, 'Tha'll afta suck it and see, 'cos tha niver knows unless tha dips thi toe into t'watter.'

By the time Jack reached home, he had more or less made up his mind to take the job if it was offered. After his complete honesty about what was needed to bring the school up to standard for the twenty-first century, however, he wasn't so sure that he and the school would be joining forces any time soon.

Only time would tell. Nowt ventured, nowt gained.

"I got the job," Jenny enthused as he snecked the front door behind him. "I got the … job."

"Congratulations!" he said, drawing her excited, quivering body to his. "But I thought we were going to discuss it before you made your final decision?"

"So, you don't want me to take it, then?" she replied, more than a little nonplussed and annoyed at his response.

"Of course I do, daft beggar," he said, a grin hoping to dispel her negative take on his answer. "I just thought you might want us to talk, to calm any qualms you might have. After all, it will be your first foray into working for gain – iffen you take working in Woollies in the summer hols out of the equation."

She laughed at his caricature of temporary staff at the sweet counter doing their 'one for you – one for me' routine as they weighed out a quarter of midget gems.

"So, I can retire then," he said with a grin, "or at least do part time?"

"'Fraid not," she replied, drawing him to her, "because the job doesn't pay much, but at least it pays."

"Sorted then," he said, lifting her off her feet in a bear hug. "Life of Riley, here we come!"

Chapter 9

"That sounds fantastic," Jack enthused through his chomping a mince pie accompanied by the statutory mug of Yorkshire Tea. "Pay's none too bad, and I think you'll really enjoy yourself. There's nobody better than you at getting young 'uns to do what they need to do."

"Thank you, kind sir," Jenny said, curtseying before she joined him on the settee. "It means a lot coming from you."

"Have you ever considered doing what Ellen has done?" he asked through a mouthful of pie. "You know, learn to teach class?"

"No, thank you," she replied emphatically. "I'm not a leader. I prefer to do as I am told."

"That would be a first then," he said sliding away, anticipating her response.

"You've some need to cringe away, Buster," she interrupted, lunging for his now-withdrawn neck, a determined grin splitting her face. "I'll get you back."

"George William not around? Seems a bit *too* quiet," Jack said.

"Working with Eric," she replied, "no doubt going over some engineering malarkey that none of us mere mortals could hope to understand. He *really* is loving working and staying with your Eric. Anyway," she added after a few moments' quiet, "are you going to tell me about *your* afternoon?"

"Not keen on the motorway start to the drive," he began. His voice slid away beneath the bubbling of the kettle in the kitchen and the incessant spluttering of pellets of hard snow on the windows. The clicking of a key in the front-door lock interrupted the sounds of the weather and fixed their attention. Jack was about to intercept the interloper when the appearance of Florence May's head told them she was back from badminton.

"Is that the kettle I can hear, Daddy Jack?" she asked as she sidled into the front room.

Jack knew perfectly well what *that* meant. Living with three females for eighteen years, he had learned to communicate reasonably well in girl-speak. He was still unsure about understanding what *all* their conversations meant, though.

"Pot of tea, anyone?" he grinned when he had hugged his daughter.

"Yes, please!" two other voices echoed from the hall.

"Jessie and George?" he turned and mouthed silently at Jenny as his other two offspring poured into the room.

"Tea and a sandwich 'appence, eh, Dad?" George's urgent voice flew in after he had rushed upstairs.

"Jessie!" Jack and Jenny chorused, delighted to see the daughter who hadn't been home for the odd month or three.

Detecting a moistening in Jessie's eye corners as he hugged her, Jack raised his eyebrows at his wife to signal danger and then disappeared into the kitchen, beckoning Florence May to follow. It had always been a prudent idea to leave mother and daughter to sort out difficulties while he sorted out tea and nibbles.

"Ready for your final push towards university, sweet pea?" Jack asked his daughter as they mashed tea and made enough sandwiches to feed a regiment.

His daughter simply stared out of the window in deep thought, not really wanting to reply.

"Florence May?" Jack asked, turning towards her, confused by her unusual reluctance to speak to him. "Hearing failing you? Need to get a doctor's appointment, perhaps?"

"Not sure that I really want to go to university, Daddy Jack," she replied eventually, unusually quietly for her.

"Oh?" he replied, sliding his arm around her shoulders whilst he stirred the teapot. "Any reason why?"

"Not really," she said, resting her head on his chest. "Just a feeling that I won't like it."

"Have you thought about what you might like to do instead?" he asked gently. "You don't have to do anything you don't *want* to do."

"I'll do my best to pass *all* my exams," she replied slowly, "but I need a bit more time to decide where I go from there – and it's probably not university."

"Whatever you decide, sweet pea," he said, "is OK by me. You can, as you know, stay with us for as long as you like. I'll draw up a contract of jobs you'll need to do to—"

They both burst out laughing at Jack's weedy joke as they prepared to take their trays into the lounge.

"And you must promise me you won't tell Daddy Jack!" Jessie urged her mother. "Promise!"

"All right," Jenny promised, concerned at what her daughter had confided in her, wondering which way she was going with this and recalling the last time she'd made such a promise.

"OK, you two cherubs," Jack shouted, backing through the dividing door from the kitchen, clutching a tray full of goodies and followed by Florence May, who started to lay a relaxed and informal table.

"Excellent!" George William gushed, making his grand entrance. "Just the right time."

"Good morning, Jacky-boy," David's cheery voice accosted him as he sidled into an early classroom. "How did Friday go? Have they offered you the earth?"

"Central heating not working today, Old Man?" Jack replied, deciding not to remove his coat in the distinctly parky teaching area.

"Boiler's gone on the blink, so the kids won't be in today," David replied. "Neither will the staff, and we're only staying until noon. One or two things to talk through."

"Having given it much thought over the weekend," Jack said. "Status and salary are too good to turn down and, although it's a bit of a drive, the owner has offered me a package that includes petrol at the school's expense. Consequently, I've accepted, at almost twice what I'm getting now. Start Tuesday 24th April. My notice will go in at the end of this week."

"Snap!" David said with an enormous grin. "I've been asked to start my new school the day before. So, I'll be hanging up my Broughton keys on the same day as you – Tuesday 10th April."

"But I thought you started in September?" Jack said, frowning deeply.

"Changed their minds," David explained. "They want me to start at the beginning of the summer term – 23rd April."

"The remainder of this term is to be our swan song, then," Jack added, his grin tinged with more than a bucket of sadness.

"Do you remember at about this time, goodness knows how many years ago, when we took Lee across to Manchester so she could fly back to Canada?" David asked, a mug of tea warming his hands and his blue lips.

"How could I forget the journey *back*?" Jack replied, unable to contain his mirth. "Our walking into yon Driver's Arms at Apptipply must have been a sight and a half."

"Plus-fours, spats and a tweed jacket – a size too small – didn't quite do it for you, Old Chap," David recalled, beginning to snigger.

"And those huge Oxford bags and Fair-Isle jersey you had on," Jack replied with a hearty guffaw. "I wish I had a photograph to keep for posterity."

"We've done some stuff together, Old Man," David said, his voice reflecting the sadness at their working together no longer from the end of this present term.

"It's true we won't be inhabiting the same working space anymore," Jack added quickly, "but it *doesn't* mean it's the end of our life together."

"How about an early dinner in the Ship," David suggested, "and a shandy or two?"

"Sounds like a plan, that man," Jack agreed. "Pie, peas and the occasional chip wouldn't go amiss, I'm sure."

-o-

Mounds of dirty slushy snow had begun to melt by the roadsides as David and Jack picked their way to the Ship, although a sharp chill lurked around corners that were exposed to a stalking northerly.

The pub was warm but not especially busy, as Monday was habitually quiet after the heaving weekend.

"Pie, peas and chips, gents," Terry the landlord said, setting their 'snack' before them. "Nicking off today then, mate?"

"They can manage wi'out us today, Terry," Jack replied, eagerly eyeing the gravy oozing out of his pie's crust as he tucked his napkin into his shirt collar.

"Boiler's packed in," David added. "Menders will be in by the end of tomorrow. As usual, schools are at the bottom of the list."

"A chirpy little birdy whispers in my ear that neither of you will be here next term," Terry said, with two pints of shandy on a tray. "Is that rayt?"

"Are they pensioning us off, Old Chap?" Jack piped up, turning to David with a mock show of surprise on his face.

"Life of luxury here we come!" David said, winking at Terry as he smiled and touched the side of his nose conspiratorially. "How's Jessie these days? Not seen her for a while."

"I was about to ask you the same question," Jack replied. "We thought they had been at yours."

"Likewise," David said, a wave of concern sweeping his face. "Still, I suppose they are in their twenties and able to make their own decisions."

"Our Jess came home at the weekend for the first time in a while," Jack went on, polishing off the last of his gravy-smothered chips. "She was a little upset, I would say. I left Jenny to sort that one out. When—"

"Strange," David butted in. "Same here. But the only thing I could get out of Irene was—"

"'Women's problems', by any chance?" Jack offered.

"Something going on that we're not party to, do you think?" David wondered, becoming more than a little anxious.

"Too right," Jack replied. "First thing I'll be doing when I get back is asking Jenny to cough."

"Fancy coming back to ours for a coffee?" David offered. "Or tea?"

"I'd better be getting back, thanks all the same, Old Man," Jack said. "Can't be seen to be having too much fun. We *all* need to get together soon, at least before we leave our hallowed ground."

"Deal!" his friend replied as they shook hands before driving away.

–o–

"You're home early, Our Jack," Jenny greeted her husband. "Time off for good behaviour?"

"No heating, no children, no teachers, no point in being there," he replied with a grin. "Any chance—?"

"Just putting the kettle on now," she said making her way to the kitchen.

"And if I'd continued what I was going to say with 'of sex,'" he continued putting his arms round her from behind, "what would you have said?"

"I would have said 'Just putting the kettle on'," she repeated as they laughed together. "But you don't have to take your arms away," she said as he moved away.

"At the last count," he added, "for a cup of tea, as well as a boiling kettle, we need cups and milk and—"

"Biscuits," she added with a grin. "Instead, how about a freshly baked scone with lashings of butter and strawberry jam?"

"Had a long chat with David ower pie, peas and chips in the Ship," he started, having supped his mug of hot Yorkshire Tea. "It seems that their Jessie got home at round about the same time as our Jessie the other day, somewhat … upset."

"Oh yes?" Jenny said slowly, expecting what was coming next. "And?"

"I think you know *what*," he continued, "because David said they hadn't seen *our* Jessie for quite some time, and Jessie Aston was upset, rather like *our* Jess. Guess what Irene said to him when he asked the obvious question? Just what you said to me when I asked," he continued when she didn't reply. "Which was, now that you seem to have forgotten, 'women's problems'. Anything you want to tell me?"

"Not really," Jenny replied deliberately slowly as she continued to stare into the fire.

"OK," he said curtly, annoyed that he had been cut out once again – once about a brother he didn't know she had, and now something amiss with his own daughter. "Tell me stuff I need to know when you either want something from me or when it's convenient, eh? Enough said. I'll remind you the next time you want anything from me." He got up, leaving his half-drunk tea and scone and stomped out of the room.

"Jack!" she shouted as soon as she heard the door open. "Jack, come back!"

The door clicked shut and he was gone.

"Damn!" she muttered. "Kids and … husbands."

She'd regretted what she'd said as soon as she'd said it; perhaps she should have told him. Look where keeping an impossible promise had got her the last time. She had almost lost her husband. Now what?

"Dad not in, Mam?" Florence May's voice brought Jenny back from her thoughts.

"Gone out for a walk, I think," Jenny replied.

"I wish I'd known," Florence May said, "I'd have gone with him. He—" She was interrupted by the front doorbell's urgent insistent warble. "I'll get it," she said, already on her way.

"Hello, Aunt Jenny." A male and female duet brought Jenny out of her daydream once again. "Uncle Jack in? We have one or two things we need advice on."

"I'll put the kettle on," Florence May suggested.

"Give you a hand," Mary offered, following her cousin into the kitchen.

"He just popped out, Joey," Jenny replied. "He shouldn't be long. Anything I can do?"

"Not really, Aunt Jenny," he said, almost dismissively. "A couple of knotty questions. Not being rude, but he's the only one we can trust to give an honest, considered answer without having any axe to grind."

-o-

"Job not going so well at your present work, Joey, I gather?" Jack said, his cold fingers wrapped lovingly around his favourite mug of tea.

"How did you gather that, Uncle Jack?" Joey gasped. "I mean, I know you're a magician dabbling in the occult, but…?"

"Contacts, Joey, owd cock," Jack said, touching the side of his nose and winking. "It's all about *who* you know. So, the problem is…?"

"Too many young people in the company that are older than me," Joey explained, "and I seem to be picking up all the dead-end jobs."

"Solution's plain to me," Jack said. "But it will need a bit of creative thought on your part. You up for that?"

"You bet!" Joey replied, shuffling to the edge of his seat, an eager gleam revisiting his eyes.

"I know that your Uncle Eric is struggling to fulfil his work commitments because there is a shortage of skilled engineers in his neck of the woods," Jack started. "He has his own company, as you know, but what you didn't know is that he's asked me about you on several occasions recently."

"Me?" Joey gasped, more than a little surprised. "But I hardly know him."

"True, and you've your Dad to thank for that omission, I'm afraid," Jack said. "Because Eric and I talk on a daily basis, I know that he would snap your hand off if you wanted to join his company. My George, at seventeen, is already apprenticed to him and Eric is delighted with him."

"I'd love to work for him but isn't it a long way to travel daily?" Joey replied. "I mean, it's Normanton, isn't it?"

"Your dad does it," Jack smirked, "and if he can do it… Anyway, time to be blunt. Can you cope with my bluntness?"

"Have done for the last twenty years or so, Uncle Jack," Joey laughed, "so what's new?"

They all laughed at Joey's honesty as Florence May nipped into the kitchen to make a fresh pot of tea.

"But my suggestion to you would be for you to get a place of your own." Jack advised, "preferably in Normanton. At your age, it's time you were living independently."

"Wow!" Joey gasped. "I like the sound of that. Will you—?"

"Help you?" Jack said. "Too right I will. I still have a lot of contacts in t'owd town. Priority. Are you open to a further suggestion, Joey? A bit way out, maybe, but I'll pay something towards costs for Our George to come with you."

"George?" Jenny said, suddenly waking up to reality. "But he's only seventeen."

"I left home at eighteen," Jack replied dismissively, "and so did you effectively. He can't stay with Eric during the week for ever."

"That would be great, Uncle Jack," Joey butted in. "Can't wait. But how—"

"Leave your accommodation to me, Old Chap," Jack said, grinning as he touched the side of his nose again. "I'm sure I can find you at least a reasonable shed.

"Now then, Our Mary," he went on after a moment's pause to pour a fresh mug. "Our business lady of the year! I think you, my young entrepreneur, need to move out of your family home to stand on your own feet before your ideas and your business can grow."

"How did you know that *that's* what I wanted to talk to you about?" Mary gasped, gobsmacked at what her Uncle Jack had worked out.

"It stands to sense, Our Mary," he went on. "You, in particular, need to be on your own somewhere nearby. Somewhere you can spread out and use that creative genius of yours and not be bothered by fuddy-duddies that are forever asking you to 'clean up your room'. Know what I mean?"

"Of course I do," she said with a giggle. "But how can I do that? I don't know—"

"But *I do*," he replied. "Remember that word 'contacts'? First and foremost, you need somewhere to live that has enough space for you to breathe and to grow your business. Are you anywhere close enough to needing separate premises? You know, purely and simply for work?"

"Not yet, Uncle Jack," she replied, her excitement building.

"Let me know when you are," he offered. "And we need to decide whether you have enough money to buy your own place or to rent."

Mary sat back in her seat, sipped her tea and looked across at her brother who had a similar look on his face – a look of utter excitement mixed with a little fear. Standing on own feet time.

"Think about it all," Jack said finally, "and come back here next weekend. By that time, I will have made enquiries, called in favours, and will have more to tell you. *Then* the next exciting part of your life begins."

Chapter 10

"My God!" Mary said to her brother as they trudged through the slight covering of snow. "How did all that happen?"

"A man called Uncle Jack, that's how," Joey replied. "I don't know about you, but I am so glad he is in our lives – and I am so excited for our future."

"You can say that again," she agreed. "Everything he said makes so much sense. Why didn't *we* think of it before?"

"Because *he's* Jack Ingles," Joey sighed, "and we're not. Why can't Dad show as much interest? It's almost as if Uncle Jack's making up for his brother's inertia and inadequacy."

"He loves us as his own," Mary replied. "That's what it is. He *cares*. It's what *real* dads and uncles do."

"Are we decided, then, that we keep this to ourselves until we have something concrete?" Joey suggested.

"Agreed," she returned. "I don't think Uncle Jack will give a toss if Dad has a go at him. I'm quite sure he will put Dad in his place, big style."

"Can't wait!" Joey chortled, rubbing his hands together.

-o-

"I'm sorry I didn't tell you, Our Jack," Jenny said, cosying up to her husband when they were finally alone.

"About what?" he replied, his matter-of-fact response causing her to frown slightly.

"Forgotten already?" she harrumphed, a little irked by his off-hand response.

"What – that you wouldn't tell me about Jessie's problem?" he said briskly. "No, course not. It's just not important, that's all. If you don't think it's important enough to discuss, then it's not worth getting into bed about."

"Do you know, Jack Ingles," she started with a sigh, "you can be *so* difficult when you get on your high horse. Do you want to know about Jessie or not?"

"It all depends whether or not you *want* to tell me of your own volition, or you need to be coerced," he replied quickly.

"Oo, 'ark at 'im, wi' 'is dictionary in 'is gob!" Jenny mocked, knowing she would never get the better of his innate stubbornness. "I'll tell you anyway."

"Go on then," he urged, flopping on the settee, pulling her close up beside him. "I'm all ears."

"Never mind, my love," she cooed, quick and sharp as a tack. "They're not *that* big." Quarrels and sharp words never lasted long in the Ingles' household.

"Our Jessie had found a young man and started a reasonably stable relationship with him," Jenny began. "David's Jessie had started a relationship with *her* young man. Everything was going well until—"

"I think I know what you are going to say," he interrupted, with a knowing nod and raise of the eyebrows. "The same young man?"

"Can't get anything past you, Our Jack," she sighed, a rueful smile betraying her feelings. "Unbeknown to either of them, he had been playing them both along."

"Anything sexual involved?" he asked directly.

"Jack!" Jenny gasped in surprise at his bluntness. "You

can't ask that! This is your daughter, and you—"

"But I just did," he replied. "Straight question needs a straight answer. Did they have sex?"

"Unfortunately, yes," she agreed. "Both of them."

"I expect our Jessie took appropriate action?" he asked.

"What do you mean?" Jenny puzzled.

"Retribution?" he sighed, impatiently.

"Yes," Jenny replied slowly. "She punched him in the face. Broke his nose."

"Excellent," he said with a grin. "That's my girl. Lesson learned. Where is she now?"

"Back at work, I assume," Jenny replied. "You know what youngsters are like, only around when they need something."

A gentle snick of the front door alerted them that they had visitors. Both heads turned slowly towards the lounge door in anticipation. They knew it would be family because only a key would have made such a quiet opening, and only five keys existed.

"Talk of the devil!" Jack said, a grin growing as Jessie's head peered around the door jamb. "No work today?"

"Day off," Jessie replied as she took off her coat and sat down.

"Me too," Jack said. "Busted boiler at school."

"May I have a cup of coffee, Daddy Jack?" she asked, inclining her head slightly whilst raising her eyebrows in the time-honoured way she had learned from her dad.

"Of course you may," he replied, squeezing his body reluctantly out of his comfortable seat next to his wife. "Jenny?"

"Tea for me please," she said, "and there's—"

"A scone or two in the tin?" he said, smiling his joy at her full baking tin.

"I should have known," she tutted, raising her eyes in supplication to the heavens.

"Did you tell Daddy Jack about … you know?" Jessie asked quietly, once Jack was in the kitchen.

"He knows, Jess," her mother warned her.

"Mother!" Jessie gasped, alarmed. "You promised."

"I didn't tell him, Jessie," Jenny assured her daughter. "You should have known he would work it out. He's no fool, you know. He won't let on, but you might as well tell him."

"Coffee and tea and freshly buttered scones, mi ladies," Jack's cheery voice followed the tray he so deliberately laid on the coffee table.

"Not fresh, dear man," Jenny smiled. "I made them yesterday."

"I know," he replied, "but they *are* freshly buttered, as I said."

"Smart arse," Jenny muttered almost inaudibly.

"You know that I was upset the other day, Dad," Jessie started, once tea and coffee and scones were on their way down. "I should have—"

"I know about it, Jess," Jack interrupted. "Worked it out. How many years have I known you? It was quite simple really, so there's no need—"

"He's threatening to sue me for assault," she blurted out, a tear making its way slowly down her cheek.

"Is he local?" Jack asked pointedly.

"You can't go visiting," Jenny said. "I know you, Jack. You'll 'have words', and you can't … *do* … that."

"There are other ways and means," he explained, his forefinger touching the side of his nose. "I simply need a name. If you won't give it, end of story and you will have to suffer the consequences."

"Simon Ridley," Jessie muttered reluctantly. "He's a twenty-three-year-old teacher in Leeds."

"That's all I need," Jack replied, a triumphant grin covering his face. "Just leave it to me. You have no need to worry, my sweet pea."

"I love you, Daddy Jack, my champion," Jessie sighed, throwing her arms around his neck. "Why is it you always sort out our problems and know the right things to say?"

"It's what dads were invented for," Jack answered with a sage nod. "My family has to be safe and secure, otherwise I wouldn't be doing my job properly and you would be looking for another dad."

-o-

"Uncle Jack?" Mary asked, a slightly puzzled look on her face that Saturday morning. "Where are you taking me and why did you need my business plan?"

"Can't I take my favourite niece out for a Saturday morning coffee once in a while?" he said, trying to suppress a sheepish grin.

"But I'm your *only* niece – and you don't *like* coffee," she explained, bursting into a fit of giggles.

"You found me out at last!" he exclaimed, joining in with her mirth as he pulled up outside a line of outlets across the road from green fields and a magnificent oak wood. "I just wanted to show you something and then speak to a friend of mine."

Getting out of the car, he ushered her across to some empty commercial premises. He produced a key and began to open the door.

"What's this, Uncle?" Mary asked slowly, a little perplexed. "This isn't a coffee shop."

"Oh, didn't I tell you?" he chuckled, a wicked gleam in his eyes. "This is the sort of outlet you need for your business. It has this space and another work room and kitchen area behind. But the most exciting thing is that upstairs … there is a self-contained flat. The whole building is owned by a friend of mine who is a very well-respected businessman, and who is just walking up to the door round about … now."

"Mary," the newcomer announced offering his hand. "My name's Alan, Alan Cliff. Jack has told me a lot of exciting stuff about you, so I wanted to meet you."

Mary looked round at her uncle, her mouth open and a look of shock on her face.

"Your business idea sounds intriguing and very exciting, and I think I may be able to help you along with your venture," Alan Cliff went on. "Oh, by the way, I think you'll like the one-bedroomed flat that comes with the premises."

"But how—?" Mary stammered, overcome with what her Uncle Jack had managed to arrange in the few short days since they'd last spoken.

"If you'll allow me to take a copy of your business ideas and plans," Alan suggested, "and you take this envelope, which contains all the details of the premises and their rental, I'll phone you in a day or two, hopefully to finalise. I think you'll see that your business, even now, is well able to sustain your move."

"Thanks a lot, Alan," Jack said to his friend as they shook hands and Alan turned to leave. "I owe you. You all right, Mary?" he asked, turning towards his niece.

"I'm gobsmackingly shocked, Uncle Jack," she said in a hoarse whisper, flinging her arms around his neck. "You've done all this … for me? I don't know what to say."

"Then say nothing for now," he said, sliding his arm around her shoulders. "Because, if you look out of the window, you'll see somebody you know."

"Joey?" she said, puzzled to see him.

"Ey up, you two!" Joey shouted. "What are you doing here, Mary?"

"Looking at my new premises and … my new flat, upstairs," she replied with a grin.

"Enough time to see that later," Jack interrupted, seeing the very puzzled look invading Joey's face. "But for now, coffee and a Danish pastry at Betty's around the corner."

"I'll get these, Uncle Jack," Joey offered as they sat down in the café after ordering.

"No, you won't," Jack replied. "They're already paid for. Anyway, as I promised you both the other day, I've been sorting out options for your futures. Mary's sorted – she'll tell you later, Our Joey – and now for you. I've spoken about you to my brother, Eric, and he's made enquires of his own. The upshot is that he would love to talk to you with a view to bringing you into his engineering company. He asked if you'd like to take George William across with you on Monday to his office in Normanton to talk things over."

"Wow!" Joey whistled softly through his semi-clenched teeth. He sat back on his chair, overcome with surprise at the speed with which his uncle had sorted stuff out – true to his word.

"And that's not all," Jack went on, chomping into his Danish. "I've called in another favour from a good friend called Bernard Peters, who owns several rental terraced houses overlooking the bottom of Haw Hill Park in Normanton. They're all very well-maintained, so there'd be nothing to do to them. He's offered you an empty one – two-bedroomed with an internal bathroom – so you'd be close to your work should you decide to take the job I'm convinced Eric will be offering you."

"The only thing I would love to ask, Uncle Jack," Joey gabbled, stunned almost into silence, "is will I be able to afford it?"

"If you noticed," Jack replied, "I said the house on offer has two bedrooms. Consequently, as Our George will be working with you on his apprenticeship for another year or two, I propose that he lives there with you during the week.

To allow that to happen, I will pay his half of the weekly rent and food. How does that sound?"

"That sounds out of this world, Uncle Jack," Joey said, once he had overcome the shock that somebody had given him such a wonderful opportunity. "I don't really know what to say."

"All I want you both to do is to think long and hard about what these offers could do for you," Jack explained. "No strings, no conditions – just think things over and arrive at a decision that suits *you*. If you do decide, Joey, let me know and I'll put things in motion with Bernard Peters. But first give your Uncle Eric a ring. He's dying to see you. As far as you're concerned, Our Mary, Alan Cliff will phone you in a day or two."

Brother and sister sat looking at each other while they drank coffee and munched Danish pastries, unable to believe that someone had not only taken an interest in their future but had carried through on the promises he'd made. No-one else had *ever* done that before.

"Well," Jack said, when he'd finished his cup of Columbian, "I'm off now. Got stuff to do for school next week. Want a lift back? I need a cup of Yorkshire Tea to tek off the taste of this coffee muckment."

"No thanks, Uncle Jack," Mary said, laughing at the face he pulled. "I think we'll stay a while longer and have another cup of coffee. If that's all right with you."

"Thank you for doing all this," they both said as they hugged him. "You are definitely our favourite *full* uncle."

"And I'm—"Jack started to reply.

"The only one we've got!" they chorused, laughing excitedly.

-o-

"My God!" Joey gasped, once his uncle had gone. "Do you realise what he has just done for us?"

"Only laid a positive path for our possible futures directly beneath our feet," Mary replied, almost in tears. "Why would he want to do that?"

"It's up to us to make sure we make his sensible suggestions work," Joey insisted. "For me, if all goes well in discussions with Uncle Eric, I will be moving to Normanton."

"I won't be moving to Normanton," Mary laughed, "but hopefully this here will be my new home and business very soon."

"I think," Joey suggested, "we owe it to Uncle Jack to have another coffee and to propose a toast to him. And I think we need to keep things to ourselves until it's all a *fait accompli*. You know what ructions it will cause with Dad if we don't."

"Ey up! Listen to you!" she whooped. "Since when did you learn how to speak French? You'll be taking your skills abroad next."

"No fear!" he replied. "It's far enough to take them to the old town."

They laughed that palpitating, excited laugh that only those experiencing such emotion would understand. They set off home slowly, each in their own world of promise, trying to second-guess when they would know for sure if Uncle Jack's labours would come to fruition and what else he might have in mind.

He was a dark horse was that one!

Chapter 11

“I take it that *this* is your doing then, Jack?” William harrumphed sharply.

“What is … '*this*', then, Bro?” Jack replied with a defiant smile.

“The fact that two of my children are moving out,” his brother said accusingly.

“And why shouldn't they move out?” Jack came back at him quickly. “Do they need your permission?”

“No, but they might be wanting … money,” William replied, parsimonious to the last.

“How do you arrive at that assumption?” Jack started to spring his trap on the poor unsuspecting sap that was his hapless brother, much to the amusement of Jenny and Val who were sitting not three feet from this assault. “Joey is going to a well-paid job with *our* brother's successful company, getting his own living space into the bargain. Our very smart Mary has so much cash from her successful business that I can see her offering *you* a loan at some stage in the future. No, Old Man, neither will be asking you for a hand-out any time soon.”

“They ought to be at home with us,” William said, trying valiantly to maintain a coherent argument with his brother, “until they get on their feet.”

“And how is staying with you going to 'put them on

their feet', William?" Jack asked, drawing his noose even tighter around his brother's neck. "You've always abdicated responsibility for their growing up in a difficult world."

"I beg your—" William blustered.

"You've never offered them either advice *or* guidance," Jack went on, sweeping his brother's weak arguments aside. "Why do you think they've always come to me when they needed help? Do I need to give you some of the many examples floating around in this useless brain of mine?

"Rhetorical question for you … Bro," Jack went on after a moment's silence to allow his brother to catch his breath. "When did *you* leave home to stand on *your* own two feet? Eighteen? That age for them has disappeared into the mists of memory, Old Chap. No matter what you say, they will both succeed – and if they need a hand at any time, *I* will always be there. Pity it wasn't *you*, their dad, they felt they could turn to. Cup of tea, Val?"

"Yes please, Jack," Val replied, trying hard to cover the amused pity she felt for her husband's moral destruction at the hands of his much wiser little brother. "And any chance of one of those gorgeous buttered scones that my clever sister bakes?"

"Your wish is my command, O beautiful and bounteous one! William? Jenny?" Jack added with a flourish.

"I'll come and give you a hand," Jenny offered, following him to the kitchen.

"You walked right into that one," Val said pointedly, once she and William were alone. "Will you never learn not to cross swords with your brother? He *always* has the ammunition to back up his arguments because he thinks things through long before he opens his mouth. And I have to say that I totally agree with him."

William rose from his usual chair. He accidentally stubbed his toe on the hearth corner, knocking over the small oak occasional table next to it before he hopped out of the room, trying to balance on one foot whilst holding the other. The outside door slammed shut in his wake.

"No tea and scones for brother, then," Jack said as he brought the tray into the lounge. "Something wrong with your scones, Jenny? Never mind. There's them on us 'ere as'll see 'em off in no time."

They all laughed at Jack's antics and dialect – from t'time spent wi' 'is Granddad Jud, no doubt.

"You have my total support, Jack," Val mumbled through a mouthful of home-baked buttered scone.

"They'll both need looking in on periodically, in a surreptitious sort of a way," Jack advised, "to show interest and give praise – particularly Mary on her own. I trust Eric implicitly to give Joey a fair crack. *He's* old enough to keep an eye on our George William, as they'll be billeted together. For the most part, they need to be left alone. They'll ask when they need advice or help. We're onny an hour away."

"Thank God they've got you," Val added, kissing and hugging him when she got up. "And, now I must away either to massage my husband's bruised ego or to remind him of the kicking you just gave him."

-o-

"That was some performance, Our Jack," Jenny said, once her sister had left, "but well-deserved, I'm afraid."

"I don't give a cat's about *his* sensibilities," he replied quietly. "I simply want two talented young people not to miss any opportunities for lack of a bit of support and a helping hand."

"Do you think our George will be all right," she said, "living away from home, I mean?"

"He's been living away from home for quite some

time now, Our Jen," Jack said. "So why should living in a house overlooking a lovely park with an adult I trust be any different? I *will* keep an eye, don't worry on that score, and—"

The slightest click of a key disturbing the tumblers in the Yale lock on the front door stopped Jack in mid-speech. He had been paranoid about security all his adult life and could detect and recognise any noise in his house that wasn't normal.

Jessie's cheery face popped around the door. "It's only me," she said quietly, not wishing to disturb.

"Hello 'only me'," Jack replied, his usual cheerful greeting bringing a brief smile to her face. He noticed she was still worried. He got up and drew her to him. "Would you like some good news or some even better news?"

"Go on then," she replied with a little nervous giggle, knowing there was likely to be only one piece of news anyway.

"Simon Ridley will not be causing you any problems, ever," he said.

"But Daddy Jack, how can you be so sure?" she replied, a nervous twitching frown showing she was still upset.

"I found out that a very good friend of mine is his head teacher," Jack explained, "and he has had a 'word' with him about his behaviour, because apparently he has done this sort of thing before – several times. My friend warned him it wouldn't be tolerated. He let him know that if he continued with any action against you, his job would be on the line and he would find himself out of teaching – permanently. Besides, he would become a laughing stock. Let's face it, which young man would want it known that a young, frail woman had broken his nose with one punch?"

"Not so much of the 'frail', if you don't mind, Daddy Jack, Mr Fixer!" Jessie laughed, brightening up at last. "I knew I could rely on you. Now, where's that cup of tea?"

"So that situation doesn't happen again," Jack offered, suppressing a smile and putting on his most serious face, "would you like me to 'vet' your prospective young men in future?"

"I don't think so, Daddy Jack!" she replied forcefully with a laugh. "I think I'll be able to manage next time – if there's going to be a next time. Tea? Would you like a hand? I know you're getting on a bit and might forget again before you reach the kitchen."

"On my way," he said, laughing heartily at her funny. "On my way."

"Good news and not so good news, I think, Mam," Jessie whispered once Jack was out of the room.

"Good news first, then?" Jenny asked.

"I've been offered a new job," Jessie replied quietly.

"Well done," Jenny said. "Better status? More money?"

"Both," she replied.

"And dare I ask you about the bad news?" her mother asked tentatively, not really wanting to know.

"It's abroad, isn't it?" Jack butted in, carrying a tray of tea and buns from the kitchen.

"How do you make that out?" Jenny gasped. "The world isn't so small that you can predict that with any accuracy."

"The States, I should imagine," he went on, pouring the tea. "Probably—"

"New York," Jessie said, filling in the gap. "I've got a new job in New York."

"One you couldn't afford to miss?" he asked, pragmatic to the last.

"I've given up wondering how you do that, Daddy Jack," Jessie sighed. "You really do know—"

"Not everything, my sweet pea," he replied. "Just a process of deduction, that's all. It's the Sherlock Holmes process of deduction."

"Sherlock—?" Jenny said.

"When you've eliminated all the possibles, whatever is left, no matter how improbable, has to be the answer," Jessie replied. "Or something like that."

"Elementary, my dear Ingles," Jack said, with a triumphant grin.

"How did you know that?" Jenny asked, astounded at her daughter's knowledge.

"I didn't just listen to children's fairy stories on Daddy Jack's lap when I was five, you know, Mam," Jessie replied with a toss of her hair. "I know all about *The Study in Scarlet* et al."

"Staying over, love?" Jenny suggested, more in hope than certainty.

-o-

"Well, Jack-boy," David said as they walked through the staffroom. "Not long to go now."

"One week and four days," Jack replied with a sigh. "Nine school days, and then…"

"The end of an era," David said quietly, "but one that has seen massive changes in this school and the area it serves."

"I hope we're not having a do next week," Jack harrumphed, "where dignitaries from far and wide are dragged in to trot out their insincere platitudes about how wonderful we have been, and—"

"Don't worry, Jack," David laughed. "The Queen has another engagement she can't cancel, but she sends her regards and best wishes."

They both laughed as they walked into his office for their last-but-one early-Monday chat.

"How's your Jessie?" David asked as they sat down with

steaming mugs.

"Strange you should bring that up," Jack replied with a warm smile. "You took the words right out of my mouth. You know about the business with the young teacher, Simon Ridley?"

"Yes," his friend added, "she told me eventually, and a little bird told me someone who is not a million miles away sorted him out, for one reason or another."

Jack explained the reason for his intervention and David grinned his approval at Jessie's response. "Good girl!" he added. "He deserved it. A punch in the nose is definitely much more of a deterrent than a slap across the face. How are your brother's children these days?"

Jack's brief explanation faded into the background shushing noise of teachers heading into the staffroom for a stiff mug of tea or coffee to fortify them against another busy Monday's onslaught. Mixed with the occasional clacking and hissing escaping from the kitchens, it heralded the beginning of the penultimate week of the spring term. Soon it would be summer!

"Bernard Peters?" David's voice urged its way back into reality. "Don't think I've heard *that* name before."

"Getting on a bit now, but I believe he was the original Casey Jones," Jack began. "You know the last engine driver in the earlier days of modern steam trains. These were the sorts of engines that had a small open cab behind a huge cylindrical boiler where the steam engine was fired and fed by a stoker who kept the coals burning at an extremely high temperature to generate the steam needed to keep the wheel pistons driving."

"Wow," David said, a soft whistle through his teeth showing his awe. "Never ever seen a steam engine up close."

"You've never lived, Old Chap," Jack replied. "Bernard once told me about the times he used to drive an engine pulling goods wagons. When they got out into the countryside on a particular run, he would stop the engine close to where he knew a huge patch of mushrooms grew. He'd send his stoker off hot foot across the field to gather as many mushrooms as possible and bring them back for breakfast."

"Breakfast? On a goods train?" David said, a disbelieving look in his sceptical eyes.

"Aye," Jack replied, a laugh threatening to burst out. "Then they'd set off again and Bernard would cook mushrooms and an egg or two in a liberal smattering of engine oil on the stoker's coal shovel in t'fire box."

"Is that true?" David scoffed, disbelievingly. "Only I know you of old, Jack Ingles."

"Yes, it is, *mon capitaine*," Jack replied. "I didn't believe it at first when he told me, but I know Bernard doesn't fib."

"I'm going to miss all this frivolity, you know, my old friend," David said quietly, after a moment or two of silence.

"Ey up, Old Man," Jack urged, "don't forget tha's family. We will just have to compensate by having more family get-togethers – or is it gets-together?"

"You and your precise language, eh?" David said, grinning. Nobody would ever appreciate Jack's professional support like *he* did. He knew that it would be unlikely he would be fortunate enough to find someone else he could rely on to be there, to stand up and be counted without having to be asked whenever problems arose.

He was a one-off, was Our Jack. Fractured the proverbial mould when he joined the world.

Chapter 12

"Are you sure you wouldn't rather *stay* at this 'ere school?" Jenny said about his very early morning start. His five o'clock get up didn't fill her with awe.

"How many times have we not slept in the same bed since we've been together?" he replied.

"None," she said with an appreciative smile.

"Then I've no intention of starting now," he answered her. "The only time I would stay in yon school would be if we *both* stayed there. Quick breakfast, then I'll have to be off."

"Looking forward to it, Our Jack?" Jenny asked tentatively.

"I've no idea what to expect," he replied through a slice of toast and a mug of his favourite. "Today's the day before the lads come back after Easter, so it should be … interesting."

She recognised that 'I'll give it the benefit of the doubt' look on his face. He wasn't prepared to either express an opinion or to damn without testing the water first. T'proof in t'pudden, as his Granddad Jud allus used to say.

"Take care," she whispered as they embraced before he sought the car. "And come back safely."

"You too," he replied, hanging on to their last few moments before his leap into the unknown. "Particularly on the first day in your new venture. I'm sure you'll love it."

Outside his comfort zone and his known educational universe, Jack had serious reservations entering the busy motorway on his way west. Fortunately, he had given himself ample time to reach his journey's end, but would he need to set off this early every day? Doubts began to crowd his usually clear and decisive mind. Was his successful and comfortable life about to change?

"Stop ower-thinking it, daft bugger," he muttered, when he reached the bottom of Pexwood Road in Todmorden. "Ey up?"

The road surface had become pitted and worn following the vicious floods and snowfalls this area of the West Riding historically gloried in. Significant care was needed if Jack wanted to guard his tyres and wheel rims from damage.

Now the snow had disappeared, faint glimmers of a belated spring were starting to push through in gardens and fields, bringing joy to the heart and uplifting the spirit. However, Jack wasn't sure how the onset of spring was about to help him now.

Although the school building was crenellated, it bore no relation to its medieval forebears, and had been built in the late-nineteenth century by some local industrial grandee with delusions of grandeur. It was certainly an impressive sight – set in twenty or so acres with wonderful views on a sunny day across the Calder Valley to the crags beyond.

"Well, here goes," he muttered to himself, as he shouldered his way through huge, heavy, oak double doors that had seen better days.

At some time in its illustrious life, the atrium had been a truly awesome and breath-taking place, the central feature of which was a U-shaped stairway leading to the one upper floor. Its once ornate wide marble treads and intricately carved balustrades now betrayed years of use and abuse by countless cohorts of emotionally and behaviourally disturbed adolescent boys.

"Jack—" he announced as the secretary opened the door to her long, narrow office.

"Ingles?" she interrupted with a smile. "Come in. I'll let Mr Buckby know you're here."

Mrs Barber was a good-looking lady of about Jack's age, with a full figure and a ready, attractive smile. He could tell she was an organised and efficient secretary because her room was tidy and all her shelves were straight, with identical box files in both alphabetical and date order. Her well-used desk was clear, save for a huge mechanical typewriter that was probably new thirty years before.

"Now then, Chief," Mr Buckby's bluff Yorkshire voice greeted Jack when he entered the office. "Sit thissen down and we can have a chinwag. Then I'll show thi around and introduce thi to t'teaching staff."

Designed as a late-Victorian drawing room in the home of a rich industrialist, this 'office' was enormous. It had views through stone-mullioned windows to what would once have been manicured and geometrically designed gardens that stretched almost out of sight. Now time and neglect had ravaged those beautiful havens of nature! All that could be seen was rampant couch grass and dense, uncontrolled brambles. An ornamental pond, where once luxuriated mature Koi carp, lay under all that undergrowth – somewhere.

One very large oak desk with a faded green-leather inlaid top dominated an otherwise empty room, save for a matching swivel chair and an outdated locked cupboard with a large Edwardian BENT STEEL safe close by – and *that* had also seen better days.

"As you can no doubt see," the gaffer started, once

they were seated by the desk, "no lads in today. They'll start arriving tomorrow afternoon, about four o'clock. I've asked—"

A knock on the door stopped him mid-flow and a short, gruff-voiced, middle-aged man stepped over the threshold.

"Mr Dyer's here to show you around and tell you how we go about things hereabouts. Mr Dyer?"

"Mr Buckby," the man replied in a deep Barrow-in-Furness accent, beckoning Jack to follow when he had turned to the door. "Follow me, please," he said, his rough voice dragging along the worn corridor's once-beautiful marble surface, where here and there broken and gouged areas had been filled with smooth-surfaced concrete, giving that depressingly shabby-chic effect it was never meant to have.

Although he was used to the dilapidated appearance of most ageing schools because of a lack of supporting funding, Jack was taken aback at what he saw during this short walk towards the education end of the building. "Hmm," he muttered as they reached the outer enclosed courtyard.

"Surprised at what you see?" Mr Dyer asked, a knowing smile growing. "Or shocked at what you *don't* see? The name's Mick, by the way."

"Well, Mick," Jack replied slowly. "Yes and no. I've seen a lot of this sort of decrepitude in state schools, but never expected to witness it here in the independent sector where folks are supposed to have a licence to print money. Aren't they?"

"Money's coming in all right," Mick agreed, "but buggers like yon in t'office, are loath to spend it."

"Met that before as well," Jack said, with a disappointed sigh.

"Any road," Mick said finally, "I'll leave you to t'teachers. They'll introduce their sens. I've some business to attend to. I'm not supposed to be on duty until five tomorrow. See you." With that, he turned on his heels and fair sprinted around the back end of the building to his house amidst the – at the moment – empty dormitories.

"I know you," a deep male voice accosted Jack, dragging him back to reality.

"And I know you, too," Jack replied, spinning around to greet the newcomer. "You're Peter Shackleton from Merton Grange Middle School. Woodwork and Metalwork, wasn't it?"

"Technical Science, they called it," Peter replied with a derisory laugh as they shook hands. "Your description will do fine.

"Irvine! Brian! John!" he turned and yelled after a moment or two's quiet. "Irvine Wright, Brian Jenson and John Hodgson, I'd like you to meet Jack Ingles, the straightest talking bad-ass *I've* ever met."

"An accolade coming from you, Pete," Jack replied with a nod. "So, what are we going to do for the rest of the day now I've seen everything? Sit with our feet up drinking tea and swapping anecdotes?"

"I'll just show you your office in the education block," John added as the others smiled at Jack's directness, "and then it will be time for home."

"What time will the lads be in tomorrow?" Jack asked, giving a curt nod at the office, looking around it briefly before closing the door and wandering back to his car.

"They'll start arriving in dribs and drabs at any time from around eleven," John replied. "Be warned, too, that Mr Buckby won't want you teaching… He'll—"

"Then what will he be paying me for?" Jack harrumphed. "Making the tea? Good luck with that one. I'm a trained teacher first and foremost, and an organiser and administrator a distant second. As no doubt I will be responsible for the timetable, I'll be putting myself both on the teaching timetable, on cover for absentees and on playground and lunch duty."

"He won't like that at all," John said with a welcome raising of the eyebrows. "But I suspect the teachers *will*."

"Then Mr Buckby will have to lump it," Jack replied with a defiant grin once he had opened his car door. "See you tomorrow bright and early, John."

-o-

"I'm not sure, Our Jack," Jenny sighed as they sat with their afternoon cup of Yorkshire Tea.

"I'm not sure either, Our Jenny," Jack grinned in response as he explained what would be expected from him. "Bit of a Mickey Mouse affair really, if you ask me. Not sure I will last very long there. Not convinced, either, that *it* will survive as a thriving entity. You?"

"I'm not sure I will be able to stand either the boredom in some classes, or the response from some teachers to my being there," she explained.

"If they resent your presence with the common sense *you* bring," he replied with a sneer, "then they don't deserve you. Teachers can be arseholes when it comes to embracing change, I'm afraid. Seen a lot of bigotry in the schools I've served in. Can't do wi' it missen. You stick at it, Our Lass, and ignore what they have to say."

"Oh, it's not what they say I can't do with," she explained, "because they don't say anything. It's what goes on when I'm not there to answer back."

"As far as I am aware," Jack went on, "there are only twenty-five lads in the school designed to take fifty. Now that's got to be a concern on two counts – firstly, maintaining a reasonable level of educational and care cover, and secondly, how long unsustained cover can last.

"Does that mean you might be out of a job?" she asked, a serious depth of worry darkening her face.

"I honestly don't know," he told her quietly, now beginning to regret his rash move away from relative security in Leeds. "It shouldn't, but I don't trust this man. You see, the secretary told me in confidence that twenty-five referrals for places in this school arrived recently, seeking firm placements for twenty-five pupils. If the owner were to accept them, the school would be full, and everybody's job would be secure. The worrying thing, however, was that she warned me that he'd sworn her to secrecy about those referrals and he had locked them away."

"What's going on then, Our Jack?" Jenny asked, a concerned edge to her question. "Does he want to close the school and—"

"Sell up?" Jack interrupted, eyebrows raised and head tilted with his usual quizzical expression. "You can bet your bottom dollar I'll be asking him tomorrow."

"It looks like we need a serious re-think," she answered, mind leapfrogging back to the days they had nothing. "Belt-tightening time, perhaps?"

"If the worst came to the worst, I could always sell mi body," he replied with a chuckle.

"And what would you do when people demanded their money back?" she quipped, drawing a great guffaw out of him.

-o-

"I'd like you to meet Mike Gore," Ivan Buckby growled at Jack in a voice that was almost close to friendly. "He's our adviser."

"Now, Boss? Or when we've got the lads in?" Jack asked,

unsure of procedure and protocol.

"Now's as good a time as any," Buckby replied. "T'lads won't be in completely until late afternoon. It's up to t'care staff to amuse 'em today."

"Meeting Room One, then?" Mike Gore suggested briskly.

"Aye, rayt," Buckby agreed. "I'll get Maureen to bring you some coffee and cakes. All rayt?"

"Yes, Mr Buckby," the adviser said, in his clipped officiously official tone, leading Jack out to Meeting Room One, which turned out to be aptly named – big enough for only one person and the only one of its kind.

They squeezed in and sat, one either side of a small yellow Formica-topped table that had seen better days and would have been more comfortably placed in a kitchen.

"The one driving force you will have noticed about Ivan Buckby, no doubt, Jack – I can call you Jack? – is that he doesn't believe in extravagance or ostentation," Mike Gore observed. "Everything here has either seen better days or will have been acquired at minimal cost."

"I had rather noticed," Jack said, a smile spreading. "Still, there's not much wrong with that philosophy as long as things are fit for purpose."

"Very true," Mike agreed. "But quality will show education authorities that here's the place they would have no qualms about paying £20,000 per year for each child placed. It's the difference between a full school and a failing school."

"Wow!" Jack whistled silently through his teeth. "I've got my work cut out, then."

"Very true," his companion replied. "And to help you a little, because there is no educational documentation here – one of the reasons this establishment almost failed its HMI inspection recently—"

"Woa! Now hang on a bit," Jack butted in, an incredulous gasp escaping. "Nearly failed? I wasn't told that."

"Well, that doesn't surprise me," Mike harrumphed, a rueful smile hovering. "Would you have come had you known beforehand?"

"Possibly not, but—" Jack answered, with a disbelieving shrug of his shoulders.

"Then that's why he didn't tell you," Mike replied. "Even he, dour non-professional Yorkshireman that he is, could recognise your enviable qualities and qualifications."

"Flattering though all that bullshit might be," Jack pointed out bluntly, "it was dishonest of him – and you, by association – not to tell me. You never know, it might have been one of the things to draw me in."

"You're honest, I've got to give you that," Mike replied with a laugh. "So, what are you going to do?"

"What do *you* think, Mike Gore, Special Education Adviser man?" Jack responded sharply. "I'm going to turn things around here – if the boss man will allow it."

"I wasn't sure if that would be your answer," Mike said, happy at what he had heard, "but I'm glad, otherwise I'm sure the place will close. I think you'll do a great job and you will have my total support."

"I think I'm going to need it," Jack replied, "particularly with Mr Buckby."

"You will need this," the adviser continued, passing Jack a bulky brown envelope. "It's a copy of my Local Authority's special education policy for residential EBD schooling. It's been well-received by the national inspectorate. I would suggest you could do worse than to 'consult' and use it as the basis for the school's policy. You'll need it very soon, as HMI *will* be back in the very near future."

"No pressure then," Jack muttered as they left Meeting Room One and Mike Gore headed for his expensive car.

It was obvious where he got the money to pay for *that* one.

-o-

The education office where Jack was supposed to be based was cold and smelled of damp. The only window was small and north-facing, so sunlight never ventured beyond the outside sill. It was the most uninviting tiny room he had ever set foot in, and he was convinced that it would rarely experience his footfall in the time he had in this organisation. He wasn't an office person to be shut away from all the action, unlike his predecessor Mr Hamish McDoogal apparently.

McDoogal wasn't a teacher. Never had been; didn't ever want to be. He was an administrator and enjoyed 'arranging and sorting out'. Might as well have organised the flowers at the local church for the good he had done. For the life of him, Jack couldn't understand how a non-teacher could know teaching well enough to become a Head of Education. He could only think that it was a matter of financial expediency on the owner's part.

Mr Hamish McDoogal's favourite saying? "Ar much, Chief?"

Enough said.

Chapter 13

"And the winner of this week's poetry competition is," Jack's booming, enthusiastic voice during morning assembly in the tiny hall cut in, "Mark Stembridge. So, he gets to wear the Bard's Crown for the second week in a row. Mark?"

A small wave of applause broke out from the gathering as a slim fifteen-year-old made his way to the front, a slight swagger of pride helping him along. A smile of satisfaction decorated his face as he received his crown, his certificate and an envelope containing a winner's card and extra pocket money.

"I've got to hand it to you, Jack," Irvine Wright said, once the lads had dispersed to their respective classes for the first session of the day, "I thought this Poet of the Week competition would fly like a fat wingless duck. I never had young Mark down as a sensitive poet because the only thing he was ever good at was absconding. Now where are we? Second week in July and only one sneaking off to London. I can only guess at what funded *that* escapade. Came back when t'funds dried up, I suppose."

"You're an incorrigible cynic, Irvine Wright, but I like you," Jack said, a satisfied smile growing as he slapped him on the shoulders, Dick Emery style. "All of these lads have a back story, I know, but there's always 'something' lurking in there that needs teasing out. Just a certain small piece of the jigsaw that has to be eased into place to complete the overall picture."

"Bloody 'ell!" Irvine gasped. "Tha can't 'alf talk, Jack lad."

"Part of the job, Old Chap," Jack replied with a grin.

"Nay," Irvine said, "wi'out tekin' a breath or seeming to think? That's a skill *I'll* never master."

"Wi'out folks like thee, Irvine, mi owd cock," Jack replied seriously, "t'lads in places like this'd never stand a cat in 'ell's chance. Tha's giving 'em a crack at reality, a skill that can't be taught by t'likes o' me. I'm good at spouting hot air and organising around it. Thy's good at turning yon hot air into solid reality – thee and folk like Peter Shackleton over yonder."

"Never thought on it in those terms," Irvine replied, scratching his head as a grin forced its way through. "Like I said, tha can talk but t'difference between thee and others like thee? *Thy* talks sense."

"I'll tek that as a compliment, Irvine," Jack laughed. "But now, if you'll excuse me, I need to try to pick Ivan Buckby's pocket."

"Good luck wi' that one," Irvine replied. "Best think on a good diversionary tactic before thy enters yon holy of holies. He doesn't tek kindly to folks asking him for money and it nigh on gives him apoplexy to shell it out."

"Two questions you'll always have thrown at you when seeking to filch his cash," Peter Shackleton added when he had joined the group. "One, what's it for?"

"And the other?" Jack asked after a moment's pause.

"Ar much, Chief?" his companions chorused, guffawing, putting as much feigned pained expression into the question as they could muster.

-o-

"'Ow much, Chief?" Mr Buckby gasped, eyes almost popping out of his head at the thought of relinquishing even one of the pound notes he had built such a close relationship with over the years. "Let me think on it for a while and see if'n we can afford it. Is it really necessary?"

"Just bear in mind, Mr Buckby," Jack warned, "that HMI *will* fail the school if a proportionate level of support for its organic development is missing and they don't see the mechanisms in place to encourage the lads' realistic social, intellectual and personal growth. Unfortunately, those necessary elements are woefully inadequate here."

"Tell it as you see it, eh Jack?" Ivan growled.

"What did you expect?" Jack harrumphed. "A sycophantic arse-licker? I'm a Yorkshireman, so you're never going to get that. Now, here's another home truth. If you don't put into place the suggestions I make, yon school *will* close within the year!"

"Bloody 'ell!" Buckby gasped. "Don't soften the punch, will yer!"

"I know these inspectors," Jack replied quickly, to drive home his initiative. "In fact, *I've* been inspected by at least one of them before, and *he* is thorough. No stone unturned and all that sort of stuff."

"How much, then?" Buckby asked, taking Jack by surprise.

"How much what?" he replied.

"Does tha need for t'purchase," the boss went on, "o' yon books?"

"I can order and ask for an invoice," Jack suggested, his explanation beginning slowly to excite his boss's attention. "That will mean you don't have to pay until thirty days later."

"Bloody 'ell!" Buckby gasped. "I like t'sound o' that."

"You still have to pay," Jack advised with a grin, "but not straight away. It's a newer, better way to settle."

"Gerron wi' it then," Buckby urged, "but tha'd best keep track on t'order."

"Been doing this sort of ordering for years," Jack said, "so you've no need to get into bed about it."

A loud banging at the office door urged Buckby to attend to the clamour. "What the…!" he growled. The large – but limp – body of one of the new thirteen-year-old lads was prevented from collapsing by two burly care workers, his seriously bloodied face only hinting at what might have happened.

"New lad, Mr Buckby," the tall, bearded care worker explained, "by the name of Keith Henson."

"Why the blood?" the owner of the school asked.

"It's a new game," the deep raspy voice of the short, stout worker continued the explanation. "They stand the unsuspecting sap with his back firmly against the wall."

"They tell him to breathe in deeply," his mate continued, "and to hold his breath and close his eyes."

"Several of them press very heavily on his chest," the tall bearded care worker added, "which causes the victim to hyperventilate and lose consciousness."

"Which, in turn," his mate added, "causes him to fall flat on his face. Hence the broken nose and significant gravel-caused lacerations to his face and head."

"Better get him to hospital then," Buckby said, "and—"

"Ambulance is on its way," Tall Beardy replied. "The nurse has been told to be prepared for when he returns."

"Nurse finishes tomorrow," Buckby replied.

"Her replacement, then?" Shorty Rotund asked.

"There won't be one," Buckby said with finality.

"We'd better take him round to see her now, then," Shorty Rotund added, as they turned to leave. Such a scene could only have been more comical if it had been shot in a movie – two burly guardsmen 'helping' along a semi-conscious, much slighter body, head lolling uncontrollably, toes barely touching the floor, to an uncertain end.

-o-

"Does stuff like that happen often, John?" Jack asked one of his fellow teachers.

"Pretty much," John replied, a resigned shrug betraying his frustration at what was an all-too-frequent happening. "The Occurrence Book is full of it."

"Occurrence Book?" Jack asked, puzzled at an expression he had not come across before.

"Something he's not explained to you, then," John noted with a grimace. "Typical. Let's go down to the day room and I'll explain."

The school and its grounds, imposing and elegant in their heyday with sophisticated, cultivated gardens bearing the stamp of top Victorian designers, were now in a frighteningly dour and dilapidated state that no-one in their right mind could find exciting, attractive or inviting. The last thirty or so years, since the local authority had bought and turned the estate into an approved school for delinquent boys, had witnessed a seriously rapid deterioration. Now, although there was still a market of sorts for what it offered, the demand for such an expensive provision had been reassessed by a reasonably large number of former client education and social authorities. Mr Buckby, unfortunately, had done nothing to make the establishment more attractive to interested organisations.

Unfortunately for him, Jack had become aware through various covert investigations that he had been used – big style. Several things had drawn him to this conclusion: the hidden applications for places; the secretary sworn to secrecy; Mike Gore's comment, almost as an aside;

the deplorable state of the whole estate, and the woefully inadequate provision for the training of staff to meet the profound needs of their youngsters as they headed towards the twenty-first century.

"Are you not concerned with the state of this … this apology for a school, John?" Jack asked, when they were outside and out of earshot. "I mean, the worst down-town, run-down schools I've been in are palaces compared with … *this*. Had he been honest with me when I came for interview, I wouldn't have touched this place with the proverbial – unless, of course, he had guaranteed we could work together to bring it up to scratch."

"No chance, dear boy," his companion sighed with a disdainful grimace. "Don't forget I was here when it was an approved school funded directly by the government. It was poorly run then – with little change now – and things won't improve. Mark my words, you need to make your own decisions based on that."

-o-

Jack's journey home at the end of the day was a sobering one. Where was he to go from here? He was convinced the school's closure was imminent, and the lying cheapskate whom he had taken on face value was about to walk away with a small fortune once the place had been sold to the highest bidder. At 1990s' values, the million pounds Buckby expected to realise was a king's ransom. *That* scenario wasn't official, but clandestine muttering from secretive sources had crept Jack's way.

Was there any way he could stave off what seemed like the inevitable fate that would be shared by the whole estate? He didn't have an answer for that one – not yet, anyway. But, knowing Jack, *his* solution wouldn't be far away.

"I can smell a pot of tea mashing," he called out, locking the front door behind him, "and a slice of lemon-drizzle cake. How did you know when I was going to be back?"

"I didn't," Jenny replied, flinging her arms about his neck and kissing him. "It wasn't entirely for your benefit. We have visitors."

"Visitors?" he puzzled, striding into the lounge. "At mi teatime? Jessie Ingles, what are you doing here? I thought you were preparing to launch your invasion of New York. And who's this ridiculously good-looking young man?"

"This is Brian, Daddy Jack," Jessie replied directly. "My husband."

"Hello, Brian," Jack said without thinking. "Pleased to… Sorry, I could have sworn you said—"

"We got married yesterday," Jessie interrupted, "because—"

"You didn't think it might be just a little bit important to let us know?" Jack interrupted, as Jenny's eyes warned him to go easy. "Hey, you're old enough to make your own decisions and be your own person, but didn't you consider your mother, at least, might—"

"She knew – yesterday," Jessie explained quietly, "after the registry office ceremony."

"You—?" Jack said, turning towards his wife, needing a look of confirmation, and expecting an answer and a reason. "Is there a reason for the hurry? Are you—?"

"No, Daddy Jack, I'm not pregnant," Jessie continued. "I had my passport stolen from my hotel room while we were out eating. I couldn't travel without it and, as I no longer wanted to leave Brian without me, we decided to get married and stay in this country."

"Wow," Jack said, a soft whistle betraying his shock. "So, Brian, can I assume you will be giving my daughter a bit more than your surname – which is, by the way—?"

"Wainwright, sir," the young man replied, a note of uncertainty licking the edge of his words. "And I intend that we shall find a place of our own pretty soon when—"

"Have you somewhere to stay in the meantime?" Jack asked, concerned about his daughter's security as any father would be. "There's always your old room until you find the right place. We could even find somewhere for your young man, at a pinch."

Brian cast a sharply worried glance at Jessie, not sure how to take what Jack had said.

"You'll come to learn – but *not* understand – Daddy Jack's sense of humour, Brian," Jessie explained with a knowing smile.

"Wainwright, eh?" Jack said, his usual raised eyebrow and slight head inclination betraying his intrigue. "Any relation to—?"

"Grandpa Jim?" his daughter suggested. "None."

"And does your grandma know yet?" Jack continued.

"Tomorrow," Jessie replied. "We'll be telling them tomorrow."

"And tonight?" Jack asked.

"We have the prospect of a rented flat for a month or two," Brian said, quickly, "until we can find somewhere of our own."

"And what are you doing for money?" Jack said, the concerned parent underlining his words.

"I've been a teacher for two years, sir," Brian assured him. "So, we're all right."

"Incidentally, Brian," Jack asked his new son-in-law, "do you know something I don't?"

"How do you mean, sir?" the young man replied hesitantly.

"Well, you've now called me 'sir' three times," Jack said. "What do you know that I don't? Are you related to some profligate politician that has knighthoods to give away, or have they started putting them on cornflake boxes?”

“Jack…” Jenny’s gently warning voice cut into her husband’s mild fun poking.

“So, you’re at work tomorrow, then, Brian?” Jack asked. “Anywhere I know?”

“Methley?” Brian replied. “Ever heard of Methley?”

“Have I ever heard of Methley?”Jack said straight-faced, tapping the side of his cheek rapidly with his forefinger, a slight smile beginning to grow. “Now, let me see…

“Where are you living now?” he continued, after regaling the young man with his exploits as a rugby-playing youngster down Pinfold Lane in … Methley.

“One-roomed bed-sit off Stock Lane, sir, er, Mr, er,” Brian stammered, quite embarrassed.

“It’s Jack, Brian,” Jack urged his new son-in-law with a smile. “Call me Jack.”

Chapter 14

"Is your dad serious?" Brian asked, once they had settled down in Jessie's old room. "About our staying here to save money, I mean?"

"Two things you'll learn about my dad," Jessie replied, a serious smile reinforcing her words. "He doesn't make idle promises, and he never forgets."

"What do *you* think then?" he asked quietly, unused to the sort of support that Jack was offering.

"If you wouldn't mind living with your in-laws until we've saved enough for a deposit wherever we decide to live," Jessie said, "then it makes complete sense. After all, we have our own bathroom here, and *their* bedroom's at the other side of the house. No brainer, really."

She looked over at her husband's head on the pillow; his chest rose and fell slowly, and the air from his nose made tiny whistling noises as it ambushed the hairs in his nostrils on its way into the bedroom. She smiled to think that they hadn't convinced Daddy Jack for one moment over her 'missing' passport, although he hadn't let on. A clever man was Daddy Jack, whose eyes were proof against any amount of wool you might try to pull over them.

"Tomorrow, then, my lovely," she whispered as *she* started to drift.

"Stolen passport?" Jenny puzzled over a post-breakfast cup of Yorkshire Tea, once daughter and son-in-law had set off to see Grandma Flo and Grandpa Jim. "Surely that—?"

"Can't be true?" Jack replied. "Of course it's not. They wanted to be together, which they couldn't be with her in America and him in … Methley. She knows I know, you know."

"Then why didn't you say so?" Jenny asked. "You are the one who says it as he sees it. Aren't you?"

"There's a time and a place to bust folks' bubbles," he replied with a shrug, "and this is not one of those. Think back to when *we* wanted to be together and what *we* did. We were lucky the wherewithal fell into our lap, really, and—"

"You made sure I didn't forget," she said, snuggling up to him, a suggestive smile leaving him in no doubt. "But perhaps you might like to give me a little reminder?"

"Any time, you sexy little minx," he replied drawing her close. "Shall we—?"

"Uncle Jack?" a familiar voice burst over them like a cold shower. "You here?"

"In here, Joey," Jack replied, sliding out of Jenny's clinch with a shrug, a disappointed look dancing in his eyes. "Coffee or tea, Old Chap?"

"How could it be anything but—?" Joey replied, sharp as ninepence.

"Yorkshire Tea and a chocolate digestive – or two," they chorused together, grinning widely.

"I'll get them," Jenny said, with her hand on Jack's elbow as he moved to get up. "You stay and chat with Joey."

"Long time no see," Jack greeted his nephew. "Come to that, not seen my favourite niece, either. And how's the old girl these days, and the Rover?"

"Both been unbelievably busy," Joey said, grinning at the reference to Jack's sister and his mum. "Mum's good and so's the Rover, although about to upgrade soon – the Rover, *not* Mum."

"Come on then, spill," Jack added, eager to hear what had been happening in the wide Ingles' world.

"I wanted you to be the first to know," Joey began with a self-satisfied grin. "Uncle Eric has offered me a partnership."

"A par…?" Jack gasped, a look of admiration for, and pride in, the lad.

"Aye," Joey went on. "He said he wants to spend a bit more time wi' his family. Says he can trust me to keep the cart on the wheels when he's not there."

"What did I tell you about your talents, Old Chap?" Jack gushed, wringing Joey's hand in congratulation.

"Uncle Eric says that when young George has finished his apprenticeship in a couple of months, along with his sandwich course at Whitwood Tech," Joey added, "we'll have the complete engineering company to tackle anything. I take it you didn't know about George?" Joey said, gleaning his uncle's ignorance from Jack's lifted eyebrows.

"He doesn't often communicate," Jack replied softly. "Where is he now? Do you know?"

"I'm right here, Dad," a deeply gravelly voice attacked him from behind.

"Jenny!" Jack shouted to his wife in the kitchen, a grin spreading across his face. "Quick! A huge interloper I don't recognise has burst into our home!"

-o-

"I tell you what, Our George William," Jack said over a mug of Yorkshire Tea and Danish pastries, "if I give you a couple of sheets of paper, envelopes and a postage stamp or two, do you think you might drop your mum a note or two every couple of years or so?"

Joey burst out laughing as George smiled sheepishly.

"There is a phone box at the bottom of our street," Joey chipped in.

"OK, OK, OK," George added, throwing his hands in the air in surrender. "I'll phone you – but I *have* had a lot of work on, what with my apprenticeship and the sandwich course I'm doing at the Tech."

"Your dad's having you on, love," Jenny butted in with a smile. "Take no notice of him. Now you're here, any chance that you might be staying for a bit?"

"I've a few days off," he replied. "Is it all right if I stay until next week?"

"Your room's always made up, as you know," Jenny said, "so stay as long as you need."

"I'll leave the bill for your keep on the bedside table," Jack said with a guffaw.

"I've also put an offer in for the house we are living in," Joey added with a self-satisfied grin.

"Wow," Jack gasped. "A man of substance at last, eh?"

"There's quite a bit needs doing to bring it up to scratch," Joey went on. "But who wouldn't want to continue waking up to a view over a fantastic stretch of open greenery – Haw Hill Park. What an evocative name. Did you know—?"

"The origin of the name, and that it's in the Domesday Book of 1086?" Jack interrupted with a knowing grin. "Aye, Old Chap, I do."

They all laughed together with that easy humour all families ought to share, comfortable in each other's company.

"Have you brought an overnight bag?" Jenny asked her son.

"And your weshin', no doubt?" Jack added.

"Well—" George started.

"Then empty your bag into the wash basket under the stairs," his mum advised. "All of it, mind."

"Then you can treat us to tea," Jack added quickly. "Scribes and pharas, from t'local chippy."

"Scribes and—?" George repeated, puzzled at the name.

"I once had a pal at college called Tony Stathers from Skefling, close to Spurn Point, and he called fish and chips 'scribes and pharas' – a biblical reference to the Scribes and Pharisees. Strange lot in t'East Riding," Jack explained.

-o-

"I told you!" Jack announced to the gathered group of teachers at briefing the first Monday back after Whitsuntide.

"Told us what, Jack?" John asked over a mug of strong tea. "You've told us all sorts since you've been here."

"This school won't be open in September, that's what," Jack stated, annoyed that he had been used. "We've been led into a dead end by yon unscrupulous charlatan."

"It's true," the secretary agreed as she dropped into the teaching staff room to deliver the morning's post. She looked over her shoulder to make sure no-one else could overhear. "I got to know that *he* is trying to sell, whilst saying that we have no requests for placements for September."

"And is that true?" Peter asked.

"No, it's anything but," she replied. "I have enough requests locked away in the office to make sure the school will be full in the new term, should they all be accepted – and there's no reason for their not to be."

"The lying bastard!" Irvine growled, "and I'll tell—"

"No, you won't," Jack warned. "Because if you do, Maureen here will be sent down the road sooner than she ought. And we've only got six lads left for the remainder of this term."

128

"How come?" Irvine asked, an annoyed frown invading his face.

"My guess would be that he's had to inform the local education authorities and social services," Jack butted in, "who, no doubt, have left only the lads that are with us for fifty-two weeks of the year. They are difficult to place because there are very few educational establishments that can take them after the last round of cuts."

"Once the kids get to know," John added, "it's likely we'll have even fewer. Anything about our jobs, Jack?"

"I have no idea, John," Jack replied, shrugging in frustration. "Buckby tells me nothing, probably because I'm only the head teacher. *You* know him better than I do."

"He tells nobody anything, to be honest, Jack," John said, a wry smile decorating his craggy features. "The one thing I do know, to my cost, is that if he decides on a course of action, he won't be deflected from it. And he will never admit he has made a mistake."

"Character faults as well as all his other stuff, eh?" Jack replied. "So in default of any definitive edict from above, we all need to start looking around for another job."

"About the top and bottom of it, I'm afraid," John agreed reluctantly. "I suppose I should have seen it coming, really, as there have been subtle signs for a month or two that all is not as it should be."

"Signs?" Jack puzzled.

"Repairs not being done to the infrastructure. Just look around, the signs are all there," John explained. "Curriculum stagnating, inappropriate staff appointments – present company excepted, of course – hence the appointment of Mike Gore, Cheshire's adviser for special education."

"Then why has nothing been said before now?" Jack harrumphed.

"Oh, but it has," John grimaced. "Twice HMI has issued

warnings. Their next visit they've threatened to close the school. Why do you think he was *so* happy with the policy document and the school's curriculum development plan you produced, along with your introduction of a modern foreign language teaching? Had it not been for you, the school would have been closed just after Easter. He only needed another term's funds to make it worthwhile to stay open until the end of the autumn term."

"Well planned and in secret," Jack added, a thunderously angry demeanour overtaking his body. "I need to speak—"

"I wouldn't," John interrupted. "Don't forget that he stands between you and your next job. Above all else, he is a very vindictive man who will not tolerate dissent or demur."

"In that case," Jack replied after a moment or two's thought, "I won't forget, either. Retribution will descend upon him from an unexpected source – and he *will* be sorry."

-o-

"And consequently, I need to be looking for a new job," Jack warned his wife, once he had explained their now-difficult position.

"The—!" she replied, ready to heap hellfire and damnation onto Buckby's shoulders and upon his line for eternity.

"Don't worry," he went on, drinking his mug of Yorkshire Tea. "I have until January to reconnect with the real world and pay him back as a consequence. I have a number of sound options that I've started to pursue already."

"It's a good job our kids are off our hands," Jenny said, "and I have *my* job."

"If I'm not connected permanently by next January," Jack continued, "I can always pick up supply schoolwork in local schools. Fortunately, my experience of teaching secondary

French to a high level will be invaluable in finding schools. I have already spoken to the powers that be in the LEA, and they suggest there are several options hereabouts that they'll tell me about when we reach the autumn term. Your wage will keep us ticking over nicely."

"Do I need to be concerned about anything?" she asked, fearing his response.

"What, as far as poverty and not knowing where our next meal is coming from?" he quipped again, a grin emphasising his humorous response. "Nothing to worry about, my lovely. Everything is in hand. If the worst came to the worst, I could sell mi body."

"That'll keep us in Yorkshire Tea and digestives for a few days only," she bantered, her sharp reply making them both laugh.

–o–

"Has somebody here won the pools?" Jack gasped as he left his warm and comfortable chair to make a fresh tray of tea and coffee and buttered scones. "Never seen so many people. All wanting a piece of my hospitality, no doubt. I knew I was popular, but—"

The gathered throng burst into hearty guffaws, knowing how affable he was, and enjoying the genuine welcome he always extended.

Looking around, he couldn't believe how big and grown-up they had all become, but then he had known them all since birth – except, of course, for Mary's boyfriend, Jake. Florence May's boyfriend, Billy, was Joyce and Stick Walker's son. Why on earth were they all here, dropping in unannounced? Not that Jack minded – the more the merrier, he always said – but he liked control and to be in charge of invitations.

"I'm not trying to vet you, Jake," Jack said with a smile, rounding on Mary's boyfriend, "but I have to make sure you're good enough for our Mary, and not after her for her money."

"Uncle Jack!" Mary gasped.

"Just saying," Jack replied with a shrug. "Jake?"

"I'm really rather keen on her, Mr Ingles," the young man answered. "And I think we make an excellent match because she's a businesswoman and I lecture in Business Studies at university. So, this would be a good marriage … in all senses of the word."

"Would that be a proposal, young man?" Jack asked, jumping quickly back into the conversation.

"Actually, it is," Jake replied confidently, pulling out a small maroon-coloured box bearing the well-known name 'Dysons' from his pocket, and turning towards Mary. "Will you marry me, Mary?" he asked, opening the box with a light snick as he held it out to her. "And make me the happiest man alive?"

Mary gasped when she saw the huge sapphire and diamond cluster engagement ring resting on the white-silk cushion in the box.

"I don't know what to say," she stammered, unable to take her eyes off the ring.

"Say yes!" the others in the room chorused happily.

"That does it, then," Mary responded, clapping her hands quickly in excitement, an ecstatic grin enlivening her features. "I accept. Yes, I *will* marry you."

"My God!" Joey gasped. "I'm going to have another brother! How did *that* happen? And do I really *need* another?"

Cheers and excited clapping and slaps on backs abounded as the room filled with good cheer and congratulations. Nobody would have believed what they had seen if it hadn't all unfurled before their eyes.

"I think I need to ask your father's permission next, Mary," Jake observed. "Don't you?"

"The one person you need to convince, Jake," Joey said seriously, "is standing in front of you."

Jake remained silent, puzzled, with no idea what they were talking about. He turned towards Joey, shaking his head almost imperceptibly, a frown underlining his ignorance.

"Uncle Jack!" they all chorused.

"He's the one who will give you gyp if anything goes amiss with your intentions," Joey pointed out. "So, you'd better be serious."

"Then, Uncle Jack," Jake said, a huge grin bursting across his face, "may I?"

"Mary," Jack replied slowly, turning to her eagerly nodding head, "has chosen to start her journey. I am merely the boatman. Hopefully, *not* the boatman over the River Styx. This calls for a toast. A cup of Yorkshire Tea all round!"

"Don't forget the chocolate digestives, eh, Uncle Jack," Joey pointed out.

"Nope," Jack replied, a serious look on his face. "Superseded by Hobnobs. I'll have you know that *they* will stand up to five dunks in your Yorkshire Tea before they start to become too soggy to maintain structural integrity."

"We know that, don't we, George?" Joey laughed. "Been running engineering tests on their relative merits and Hobnobs win hands down."

An engineering field study *worth* undertaking.

Chapter 15

The sharp practice engineered by the school's owner rankled seriously with Jack. He knew there was no chance of getting Buckby to see sense and allow him to guide and develop the school's future. He understood the man's devious ploys well enough to know there would be no point in trying to appeal to his better nature because Buckby didn't have one.

It wasn't in Jack's nature to seek revenge, both because he didn't see the point in trying to change the unchangeable, and because Buckby wouldn't be affected by anything Jack could do. No doubt he would come up with some token that would let Buckby see what he had done, that would no doubt cause the man no harm at all. Jack would have to bide his time; at some stage, that would allow him to have his say.

Buckby was another megalomaniac who thought he could trample on lesser beings in his race to become one of the idle rich who had ploughed this furrow before him. This not only incensed Jack, it made him stop and think about what he might do to redress the almost impossible balance.

-o-

"So, what are you going to do now, Our Jack?" Val asked over coffee the day after his birthday. "Your school's closed, isn't it?"

"It is, and I no longer have to work for an empty-head that thinks of nothing but money," he replied. "Fortunately, two jobs have raised their heads over the parapet, one of which my colleague John has applied for and has secured. I have my shout in three days' time."

"What about your salary until the end of this month?" Val asked tentatively, rather concerned that he and Jenny wouldn't be able to manage.

"I won't get paid because I won't have worked," he replied openly. "We'll have to tighten our belts, that's all."

"But—" she started to point out.

"We won't starve, Val," Jack said with an indulgent smile. "Fortunately, our eating machine is earning his own money as a fully paid-up member of the working classes, and the other two are spoken for. So, Jenny and I will be fine, won't we, Jen?"

"What's that?" Jenny asked, backing her way through the doorway bearing a trayful of goodies with – most importantly for Jack – a fresh pot of Yorkshire Tea.

"We were saying that it's a bit of a bugger being out of work at forty-five years old," Jack replied, knowing what her response would be.

"One of those things," Jenny said, right on cue. "You'll get another job I have no doubt. Until then, we'll manage."

Good old Jenny. He knew her so well – just as she knew he wouldn't let *her* down.

"I never liked the sound of him, anyway," Jenny went on.

"If you ever need—" Val offered.

"A cup of tea and a scone, Sister?" Jenny butted in, deliberately ignoring Val's words.

"OK, OK," Val said, shrugging her shoulders and raising her hands in supplication. "I get it. Your brother not been to see you?"

"One of them has," Jack replied, "but not the one you are tentatively married to."

"You know William," Val said, a look of apology leaping out to him. "Never—"

"In the loop with family, eh?" he smiled ruefully. Although he had little time for William, he was still his brother and brothers usually had each other's backs – or so Jack could hope.

"When are you hoping to start – if the job's right for you, that is?" his sister-in-law asked, genuinely concerned that nothing really would match his exacting standards.

"Worried I might not like what I see, Val?" Jack replied with a chuckle.

"You know me so well," she laughed. "It had crossed my mind … a little."

"I know perfectly well that these jobs might not fulfil *all* my criteria," he went on, "but I have to be pragmatic and go for the one that's going to give me the best return. So, I'm not holding my breath for job satisfaction here, Val. Perhaps one day…"

-o-

Crowthorn School was a residential establishment looked after by the National Children's Homes for children with emotional and behavioural disorders brought about by a variety of factors. It had begun life in the early 1870s as Edgworth Home on seventy acres of bleak, wild Bolton moorland, where its latter-day roads, streets and stone buildings had been fashioned out of an exposed landscape by the children, guided by their supervising adults.

Built entirely out of stone quarried locally by the residents themselves, the living accommodation was organised around individual detached 'Houses' bearing the names of local dignitaries who had been involved in the growth of the organisation.

The school's residential buildings looked like most moorland villages – dour black stone topped with patchy white snow that allowed the deep-blue Welsh slate to creep into the biting mid-January air. Thick hoar frost coated the spikes of the hawthorn hedges that surrounded each building, allowing a little light to creep into an otherwise darkly forbidding place.

Both sides of the single wide road were lined with cars pointing the way they had come into the village, because this 'village road' ended just round the last bend, effectively making it a rather lengthy cul-de-sac. The only car different from the others was … Jack's, because he believed in parking his car on the side of the road pointing in the legally correct direction.

"Good morning, Mr Ingles," a deep voice punctuated the hissing silence of the office waiting room. "Please come through. My name's Foster and I'm principal and head teacher of this wonderful organisation."

Expecting a large body to go with the rich deep tone, Jack was surprised to encounter an incongruously tall, slim frame that didn't fit the voice at all.

"Your experience and qualifications are impressive," the head said, as he flicked through Jack's application again. "I'm sure you will be able to cope with our sometimes-trying youngsters. I'm sure you've met their type in your illustrious career – but will you enjoy doing what you will be expected to do?"

"That depends entirely on *what* I will be expected to do," Jack replied, smiling at the head's nebulous question. He realised straight away that Mr Foster had started to struggle with the concepts and language needed to persuade folks that he understood the whys and wherefores in this particular educational climate.

"Well," Foster said, after a moment or two of head-scratching and tie-tightening, "I believe you have all the attributes you will need to succeed here. The job's yours, if you want it."

"Then I accept your offer," Jack said confidently.

"Two terms in the first instance," the head replied, "until August 2nd. We'd like to keep you permanently, but it depends on pupil numbers, which are a bit low at the moment."

Job done, Jack ambled out to his car to a light dusting of snow and black clouds threatening more. "Oops," he muttered, drawing his scarf tighter round his neck. "Better get a shift on. I could do wi' mi Yorkshire Tea and—"

"Jack!" a familiar voice accosted him from behind a huge spiky bush.

"John!" Jack replied with a grin. "I'd recognise *that* voice anywhere. Working?"

"Yes, it is," John answered with his usual acerbic humour and a grin to match Jack's. "Good to see you. I hesitate to ask, but has Stan Foster done the right thing and offered you a job?"

"Strange man," Jack replied with a nod and a puzzled frown. "But yes – two terms in the first instance, with a possibility of longer depending on pupil numbers."

"Same here," John said. "Should be OK, following on from what you were saying before *we* closed before Christmas. Should be no shortage of customers, I would say."

"Anyway," Jack said, "good to meet you, Old Chap, but I need to get back before this lot drops on us and mi mug of Yorkshire Tea goes cold."

They both laughed and made promises to get together soon as Jack drew away slowly from the pavement. The long trip back home didn't fill him with pleasure and the drive through gathering snow encouraged doubts to grow in his mind.

-o-

"What *are* we going to do, Jack?" Jenny asked over tea, a worried frown betraying her concern over his – their – future.

"Fortunately, I have a job … for now," he replied quietly. "With a bit of luck this one at Crowthorn will bring home the bacon – for a while at least. Don't care much for the driving, but it will be a necessary evil, at least until I get another job. I've also been offered a couple of hours a week at St John's Youth Club. It's not a lot of money, but it all adds up."

"Youth Club?" she said with a frown. "Have you ever done that sort of stuff *before*?"

"Almost did it once when I was at college," he replied with a laugh, "but thought better of it. Did a stint at Dunlop and Rankin Steel Stockholders in Farnley during the summer holidays instead. I got ten quid a week. Done a lot of stuff like that to mek ends meet. Pea picking when I was sixteen – three and thrippence a hundredweight bag. Gibbs Proprietaries in Leeds when I'd just started college, wine waiter at the Griffin Hotel on Boar Lane, Leeds at weekends. I had just started teaching on a salary of £1670 per annum – getting on for £200 per month before tax. Fancy giving yon youth club a go?"

"We can but try, I suppose," she added with a non-committal shrug. "Have a go at anything once. When do we start?"

"Monday of next week," Jack said. "Day before I start my new job."

"Tuesday?" Jenny puzzled. "Starting your job on a

Tuesday?"

"Fifteenth of January 1991," he replied with a heartfelt sigh. "And then it's only temporary part-time until I've proved my worth, I suppose."

"Proved your worth?" Jenny exploded. "Who do they think they are? You're worth—"

"I know, my little pigeon," Jack said, trying to soothe her outburst, "but *they don't*. After twenty-three years, once again I have to prove myself to somebody who very likely knows nothing about what's involved in being a good teacher. This is probably the most uncertain part of my professional life since I joined Merton Grange."

"Diabolical," she harrumphed.

"I know," he said quietly. "And I would likely be able to do a better job than the present head, Mr Stanley Foster, but this is how it is. They don't know me or my way of thinking – but sure as hell, I know theirs.

"We need to put all else behind us," he continued, "and move on. No use mekin' a bugger out on t'rest on our lives, as mi granddad would a said."

-o-

The children at Crowthorn were similar to those he had already met previously but with one main difference. Their parents had left them to make their own way in the world at whatever age and so they had become fully paid-up members of NCH – The National Children's Homes. Consequently, as victims of circumstance, they had no choice in what their lives might hold for them.

A disparate bunch of youngsters with a multitude of special needs, they had encountered nothing remotely normal, usual or ordinary, up to walking through the organisation's door.

"Why are we here?" the occasional disarming request fell from questioning lips, "when we ought to be in an ordinary school? I don't *feel* un-normal."

"That's because you're not," Jack would reply earnestly. "It's just that you have certain educational needs that most 'ordinary' schools don't have the expertise to address."

"Oo, I do like how you talk, Mr Jack Ingles," nine-year-old Christine said. "You say it so even *I* can understand, and that makes me *feel* special."

"That fact alone – that you *are* special," Jack replied, "is the reason I wanted to come here to work with you."

"Is that *absolutely* true, Mr Jack Ingles?" little Henry asked, an earnest frown creasing his brow. "Only—"

"You are a smart young man, Henry Webb," Jack said, "who can tell a truth when he hears it. Do you detect truth in what I am saying?"

"Ye…es, I do, Mr Jack Ingles," Henry replied. "I don't think you would ever lie – not to us anyway."

"I don't lie … full stop, Henry Webb." Jack's reassertion came back slowly to emphasise his words. "Ever."

He smiled inwardly as he left the youngsters to 'sign in'. Special needs? These sweet youngsters needed understanding and honesty in their lives where both had been lacking. These two values brought trust and co-operation from them where genuineness and respect for them were obvious in the adults. Mutual respect had to be earned and, wherever it manifested itself, it would last forever.

He loved these youngsters, did Our Jack, but, as with most other educational establishments with which he had been associated, he wasn't overly keen on many of the adults – particularly the teachers. During this, his second term at Crowthorn, he had to keep reminding himself of the two reasons he'd accepted the post. As usual it came down to children and pay, without which Jenny and he wouldn't have been able to live.

Whilst he gained a certain degree of satisfaction from teaching vulnerable children, it wasn't really the place for him. Nothing and nowhere would come close to Broughton and his language experience there. Woolly-minded and short-sighted politicians, eh? Where would he be, and what could he achieve, without them?

"Jack?" the head's nondescript voice beckoned him from across the staffroom one morning break towards the end of June. "A word?"

Mr Foster's office was huge but sterile. His large desk was clear of all but an ancient inkstand and a St James' Bible. He was neither intellectual nor religious but, to his mind, those artefacts seemed to add gravitas.

"Not good news, I'm afraid," the head droned as he beckoned Jack to a chair. "The interview for head of section you had with us yesterday was superb – a headship interview, in fact, with *all* the right answers to some difficult questions. Unfortunately, I don't want to employ another head teacher. I need someone to make his own mistakes and learn by them. I am sure you did *that* some time ago, so I won't be employing you for that post. Also, we have a significant number of sixteen-year olds leaving this term, but only a quarter of *those* numbers are being replaced by new entrants in Years Seven and Eight. So unfortunately, although you have done an excellent job, we won't be able to renew your temporary post after the summer break."

"Thank you at least for your candour, Mr Foster," Jack replied, taken aback at this late stage in the term. "When do I get my marching orders?"

"Your contract will be terminated on August 2nd," Foster said with a shrug. "We'll send your P45 by the end of that month."

"Hello, John," Jack said, opening his car door at the end of his extra-curricular shift. "Just got the push for the end of this term. Turns out inexperienced Steve Smith got the senior's job and—"

"Numbers are falling?" John interrupted, finishing off Jack's words. "Me too. Job-hunting time again, I'm afraid."

"See you on Monday, then," Jack replied, "for the final canter to the finishing post!"

Chapter 16

"And the next job is?" Jenny smiled ruefully as they settled shortly after his mug of Yorkshire Tea had found its way into his hands five minutes after walking in from his last day at Crowthorn. "Are we going to be able to manage, Our Jack? I mean, where's the money coming from to pay for this place, and—?"

"I've a meeting with the head education honcho on Tuesday next – the sixth of August – in Halifax," Jack began slowly in between mouthfuls of tea and chocolate digestives. "We should be able to sort something out. Schools always need teachers to fill in for lengthy absences. Don't worry. Be rayt."

"You've got one or two things up your sleeve, haven't you?" she replied with an accepting smile. "I know you of old."

"I have to make sure we have no hitches in the money coming in," he said, "even if it means two or three jobs. After all, I didn't *have* to follow this downward path. I could have – or *should* have – stayed with Leeds. I made a potentially stunningly clever move that unfortunately backfired. I have to put that right, whatever it takes."

"That's ma Jack!" she replied drawing him to her, careful that he had finished both biscuit and tea. "And I love you so much."

As usual, Jack was ahead of the game having sussed out several local Halifax schools desperately needing the disparate skills he had in his teaching armoury. Being the sort of self-confident – that some called arrogant – self-motivated chap he was, he had already made an appointment with the chief staffing inspector for Calderdale at the Town Hall in Halifax to see what he had to offer to someone with Jack's experience and qualifications.

"We've known for some time that the Royd School would close sooner or later," the inspector said, once Jack had laid his cards on the table.

"We were only informed at the beginning of the autumn term last year that it was to close at the end of *that* term," Jack replied. "So—?"

"Don't forget, Mr Ingles," the inspector went on, a knowing smile supporting his words, "that the school was under the authority's control until it was sold to Mr Buckby's consortium. At the beginning of the term leading to its closure, we still had several children there. It's funny how they are able to pick up the clues that adults often miss."

"Do you have any positions I might fit into?" Jack asked, direct as ever.

"It's not a case of you fitting in, Mr Ingles," the officer replied with a frown and a grimace, "because I have any number of senior posts you would match admirably. Unfortunately, none of them is available – posts filled you see. Permanent basis."

"Mmm," Jack mumbled, sitting back in disappointed thought.

"However," Mr Jamieson continued, "I *do* have a post in *one* school that you *might* be interested in."

"Oh, yes?" Jack said, sitting forward in his seat, a vein of interest beginning to course through him at last.

"It is unfortunately pro rata, around £8,000 a year less than you were getting as Royd's head," Mr Jamieson warned. "Whether you can sustain that—?"

"It's more than I expected and it's better than not being paid at all," Jack replied with a sigh. "What's the job, where is it and what's the catch?"

"Head of French on one promotion point at Ovenden Secondary Modern School," the inspector offered. "Temporary for two terms. The current incumbent is on maternity leave. You would have the scope to use whatever approach you felt appropriate, up to GCSE level. Take as long as you need to decide but if you wouldn't mind letting me know by—"

"I'll take it," Jack butted in quickly. "Where do I sign?"

"Excellent," Mr Jamieson said, a hugely satisfied grin splitting his shiny face. "Telephone me in the next couple of days and I'll arrange for you to see the head teacher, Mrs Derbyshire, at a mutually convenient time."

-o-

"Is this going to work, Jack?" Jenny asked slowly over dinner, once he'd had time to shake off the day's concerns.

"Work?" he replied over a dose of her home-made sticky-toffee pudding. There was nothing at large in the known universe that could hold a candle to Jenny's sticky-toffee pudding.

"This job-hopping affair you seem to have to be doing lately," she said, being careful not to cause too many waves.

"Well," he went on, dropping his clean spoon into his even cleaner pudding dish, a heartfelt sigh of contentment escaping his seriously licked lips, "we can afford to sustain our standard of living because we are within a gnat's whisker of paying off our mortgage and—"

"Paying off—?" she gasped. "Did you say paying off our mortgage?"

"Certainly did," he replied, a triumphant smile decorating his now-happy face.

"And how did *that* happen?" she said. "You're having me on, surely. Why didn't I know that one?"

"Honest injun, mi lud," he laughed until his full belly wobbled dangerously. "You remember when the interest rate went up to fifteen per cent a couple of years ago?"

"If you say so," she said almost in disbelief. "And?"

"When it came down," he went on, "we carried on paying at the higher level – even when it came down to five per cent. That means, my little pigeon, that we have been paying three times as much as we needed to. Consequently, we now have only small change left to pay before we own the property outright. Smart, eh?"

"You never cease to amaze me, my wonderful husband," she cooed, kissing him.

"Was that a grateful kiss because you felt you had to," he said, beginning to smile again, "or a passionate kiss because you can't resist my engaging charm and dashingly attractive looks?"

"Would you like me to show you the difference?" she asked, moving towards the hall door, his hand gripped in hers.

His smile of anticipation gave her the reply she sought.

–o–

"You've got to be kidding me!" Jack sighed as Val settled into a cup of Yorkshire Tea. "*Now* what's he done?"

"Decided he doesn't want to be associated with schools anymore," she harrumphed. "Decided he wants to be a therapist, looking after people who have had debilitating illnesses and injuries instead."

"I know he's a strange bird that never seems to care for his own nest and chicks," Jack scoffed, "but … this? Talking of which, how are my favourite niece and nephews lately? Not seen them for some time."

"Breathe deeply, Jack, and hold steady," Val warned, a slight smile betraying some impending gobsmacking announcement.

"You're going to be a granny, aren't you?" he replied, a look of elation on his face.

"I should have known you would work that one out," she sighed. "But which of my children is about to produce?"

"It can't be Ed," Jack replied with confidence, "because he has no idea what or where he wants to be yet – and besides, he still lives at home."

"One down," Val replied, confidence beginning to drain away, "two to go."

"Joey is in the process of setting up his success and has no time, even for courting," Jack mused, a self-satisfied look on his face. "He will, though, in the near future. So, that leaves Our Mary … eh?"

"You should know better than to cross metaphorical swords with him, Val," Jenny advised. "If he doesn't know, he will always work it out."

"And when's the gloriously big day?" Jack said, punching the air in glee. "A great-uncle, eh!"

"She's two months," Val replied, smiling in defeat as usual at the hands of her lovely brother-in-law. "They are away in the Canaries at the mo and won't be back for another two weeks."

"Then," Jenny butted in hesitantly, "you'd better know that you, Our Jack, are soon to be a granddad too, as—"

"Our Jessie's pregnant?" he gasped. "Now, that I *didn't*

know. Hoped, but wasn't aware. Is everybody hiding from me so they can spring it all on me at the same time?"

They all laughed that easy laugh they had always shared in each other's company.

"What does William think about all this?" Jack asked. "The usual?"

"Precisely," Val harrumphed. "Doesn't seem to have time for it all. New toy time, I'm afraid."

"New—?" Jenny puzzled.

"William has always been like a kid with a new toy whenever something new has appeared in his life," Jack sneered, not too surprised at Val's response. "It'll soon pass when something else needs attention that doesn't smack of the joys or responsibilities of grandparenthood most other right-thinking folks take on, I'm afraid."

"Why don't you say it as you see it, Jack?" Jenny said, more than a little uneasy at what he had just offered.

"And why wouldn't he?" Val replied sharply. "The only decent and thoughtful father in *this* family has the *right* to express his opinions. Anyway, Jack's absolutely right. I would love to have a husband like him, Jenny, who will talk and discuss his opinions and make me laugh. All I get is silence and non-communication. I sometimes wonder why I bother."

"You can come and talk to me any time you like, lovely lady," Jack said, sliding his arm around her waist. "And the first time I catch you asleep during one of my diatribes, out you go!"

"That's what I love about your husband, Sister," Val replied, laughing at his way. "And what I miss dreadfully about mine."

"Then, his post—?" Jack said, changing tack slowly.

"Has been advertised and filled," Val replied apologetically. "According to your thoughtless brother, Mrs

Silvester had asked about you and whether you might be interested. Unfortunately, he said that you wouldn't."

"I wouldn't?" Jack gasped incredulously. "Wouldn't what?"

"Be interested in either the job or moving to Normanton," Val replied, slowly drawing in an embarrassed lungful of air. "I couldn't believe what he had done!"

"Getting his own back for the business with Joey, eh?" Jack hissed, a thunderous cloud invading his brow. "He can't be *that* thick and thoughtless, can he?"

"I wouldn't know these days, really," she said, shaking her head slowly. "And I didn't get to know until it was a done deal. It was a throw away 'Oh by the way' after tea a day or two ago."

"Thanks, Bro, for being so supportive and family oriented!" Jack muttered, quietly seething. "I think I need another cup of Yorkshire Tea to steady mi nerves – and one of your luscious buttered scones, Jenny Ingles, to go with it. You stay here and talk to your sister while I employ mi culinary skills ower an 'ot stove and even 'otter butter knife."

"I didn't know that about your Mary, Our Val," Jenny said.

"And I didn't know about your Jessie either," her sister retorted quickly. "I only got to know yesterday, via a quick telephone call from Tenerife, and that was late on."

"Snap!" Jenny added. "Similarly, a brief call from their home in Brussels. Did you know she works for the EU and her Brian teaches in an international school?"

"But I thought they had settled in York?" Val said, a puzzled smile underlining her ignorance.

"I can't keep up with her," Jenny replied. "And it was only a brief call. A case of letting us know before someone else did, I suppose. And, as you might have gathered, Jack only got to know about the baby a few moments ago. Although you have to let your children get on with their lives, it would be nice to see them a bit more often."

"You're lucky, my girl!" Val replied sharply. "You've got your Jack to keep you occupied and alive. What have I got? A boring dreary life with no-one to talk to or do things with."

"You ought to have an affair," Jenny quipped naughtily. "That would make him sit up."

Val looked at her sister quietly over the rim of her china mug, a non-committal glint in her eyes. Jenny caught that tell-tale look as she raised her eyebrows over wide eyes. "Val?" she whispered in surprise. "You … haven't!"

Chapter 17

"So, this is what a group of second formers looks like," Jack said, dropping his attendance register on his desk on his first day at Ovenden Secondary Modern School to attract attention.

He had been in similar school buildings from the 1950s and 1960s and found that they all had common characteristics. Built in a similar style that Jack called 'shoebox with windows', they represented the greatest lack in imagination allowed because they had one purpose in common – to isolate and to contain groups of potentially difficult adolescents for as little financial outlay as possible. They weren't really built to last, but they did.

"My name is Ingles and I'm here to teach you – wait for it – French," he went on, when he had finished the register, his smile daring them to comment. "My friends call me Jack but, as you're not one of them, you can call me Mr Ingles."

A gentle snigger trickled around the room as all eyes fixed on his mobile features. They might be able to get on with this one, unlike the last French teacher who had persisted in trying to speak to them in a foreign language.

"Please, Mr Ingles?" an innocent-sounding voice crept across the bare room.

"Yes?" Jack answered as he closed the register and sent off a bluff, red-faced lad to return it to the office. "And you are … Peter?"

"Yes, Sir. Please, Sir," the boy replied, puzzled that Jack knew who he was. "How did you know my name, Sir?"

"The clue lies in two places, Peter," Jack went on, a wicked smile showing he was about to teach the boy what sort of a person he was. "One, I can read, and two, I've just taken the register where I believe your name resides."

A respectful snigger or two broke out from the back of the room.

"Your initial question wasn't about that, was it, Peter?" Jack continued. "What did you want to know?"

"Please, Sir," Peter asked, "are you any good at arm wrestling?"

Although usually ready for the unexpected, *this* question puzzled Jack. A livelier outbreak of giggling left him in no doubt that there was definitely something afoot.

"Not really the most important thing that crossed my mind over breakfast this morning," Jack replied, scratching his head, unsure what his smart answer ought to be. "Why do you ask?"

Peter's answer would have to remain unspoken as bodies stiffened at the sound of the bell for morning assembly.

–o–

"Just to let you know, Mrs Silvester," Jack explained on the telephone, "that I *would* have been very interested in filling William's tiny boots with my size tens. He was wrong to say otherwise."

"And I was wrong not to contact you first," she replied. "It's a decision I hope I don't live to regret."

"Not to worry," he went on. "If your chap drops dead, give me a call."

"Gal," she corrected. "She's a gal called Jane Alison

Bradley. Says she knows *you.*"

Jack gasped inwardly, the name bringing back memories of those heady bus journeys to Broughton all those years before. "But," he stammered, "I thought she'd gone back to her roots in Sheffield?"

"I don't know about that," Mrs Silvester replied, "but her application was far above anyone else, except that—"

"I'm glad she's got the job," Jack agreed. "She's quality and will do you proud."

"Anything you want to tell me, Jack?" she asked, a slight pause hinting at another aspect to her question. "She holds *you* in high regard."

"Just that I wish I'd known about the job," he answered her firmly. "But Jane's the best of the rest and she won't let you down."

Jack replaced the receiver thoughtfully, his mind elsewhere as Jenny backed into the room from the kitchen, a tray in hand bearing a pot of Yorkshire Tea, two Yorkshire Tea china mugs *and* ... some fresh-baked scones *and* his favourite mince pies. He could never understand why mince pies and jars of mincemeat only put in an appearance at Christmas time. He had asked shops many times, and had even written to manufacturers seeking answers, but none had ever been forthcoming.

"One of your fans, Jack?" Jenny asked, putting the tray in full view. She knew how much he loved her mince pies, so she liked to tantalise him with both sight and smell. She could see his fingers already flexing and itching to feel one of them in his hands and mouth.

"In a manner of speaking, I suppose so," he replied. "It was Mrs Silvester letting me know how William had put that all-important word in for me taking on his job."

Jenny was under no illusion how Jack felt about his brother at that moment; his layers of disdain were obviously on show. She couldn't have felt sorrier for her man, but she knew his brother's betrayal wouldn't hold Jack back. He was never one to mope or complain. He was a doer, was Jack – a mover and a shaker – and there was nothing better he would have liked to do at that moment than shake his brother by the throat.

"Who got the job?" Jenny asked, genuinely interested. "Anybody I know?"

"Somebody *I* know," he replied quietly, memories crowding his head. "At least somebody I *knew*. Jane Alison Bradley was at college the same time as me."

"What, in your French group?" Jenny puzzled. "How come I've never heard of her?"

"Because, my sweet pea, you weren't there," he replied, a grin joining his words. "She was in the year below me, so our paths never crossed."

"Will she be as good as you would have been?" Jenny said, knowing what his answer would be.

"No idea," he replied to what might have seemed to be a daft question. "Never seen her function in a school. One thing's for sure, she'll be a damned sight better than mi brother."

–o–

"Arm wrestling?" Jack asked at morning registration the following day, valiantly trying to suppress a bubbling giggle while keeping a straight face. "Not done it for more years than you've all been on this earth. However, I was champion thumb wrestler when I was fourteen."

"Thumb wrestler?" groups mouthed silently to each other as they shambled out for assembly, intrigued and stumped in equal measures.

The corner of Jack's mouth twitched almost

imperceptibly as the last body shuffled through the door. Where was this leading? How long was this interaction going to last? Thumb wrestling? Where did *that* come from?

The lesson after assembly for Jack was French with his own motley crew of fourteen-year-olds who had such an inexplicable fascination for arm wrestling that they couldn't stop raising the subject with him.

"Why do you keep on asking me about arm wrestling, Peter?" Jack asked as his *parlez-vous* sashayed on to its grand finale just before break.

"Well," Peter answered, a slight smile turning up his mouth corners as he started to reel his teacher in, "Jez O'Keef in our class – you know, big—"

"I know Jez," Jack interrupted. "And—?"

"He's our champion arm wrestler," Peter went on, "and he's beaten everyone in school – teachers included. We were wondering—"

"'We', Peter?" Jack replied, a grin forming at the thought. "Are you wanting to take part in this show? Are you a champion arm wrestler as well?"

"Me, Sir? No, Sir," Peter stammered as a very large boy joined them. "Just Jez here."

Jez O'Keef was at least a foot bigger all round than Jack, with forearms any silverback would have been proud to call his own.

"Jez?" Jack said, turning towards the newcomer.

"Sor?" he replied, a deep, lilting Irish brogue rasping its way through Jack's ears.

"You're too big for me to arm wrestle," Jack said quickly, a shrug of his shoulders betraying the start of a plan. "You look much stronger than me, so we won't be wrestling today."

He turned on his highly polished heels and strode off to the staff room for his cup of tea, leaving the two open-mouthed boys in his wake. Jack's smile grew as he walked.

Was he about to hatch some dastardly fiendish plan?

Carry on, Jack.

-o-

"I think it's about time we filled this house again," Jack said to Jenny one Friday after school.

"Lodger?" she offered, shuffling aimlessly through her magazine. "Paying guests while we do a world cruise?"

"Daft bugger," he hissed through a grin. "No, we need to have a family get-together."

"And why would we want to do that?" she replied, flicking a brief, disbelieving glance at his head. "What happened to the self-satisfied 'man and his castle' of yesteryear? Are you dissatisfied with your existence now, and bored with me?"

"Course not, my lovely," he said, slipping his arm round her shoulders and drew her to him. "What on earth could I do wi'out thee, eh?"

"Then—?" she responded, a puzzled frown descending.

"I just thought as it was moving on towards Christmas," he went on, "we'd—"

"Did nobody remind you that it's only Easter just around the corner?" Jenny said.

"Well," he added, "Easter, then. Only we don't seem to have spent time with those folks dear to us for some time, and I just thought—"

"Put like that, my lovely man," she agreed, "how about we try to organise something for the summer holidays? Most education folks – like Val and David and Jessie's Brian – will be on holiday. And as Joey and our George William are their own bosses, it would be quite easy to organise if we start now. Not to mention Eric and Ellen and theirs."

"I doubt that mi brother will join in," Jack replied, "but I don't give a toss about that as long as I have time to catch up

157

wi' them that matter. Mary and Jessie should have delivered by then, so it could be a family celebration."

"Got it all planned then, my man?" Jenny said, that usual slight head tilt and eyebrow raise accompanying her rhetorical question.

"That's blood family accounted for," he replied passively. "But not mi almost-sister and *her* brood."

"Almost—?" Jenny said, absent-mindedly. "Of course! Our Joyce."

"Did I hear that we are going to have a party?" Florence May's voice wheedled its way into their conversation once she had crept into the lounge. "Can we invite whomever—?"

"Woa, Trigger!" Jack interrupted sharply with a grin. "Invitations by arrangement with the controlling committee – your mam and me!"

"And your choice of guest would be?" Jenny asked, looking her directly in the eyes, unblinking.

"I just wanted to know if I might bring my boyfriend?" Florence May replied slowly.

"If your boyfriend is closely related to the Aga Khan," Jack agreed with a chuckle, "then, yes."

"Aga Khan?" their daughter asked, confused and puzzled in equal doses.

"One of the richest men in the world," Jenny said, her explanation accompanied by a deep sigh. "Take no notice of your dad, love. He thinks he's funny."

"And your boyfriend might be…?" Jack asked as he sidled towards the kitchen to mash a fresh pot of Yorkshire Tea.

"It's Billy," Florence May added nonchalantly, as she flicked through her mum's discarded magazine.

"Billy who?" Jack asked. "Bunter? The Kid? Hickock? Billy Whizz? Billy-No-Mates? Billy Two Rivers?"

"I've no idea who any of those … people are," Florence

May said with a dismissive toss of her hair at Jack's weedy attempt at humour. "It's Billy Walker."

"What! The boxer?" Jack butted in again, dipping once again into his bottomless pit of throwaway lines, chuckling at what *he* thought was amusing.

"Joyce and John's son?" Florence May explained, one of her resigned gazes to the heavens invading her face.

"Since when?" Jenny joined in, genuinely surprised. "I thought you didn't like him when you were thirteen?"

"Well," her daughter continued, "that was *then*. This is … *now*."

"I feel sure Joyce said he was on his way to Australia in the autumn?" Jenny added, not really *that* sure of her facts.

"He is," Florence May agreed, "and I thought I would go with him."

"Oh aye?" Jack butted in when he had slid the laden tray onto the coffee table between them. "And who's laying out all that dosh to allow you travel the Antipodes in decadent luxury?"

"Well, it won't be the Aga Khan, Daddy Jack!" she laughed, trying to jest her way out of what might become a difficult conversation. "I'm on my gap year, Daddy Jack, as we discussed before, and I have a reasonable amount of money saved for just such an adventure."

"I think you'll find it doesn't rain in Australia," Jack answered with one of his usual enigmatic statements.

"What's that to do with my money, Daddy Jack?" Florence May puzzled, lips pursed and brow drawn down.

"I think the reference, oh daughter mine," Jenny butted into the conversation, "is to do with your savings being for a rainy day – that is, because you're not working or doing anything with your life yet."

"Then call my trip to Australia with the boy I love all my rainy days rolled into one," Florence May harrumphed.

"The boy you love, eh?" Jack said quietly as he slipped his arm around her shoulders. "Really? Truly? Madly? Deeply?"

"We've been going out together for almost a year," she replied, eyes beginning to moisten, "and we … love each other. I am twenty, soon to be twenty-one. You weren't much older than me, Mam, when you had Our Jess, so—"

"Fair point," Jack said with a knowing tip of the head. "But you don't want to be pregnant yet – do you?"

"No, Daddy Jack, I don't," his daughter answered him. "But at some time in the not-so-near future, I think … I might."

-o-

"But he's old enough to make up his own mind, Our Jack," Joyce's voice crackled down the phone's receiver. "And if you've no objection to their going together—?"

"We can't stop her, Joyce," Jack added, "and neither would we wish to. She insists they love each other and—"

"He's told me the same," his old friend replied, "and – I shouldn't be saying this but – he will be looking after her closely. He is a very moral boy, having said very seriously that sex for him will happen only *after* marriage and not before."

"What's he doing for money?" Jack asked, after a brief pause. "Will you—?"

"No worries on that front, Our Jack," Joyce said, with a bit of a laugh. "He's saved all his spare cash from work, and mi dad's put a dollop into Billy's bank as travelling capital, so he can draw on that at any time. Chance of a lifetime, Our Jack. His words. He has said that if the opportunity arises, he may well stay for a while, a matter supported by your Florence May, I believe."

"That's settled, then," Jack grinned as he walked back

into the lounge. "Your room, young lady, will be let as soon as your feet tread the path outside the front door."

"I love you, Daddy Jack," Florence May said, flinging her arms about him. "I will—"

"Enjoy the opportunity as it grabs you," he advised. "To make sure you have no problems wi' affording decent accommodation along t'way, we'll open a travelling account with an international bank for you to dip into when you need it, si thi. All rayt?"

Nice one Jack, mi owd cock! Granddad Jud would have approved.

Chapter 18

"OK, lads," Jack said at the start of break time on his last morning. "You've been at me about arm wrestling since I started here at the beginning of last term. Today, lunchtime start, *High Noon*. In here."

"Yes!" Peter, Jez's agent, hissed quietly, punching the air. "At last!"

"Are you wanting me to beat you first then, Peter?" Jack cajoled, a grin daring the little lad.

"Me, Sir? No, Sir," Peter gasped. "No thank you, Sir. Just Jez and … you … Sir."

"Are you feeling ready, Jez?" Jack turned to the big lad, whose grin was starting to spread. "Though you're far too big for me to have a hope of beating. We'll just get it over and done with, shall we?"

"Sor," Jez agreed, eyebrows raised in expected triumph. "I can't wait, Sor."

"Right, then, clear off and do your training exercises," Jack urged, ushering them out to the yard, "or your war dance – or whatever psyches you up for the big showdown. Don't be late or you'll forfeit the match by default."

"Are you in your right mind, Jacky-boy?" Titch Smith, his next-door classroom neighbour, gasped on the way to the staff room. "He'll beat you in a second. Jez has seen off *all* opposition, even from staff that were soft enough to believe they could beat a mere child quickly."

"Aye. All rayt, Titch mi owd mate," Jack replied, a slight smile playing round his mouth corners. "Why doesn't tha come along at noon in my classroom to give me support?"

"Not sure, mate," Titch replied with a grimace. "I don't really want to share in your humiliation – unless there's something you're not telling me, like you're a World Grand Master at arm wrestling!"

"I don't hold with all that wrangling malarkey," Jack said, sipping his break-time tea. "I believe in being smart and sharp. Intrigued?"

"Come on, Smart Arse," Titch urged, "don't keep me in suspenders. What's the plan?"

"Twelve noon. My classroom," Jack said tantalisingly as he left the room, back to class. French with the fifth formers. Who said sixteen-year olds couldn't be seduced with the love of gold stars displayed on a star chart on the wall for good work?

-o-

"And so," Jack announced to his group of twelve GCSE French pupils, "the winner of *this* term's 'cake and Coke' prize for the most gold stars – drum roll, if you please – is … Form 5G!"

Gasps and grins from all the pupils hinted at their joy as Jack dished out wrapped slices of cake and bottles of Coca Cola from the large box he had brought out of the storeroom behind his desk.

"OK, chaps and chapesses," he said, once every piece of cake and accompanying bottle of Coke had been secreted in bags for lunchtime feasting, "it's been a blast knowing you. I hope you all earn what you deserve. Now clear off. I have a competition to attend to."

Eleven fifty-five.

Almost time.

Where were those unsuspecting saps that were about to send his name into the annals of Ovenden folk lore?

"There you are," Jack called, taking his coat off and rolling up his sleeves as the motley gang filed into the room.

He had set aside a sturdy table at the back of the room with chairs facing each other, one either side of its narrower point. Jez took the seat facing his seated teacher, a smile of triumph already licking his lips. The whole class gathered around the combatants, unblinking in eager anticipation of their man's glorious victory.

As they settled, their elbows together and locked hands ready for their time-honoured joust, Jack glanced surreptitiously over Jez's right shoulder. This drew the boy's relaxed gaze for a brief instant, allowing Jack to slam down Jez's arm to the table.

"Aw, Sir!" the crowd moaned. "That's not fair!"

"Nothing in the rules to say how a person *has* to perform," Jack explained, grinning at their disappointment.

Jez stood up, a look of admiration in his eyes at his teacher's smartness and held out his arm to shake the hand of the only person to beat him in an arm wrestle this year.

"Fair and square, Sor," he said, wringing Jack's hand in genuine congratulation, before striding out – his entourage behind him – to claim his well-earned dinner.

"You crafty owd bugger!" Titch said, a grin growing as he sidled into the room. "Now I've seen everything! That's the first time I've witnessed that young man out-thought and out-manoeuvred in the time he's been in this school. He won't be bothered, because this is your last day that will be remembered only by the staff members he's beaten over the last three years."

Carry on, Jack!

My, was he looking forward to his well-earned corned-beef and chutney sandwich! He shouldered his way into the staffroom after retrieving said banquet from the car to a round of applause from virtually the whole staff gathered there.

"A legend in thi own mind, eh, Jack?" Alan Hardacre said, slapping him on the back, as Jack parked his snap tin on the table under the only window in the room. "I think everyone in this hallowed place now knows the conqueror of Jez the Gigantic."

"He's actually a good lad when you get to know him," Jack explained as the taste of corned-beef and chutney burst in his mouth.

"Aye, he is that," Albert Brahms, the music teacher butted in. "He couldn't help being born with a hefty quirk of nature in his significant physique. One day, he may end up as the Ovenden's … strongest Irishman."

"But he's the *only* Irishman in Ovenden!" Jack replied, brushing the last vestige of corned beef from his imaginary moustache. "Don't forget that he lives with his nan, who is English."

"What's next for you then, Jack?" Albert asked, cradling an enormous pint mug of steaming tea.

"2B French, and then I'm free," he replied, a cheeky grin gracing his face. "off 'ome when I'm done."

"Daft bugger," Albert chortled. "I mean job-wise, of course."

"Six weeks' worth of supply in a junior school in Rochdale," Jack said as the bell for end of lunchtime interrupted their conversation. "But as for today, my Easter hols start in an hour."

-o-

"You didn't!" Jenny exclaimed, a mist of disbelief covering her face. "But that's not—?"

"In the rules?" he laughed. "There aren't any – not in my book, anyway. You have to be smart to outwit youngsters these days. I also got a standing ovation when I went to the staffroom for mi dinner."

"You're a case and no mistake, my man," she went on, deciding to do the washing up. "Next on the agenda?"

"As I tode 'em at school when they asked," he replied, eyes half-closed and interlocking fingers supporting his head from behind, "mi Easter 'oliday will maintain mi sanity for a couple of weeks at least. And then? Who knows?"

"Not sure *that's* what you mean, Jack," Jenny answered. "Not like you at all. I'm sure you'll have something planned…"

"Aye," he said quietly, "but not just now, eh?"

"Did you get anything before you left?" she asked, genuinely interested as they sat down to a post-prandial cup of Yorkshire Tea.

"What, apart from mi P45?" he replied, caressing the large mug of hot steamy liquid. "Didn't even get a wave goodbye."

"That's a shame!" she sighed. "You'd have thought—"

"It's a job, love," he interrupted with a wry grin. "You does your job and you gets paid your dues at the end of the month. I don't think I've ever had a token of *anyone's* esteem at the end of a stint in ower twenty years in schools. All I ask is a fair day's pay for a fair day's work."

"Isn't my esteem enough, Our Jack?" Jenny asked, finishing her tea and sliding her arm about his unresisting neck.

"I assume that's a rhetorical question to end all rhetorical questions?" he replied, kissing the top of her head. "It's the onny esteem I'm interested in, you know that. All t'others

I don't give a cat's 'bout, and they can kiss my derrière if they don't like it.

"Anyway, I'm off to put t'kettle on," he said, prising himself from the warmth of his well-worn favourite chair. "Cup o' tea, missis?"

"Aye," she replied, moving quickly to the hall to answer the phone's insistent rattle. "Go on then. You persuaded me."

Although he cocked his ear near the kitchen's hall door, he was able to catch only muttered titbits of conversation about somebody called Mike, or was it about a bike that William had taken to riding? Not sure. Probably not.

There it was again! Definitely Mike. He had ears like a gimlet had Jack. Or was it eyes like a gimlet? Couldn't be definite, but—

"Tea ready yet, my lovely?" Jenny's voice squeezed through the microscopic crack between the door's leading edge and the jamb. "I'm dying of thirst in here."

"All right, Your Majesty," he replied, backing his way into the lounge, bearing a tray that was … empty. "I'm on my way."

"But…?" she said, her puzzled look adding volumes to her question.

"Just wondering how long you would take to notice," he laughed.

"We're not having a cup of tea then?" she added, not understanding why there was nothing on the tray, until a second tray pushed its way into the room, carried by…

"George William!" Jenny hooted, leaping to her feet. "What are you doing here?" She rushed over to him as he deposited the tray onto the coffee table quickly enough not to have it knocked out of his grasp by his mother's hug.

"Can't I come home to see my lovely parents once in a while?" he asked sheepishly.

"Make that 'once in a year'," she added. "What's the

matter? Run out of food? How come I didn't hear the front door? And I was in there on the phone!"

"We came in by the back door as a surprise," George said, a sneaky smile decorating his face.

"We?" Jenny puzzled. "Have you brought one of your pals with you?"

"Sandy!" George shouted, turning towards the kitchen. "You can come out now."

"Sandy?" Jenny mouthed at her husband, shaking her head slowly.

"Mum and Dad," George William said, once a beautiful ginger-haired young lady had joined him, "I want you to meet Sandy Spinks, my fiancée."

-o-

"Are you sure about this?" Val asked, not sure of the sincerity of his feelings.

"Look," Mike replied sliding his arm about her waist, "I think you know the depth of my feelings for you. Don't forget, my wife is gone but your husband isn't. Don't you need to examine what it is *you* want, my lovely lady? *I* would move in with you tomorrow."

She sat for a while on the edge of the bed, desperately trying to rationalise her thoughts and emotions. She had already accepted her husband's insincerity in his relationship with her, first with his infidelity and then with his indifference towards her, his wife of going on for thirty years. She had known that there was no way back for them before Mike had stepped into her life.

Now it was time to take care of her own future. But was it with Mike that she needed to put all else behind her as she moved towards new challenges in her life?

"Are you all right, Val?" Mike asked gently, concerned at

her quietness and the distant, pained look in her eyes.

"Of course I am, Mike," she replied slowly, a happier look relaxing her features. "Just deciding how to break my news to William."

"Your—?" Mike replied, perplexed by her change.

"My only recourse is to ask him for a divorce," she said, drawing him closer. "And to explore what *we* have between us."

"You mean—?" he gasped, an excited grin dispelling any doubts he might have harboured.

"I don't want him to be aware of *us*, you realise, until the divorce has been completed and we go our separate ways," Val explained. "I need to have enough money to provide my own space before you and I decide where *we* are. Is that all right?"

"Whatever you want," he agreed. "I'm more than happy to wait for the right moment if it means I get you at the end of it all. What's this going to do to your family?"

"What family?" she replied. "Children are all grown up and living their own lives and all that's left for me is a stale marriage that promised much in the early days but was lacking in delivery throughout. William and I have nothing left to offer each other, so it's time to move on. Can't believe I'm saying this but my brother-in-law – William's younger brother – would be saying 'way to go, Val'."

"Will you stay here with me tonight, then?" Mike offered.

"Probably not a good idea, as William's at home for a change," she warned. "Even he's not so stupid he wouldn't be able to put two and two together. So, we will need to be careful."

"Where will you say you've been?" he ventured.

"With my sister," Val assured him. "I spend a lot of time with her and Jack these days. Anyway, William won't ask.

He never has."

-o-

"And when did you become betrothed?" Jack asked his son. "And why now? No hurry is there?"

"You should know better than to ask that, Dad," George William replied, putting a protective arm around his Sandy's shoulders. "That sort of thing will happen only when we are married. I live with Cousin Joey, as you know, and Sandy lives down Ash Gap Lane with her mam. Consequently, if we can stay here tonight, I should be grateful for my old room and perhaps Jessie's old room for Sandy?"

"We offer very reasonable rates these days for B and B, you'll be pleased to know, Old Chap," Jack offered with a grin.

Seeing his fiancée was taken aback a little by this, George William had to explain his Dad's crazy sense of humour. Her sigh of relief was *tangible*.

"My goodness!" Jack gasped. "You don't need a pair of binoculars to see the rock in *that* engagement ring! It must be second only to the Koh-i-Noor."

"Koh-i-Noor?" George William repeated, not understanding the reference.

"The biggest and most expensive diamond to come out of the ground up to now," Jack explained. "Yon solitaire diamond of Sandy's is perhaps around three carats, whereas the Koh-i-Koor was around a hundred and five once it had been cut. A whopper that's in one of the Queen's crowns that she doesn't wear that often, for obvious reasons."

"A mine of useless information, your father," Jenny said with a sigh. "Have you two eaten this side of last Thursday?"

"Not for a while, Mam," her son said, feigning passing-out hunger and sitting down with a bump.

"Tell you what, Sandy," she went on, "would you like to give me a hand in the kitchen to rustle up a bite to eat and we'll leave these two to it?"

"Well then, Our George," Jack said, once the women had closed the kitchen door on their man-to-man conversation. "She's a beauty and no mistake. How did you meet?"

"Her car broke down at the front of our house opposite Haw Hill Park on her way home to Ash Gap Lane," George replied. "I went out to see if I could help. It was only a loose lead, so it was an easy fix. The next time I saw her was in the park a week or so later. We got chatting and it went from there."

"So, what's your next move?" Jack asked, as the kitchen door began to move with the promise of food at last.

"Save up for our house so that when she leads me down t'aisle, we'll have somewhere to live when it's all ower," George William laughed.

Jack joined him in a hearty guffaw.

"Wow!" was all he could say when they sat down to a sumptuously appetising spread. "Lovely grub, Our Jenny."

"Nay," she replied, "it's all down to *this* young lady."

"Learned from your mam?" Jack asked as they tucked in. "This is beautiful."

"Not really," Sandy replied. "Mum's not much of a cook, really, so I didn't learn much from her – we would probably have starved had it been left entirely to her. I'm training to be a chef."

Stunned, with his mouth full of exquisite food, the makings of an appreciative grin grew on Jack's face.

Bloomin' 'ummer! Fallen on 'is feet again! 'E were all rayt, were our George.

Chapter 19

"Of course you can, Val," Jack answered, along with a serious degree of nodding from his wife. "There's no need even to ask. *Mi casa es su casa.*"

"*Casa…* ?" she queried.

"Don't ask, Sister," Jenny advised with a condescending smile. "He's just being a smart arse. A Spanish smart arse, to boot!"

"And tell me," Jack asked, knowing already what she would say, "why isn't your husband here now, begging you to return to your marital home?"

"Because," Val replied, matter of fact, showing no concern or recrimination, "he doesn't care. He probably hasn't even noticed I'm not there. I think he's taken up with his whore, Samantha, again. I can't really do with all these shenanigans, so I've met someone else."

Silence descended like a blanket, smothering all sound, eyes casting concerned glances as the enormity of her last words started to sink in.

"Let me get this straight," Jack said quietly, surprised at what seemed like a rash and precipitate decision, when in fact he should have seen it coming years ago. "William will no longer exist once you've seen off the official paperwork, and—?"

"Oh, he'll exist all right," Val replied with a rueful smile, "just not as my husband. Well, actually, he's not been my husband for as long as I can remember in *real* terms. Time for me to start to live again."

"Which means that he will stop being my brother, in real terms," Jack replied, "because, sure as hell, he won't come here of his own volition. And your new man – Alan, is it?"

"He's called Mike," Jenny butted in.

"And how do you know that and I don't?" Jack gasped, good humouredly.

"Intuition, dear husband," Jenny laughed, her forefinger tapping the side of her nose. "He's five years older than her and he's a lovely, attentive man."

"And you know that how?" Jack responded like a flash. "Met him, have we?"

"Stands to sense," Jenny replied, equally quickly. "It's unlikely Val would fall for the same boorishness twice and she wouldn't have been interested had he not reached her exacting standards."

"Do you know," Val said with a satisfied smile, "that I love sitting here listening to you both eulogising my new exploits. Anyone would think I had taken this step lightly. I loved William to bits when I married him, but it all started to unravel when it was obvious how insular and introspective he became with time. Oh, and did I mention selfish?"

"The daft bugger niver listened to me either," Jack harrumphed. "If'n he had, you would still have been happily hitched. There's no accountin' for folk. I'll nip and make a cup of tea. Val?"

"Please," she replied, "and one of—?"

"My home-made scones?" he offered with a tiny titter and wary glance at his wife, whose almost impassive face spoke volumes to him.

"What about Mary and Joey and Ed?" Jack asked, having deposited a tray of refreshments on the coffee table.

"Do they know?"

"They've *always* known," Val replied with a heartfelt sigh and shrug. "It's testament to them – and in no small measure to you, Jack – that they've grown up to be as well-rounded and strong as they now are. Mary and Joey owe their steps on the right path entirely to you, Jack. Without your intervention and support, I've no idea where they'd be professionally."

"Just the odd pointer and prod and push in the direction they had identified and wanted was all that was needed," Jack said. "They've always been smart kids, Val."

"Don't underplay your role, Mr Fixit," she replied. "It's always been you they've looked up to and come to for help and enthusiasms. Need I remind you when—"

"OK, Val," he interrupted with an accepting shrug and chuckle, "I get your point. Still, they deserved the best and, unfortunately, latterly their father always seemed to fall short."

Saturday evening shadows crept quietly into the room on soft velvety toes, gradually filling corners where light rarely trod. Val was grateful for refuge and respite in her sister and brother-in-law's ever open and welcoming home. She would have to settle her financial affairs with her hopefully soon-to-be-former husband. Only then would she be able to get on with the rest of her life – with Mike.

Marriage? She wasn't sure. Don't rush into anything else, her mam had said, sadly. Yet she would rather her daughter was happy and could at least start to do what her younger sister had always achieved with *her* man.

Mike seemed like a genuinely lovely man who had thoughts only for her. *His* two daughters were off his hands – the one living relatively close by with her husband and four children, the other a jet-setting legal executive who might settle down – one day. They knew nothing of Val

– yet. Mike would choose his time carefully, probably when *she* had made up her mind that *their* time was imminently right.

-o-

Jack's new temporary job was relatively easy to find. A French teacher at a high school spitting distance from the now-closed residential Royd School in Todmorden had gone on maternity leave, vacating a post that was right up his street and that *he* would have no problem fulfilling. Unfortunately, she would be returning after only a term. Still, August to December allowed Jack to fulfil his financial, although not his personal, obligations.

The head teacher had offered Jack the job within minutes of his walking out of the interview room, apparently stating that there was no way anyone with half a brain would turn down *Jack's* credentials for teaching *those* children in *his* school. Mr Craven had gone on record as avowing that if he had been able, he would have offered Jack a permanent post there and then.

Todmorden High School held a special place in local folklore as it not only offered secondary education to *all* the children in the town leaving primary school after Year Six, but also had special links with *all* those educational establishments.

The only problem was that the longer Jack worked in the team, the further away from home and his wife he seemed to be. Travelling used to be exciting, a way of getting to know other areas in his Yorkshire homeland, but the constant bad weather and even worse traffic conditions had begun to pall. How he longed for a closer billet so he might get home earlier to be with his lovely wife. Perhaps one day…

Astoundingly, heart-stoppingly ordinary and mundane, Jack's everyday timetable gave him nothing to get his teeth into or to become excited about. He had been given a syllabus he *had* to adhere to so that Mrs Helsing could follow on seamlessly when she took over on her return.

There was no leeway for individuality in his teaching methods and no space for anything but his well-developed sense of humour that had, over the years, become an acquired taste that most people either didn't understand or have the desire to understand. Consequently, December couldn't come quickly enough. That third of the year certainly seemed to stretch closer to a half.

Fortunately for him, the post of Head of French and English at a residential school in South Yorkshire beckoned, which he had no problem securing – once again.

–o–

"Another residential school, Our Jack?" Jenny sighed.

"I'm afraid it's the only available job at this time for a geezer wi' my qualifications and credentials, lovely woman," Jack explained. "And unfortunately, one of the prerequisites is that I have to live in."

"And if you say no?" she countered.

"No job," he returned, uncompromisingly final. "So, either you come with me, or you get rid of me, stay here and find yourself somebody else to provide shelter and food for you."

"Don't be stupid," she harrumphed emphatically. "We'll work something out."

"Hello," a familiar voice attacked them from the hallway, when tea had finished. "Anybody home?"

"In here, Val." Jenny's voice beckoned her sister into the lounge.

"I'm afraid we've scoffed all this lovely food, sister-in-law dear," Jack said, straight-faced.

"I've eaten already," she replied, "with Mike."

"How are things?" Jenny asked. "Any further forward?"

"Well, funny you should ask," Val replied. "Mike has asked me to marry him when I am free, and I have … accepted."

"Wow!" Jack gasped. "Way to go, Our Val! You deserve a dose of real happiness. Divorce any nearer?"

"Decree absolute will be with me at the end of December," she said, an exalted note in her voice, "so we can wed any time. We will need somewhere to live, though. I don't want to live in someone else's house that I don't know, so his is up for sale and we are looking for somewhere to rent. Why the strange looks? Was it something I said – and is there anything I need to know?"

Jenny explained *their* situation, offering her their house as an interim for as long as it might take Val to find the house of her dreams. Jack nodded emphatically, punching the air in triumphant joy.

"Does that mean that you are prepared to come with me then?" Jack added, a look of mock surprise decorating his face. "Doncaster here we come!"

"William *is* back with his floozie, as I thought," Val explained, "so everything can move along more quickly. I *do* have slight qualms about what I'm about to do but I'll get over it when everything's sorted."

"And your school?" Jack asked, pragmatic as ever.

"I can stay there and simply have a stroll across King Lane to work every day," Val replied with a wide, happy smile. "You've removed a major obstacle by offering me your house."

"We'll sort out the rent situation later," Jack said, a wicked smile crossing his lips.

"Jack!" Jenny gasped.

"What?" he exclaimed in fun. "Just saying."

Chapter 20

Christmas had been a time for seriously mixed feelings. William had left their home for the last time and, as Joey and Ed and Mary dropped in to celebrate season's festivities, Val had moved back in until after Christmas when they were due to complete on its sale and the removal of her furniture into storage.

Jack and Jenny's house was full of family throughout and, as such, this was a very exciting and enjoyable but emotional time. Jessie and Brian brought their new daughter, Millie, to show off. At about eighteen months, she was gorgeous and – surprise, surprise – could say a few words for the listeners. Mary and Jake's daughter, Alice, was about the same age give or take, and the two of them played happily on *anyone*'s rug.

"Mark my words," Jack warned, "those two will be a force to be reckoned with when another year or two have passed. On your guard, one and all!"

It was the happiest Christmas ever, with one obvious omission. Despite his only grandchild being there, William didn't come near. He had other irons in the fire and this time, truly, his 'Samantha' *was* pregnant. William was going to be a dad again and this time he was going to play things differently. Even Samantha might remain faithful.

Pigs might fly and hell might freeze over!

The downside to all this merriment was that it happened only once a year and might not become a regular reunion. Still, folks had to live their lives; youngsters had to grow up and make their *own* way in the world. Where would any of us be without at least one helping hand along the road?

Mary and Joey and Jessie and Florence May and George William would heartily support that. The one serious influence in all their lives was Mr Fixit – Jack Ingles – a positive force for good for them all.

Shouldn't everyone have a Jack Ingles to call on?

-o-

"Lovely day to move house, eh?" Jenny said, watching heavy rain scything to ground into their already waterlogged back garden. "I thought it was supposed to be cold but largely fine."

"We're probably in the area that's not billed as part of the 'largely fine'," Jack replied with a resigned shrug. "Still, the removal is down to us. Our stuff's packed and boxed, the Luton van is on the drive and all we have to do is to … load it."

"Is this better than the heavy frosts we've had recently, or—?" Jenny added as she kissed her husband on the way to make a pot of Yorkshire Tea.

"Relative, I suppose," he replied. "Not owerly keen on either. Excellent," he went on when he saw his wife's move towards kettle and teapot. "Cup o' Yorkshire's just what I need before the fray."

"Hello!" a couple of very familiar male voices reverberated from the hall. "Anybody alive in here?"

"Joey? George William?" Jenny and Jack chorused from the lounge. "What are you doing here?"

"Afraid all the food's been eaten, Old Chaps," Jack added as he hugged them both.

"We've eaten anyway," Joey replied.

"Greasy caff on the way over from Normanton," George William continued. "Full English breakfast!"

"Lovely!" the young men said in unison, a satisfied smile splitting their faces.

"Something told us you were moving today," Joey said. "We knew that, as a tried and tested Yorkshireman of centuries' standing, you would have hired a Luton van to move yourselves."

"Consequently," George William butted in, "here we are … to help load and unload, so mi mam needs onny to do the … fancy stuff."

"Don't push your luck, Buster," she replied as they all laughed together. "I'm as strong as the next."

-o-

"Where are we going, Dad?" George William asked, once on the road. "Anywhere nice where we might get a good cuppa and a morsel to eat?"

"You got worms or summat?" Jack asked, forgetting that at his age *he* was no different.

"He's a growing lad, Uncle Jack," Joey put in with a laugh. "Needs regular injections of his vittels, does Our George. 'E's lucky he's got a live-in chef that feeds him four times a day."

"Live-in—?" Jack said, a slight puckering of the eyebrows betraying his puzzlement.

"Just terminology, Dad," George explained. "Sandy sometimes cooks for both of us at our place, and sometimes I get to eat with her and her parents at their house on Ash Gap Lane. Perfect arrangement."

"Doncaster," Jack said.

"Don who?" George and Joey chorused, not understanding who he was talking about.

"Your original question?" Jack continued. "Where we're going? We're off to the town in South Yorkshire called Doncaster."

"But isn't that miles away?" George William asked. "Where is it, anyway? And Doncaster, what sort of a name's that?"

"It's in South Yorkshire, as I said," Jack explained again, "about twenty-five miles down the A1. It was a Roman settlement developed next to the River Don."

"And how do you know that, Uncle Jack?" Joey chipped in. "Were you there?"

"You might regret asking," Jenny muttered, hoping her husband hadn't heard her. Forlorn hope. She could tell by his face the second she had uttered it.

"Well," Jack went on, ignoring Jenny's comment, "any town that has 'caster' or 'chester' in its name comes from Roman times. They are derivatives of the Latin word *castrium* which means 'camp' or 'encampment'. Don – caster, for example, means the camp on the River Don. Lancaster is the camp by the River Lune. Chester is self-explanatory, as is the camp at Mancunium, Manchester. OK?"

"I feel like I need something to eat and a stiff cup of tea after all that," George William gasped, shifting his backside on his cramped bench seat at the front of the Luton.

"Now *I* find that interesting," Joey smiled. "For example, Normanton comes from Norman times, the Norman Town, from—"

"The Domesday Book of 1086," George William added quickly. "Now I *do* know that one – William, Duke of Normandy, eh?"

"Well, I *am* impressed, Our George William," Jenny

gushed.

"Don't praise him!" Jack urged with a laugh. "He'll want paying!"

-o-

"This doesn't look too bad," Jenny said as they pulled into a gateway leading into a very large walled garden whose well-tarmacked driveway wound its way through immaculately tended shrubs and tall deciduous trees. "Not bad for early January."

"Wow!" Joey and George gasped as the wooded driveway spat them out on to a wide parking area as the day closed in.

"Stay here all of you until I have a key for the cottage we are to inhabit from today," Jack said, as he parked near the porticoed front entrance of the building. Almost stately in appearance, the greying façade seemed to beg for a face lift to bring it back to its late eighteenth-century birthday. Although the building's outward appearance belied its Grade II listing, it held a certain stature even in the gloaming.

"Doesn't seem to be anybody much about," Joey said, scanning as far round as he could see. There were no lights in the old house and the modern school building off to the right, but he could detect one or two dimly glowing curtained windows in a detached block of buildings close by.

"OK," Jack gasped, clambering into the van and hurriedly slamming the driver's side door. "Finally managed to find someone with a modicum of sense and a key to the cottage. Unfortunately, as I nipped in to have a recce, the lights were off, and I could hear the gentle lap of water as I walked across the first carpeted room."

"Water?" Jenny said, not quite latching on to the significance.

"The ground floor in its entirety is two inches deep in

water," Jack replied, resignation in his voice. "I'll have to try to find someone more senior to decide on our next move."

-o-

"And?" Jenny said as Jack sat down in the cab next to her after his search in this alien and alarming environment. "Did you find anything? Anyone?"

"I spoke to the same woman as before," he replied with a shrug, "and she said she had spoken to the head – a Mr Linsley – and he offered that we could unload all our stuff and store it for tonight in the main hall in the old part of the building. He also said that we should come back tomorrow and arrange to have it put into storage until they could have the cottage dried out."

"No sign of him?" Jenny replied, annoyed that they had been fobbed off. "Not going to crawl out of his warm and cosy bolt hole?"

"Nope," Jack added with a frown. "We'll have to take the Luton back to Leeds and stay the night at home. You all right with that, chaps? Tea's on me on the way back, by the way."

"Now you're talking!" Joey and George chorused.

"Mi stomach thinks mi throat's bin cut," George William continued, drawing in his cheeks in mock starvation.

"How does the Brown Cow grab you?" Jack suggested. "Down Selby Road off the A93, going on for Temple Newsam House, Whitkirk way on?"

"Painfully, I should imagine," Joey quipped, tickling everyone's chuckling gear. "Have you seen their teeth. Ouch!"

"I fancy fish and chips," George William threw into the conversation, "wi' loads of red sauce."

"Ketchup," Jenny corrected.

"*Gesundheit*, Aunt Jenny," Joey added to everyone's mirth. "Bless you."

"'Ark at 'im," Jack replied. "Speaks German now as well. Allus was a clever lad, that Joey."

"Do you speak any languages, Uncle Jack?" Joey asked in return. "You know, besides English and French?"

"I'll have you know I speak five languages fluently," Jack replied, a deadpan look on his face.

"Five?" George William gasped. "I never knew that."

Jenny tried to hold in check her broad smile because she knew what was coming next.

"Aye, lad," Jack said, dropping into Granddad Jud mode. "I do that – English, French, Yiddish, Radish and Rubbish."

Joey and Jenny burst into a rumbling chortle as George puzzled what he could possibly mean. Radish? Rubbish? How could you speak Radish and—? Finally, the penny dropped. Radish and Rubbish indeed!

"Here we are," Jack warned as he was turning in to the pub car park. "Brown Cow. Be prepared for a gastronomic treat to fill yer bellies, mi boyos!"

As they walked into the bar like four drowned rats, Jack's mind was drawn back to that inauspicious time he and David had dragged their soaked and bedraggled bodies into that pub bar on the Yorkshire/Lancashire border on their way back from seeing Lee off at Manchester Airport all those years ago. A lot of water had trickled under their 'bridge' since that day, some of it murky and not very tasty, too. His life to date had definitely been varied, to say the least.

"Pint, Joey?" Jack asked as he made for the bar.

"Shandy, please, Uncle Jack," he replied, "wi' fish and chips. Do you remember that time we had a day out in Malham, in the Rover 95? What a wonderful day that were…"

"A pretty pickle and no mistake, eh, Our Jack?" Jenny said as they sat down in a barely furnished house with a cup of Yorkshire Tea and a currant teacake to hand once George William and Joey had gone to bed. The boys had to be off at first light to return to their jobs in Normanton. Uncle Eric allowed them a certain amount of leeway, but it didn't do to try to take advantage, even though they *were* family.

"We've had worse, Our Lass," Jack replied, toasting his feet in front of their lovely log burner. "I didn't expect this, though. Here's me thinking we'd be settled about now in our new abode, looking forward to retirement together."

"Retirement—?" she said slowly, more than a little puzzled by his response.

"Just joking," he smiled, realising this was perhaps not the time to either pull her leg or make crassly unfunny comments. "A week before it's habitable, the head said, although it was through an intermediary and not from the horse's mouth itself. So, your guess is as good as mine. We need to be back there in reasonable time to contact the removal men to pack up our stuff and take it away to storage."

"Where are we going to go, then?" Jenny said, a rather concerned and annoyed frown etching her brow. "Sleeping in the dormitories with the boys?"

"B and B, I believe," he replied with a shrug, "though I don't know where."

"And who's paying for all this?" she said with a slightly sceptical inclination of the head.

"*They* are," Jack replied curtly, considering her question to be unnecessarily searching and testy.

A tense silence descended, to be broken only by one of George's squeaky night-time farts that creased Jack into a fit of laughter as such noises usually did. This caused Jenny's face to crack too and they laughed together as they had always done, although Jack would never do such a thing – not on purpose, anyway. Silence-provoking differences were *always* short-lived in this relationship.

-o-

By the time Jenny and Jack had risen at seven o'clock to start their trek back to Doncaster, Joey and George William had long gone. They started *their* day's travail at eight but felt they couldn't possibly put all their energy into work without a full English breakfast in their bellies on the way. How on earth they could function laden with bacon, eggs, beans and bread, Jenny never knew. But then she had always been worried that George William might have worms.

"Here we go," Jack muttered as they inched out of their drive and headed to the Leeds Outer Ring Road and the A93 toward Garforth and the A1 South to Doncaster. "Next stage in our stumble towards retirement."

"Do I detect a note of despondency here, Our Jack?" Jenny said, resting her hand on his thigh.

"Not really," he replied, "though it seems like these days nothing is simple. How difficult could it be to choose a productive way of living?"

"We'll get there, my lovely," Jenny soothed. "It's not like you to be concerned, because we *will* sort it out."

"It's all right for *you* to say that," Jack replied, without a supporting grin for once in his life. "*I'm* the one that cocked it all up by leaving Leeds, and it's through my obstinate—"

"Jack!" Jenny interrupted sharply. "Stop running yourself down. We're not far from Wadworth and the school, where we are going to live and do whatever it takes to make *this* posting work. All right, Jack?"

186

As they turned into the school's driveway, the sun squeezed out from her cloudy hiding place casting dappled shadows as they slowed to a crawl along the tree-lined tarmac. They drew to a halt in their dark-blue Rover 420 next to a small removal van that had reversed close to the main entrance, its rear doors open, and tailgate lowered to the tarmac. Jack and Jenny looked at each other, scowling brows lowered in surprise. There were still no children in school because of the holiday but Reg, the caretaker/handyman, stood sentinel by the door, supervising.

"You must be Jack Ingles," he said, his face raising a smile as they approached. "New teacher."

"Aye," Jack replied. "What's going on, Reg? We're here to pack our stuff up more securely for t'removers to take to storage after we dropped it off in the hall last night."

"Flooded cottage, eh?" Reg answered. "You were supposed to be moving in today, and I were supposed to have fettled it this morning."

"Why the lake in the front room, Reg?" Jack said, a slight chuckle trying to lighten the mood. "New swimming pool?"

"Frozen internal plumbing thawed, and the pipes sprang several leaks," he replied. "Unfortunately, it went undetected for over a week. Be another week afore it's fit for habitation. I told 'em last year it it wor a possibility but would they listen? Not on yer bluddy lives, they wouldn't."

He turned towards the school's main doors and ambled in, hands in pockets, to supervise in the hall as Jenny and Jack shrugged at each other and followed Reg into the bowels of this near-Neolithic pile.

Chapter 21

"I thought you were supposed to be on duty this weekend?" Jenny asked, as they relaxed in their comfy settee after one of Jenny's glorious dinners that seemed to know no bounds.

Friday evening had become a necessary oasis of relaxation at the end of a seriously busy and exacting week's toil as Jack endeavoured to bring order and education to a reluctant audience of recalcitrant teenage boys.

"I was," he replied, reaching for his dram of Laphroaig that was sitting on a small, let-downable occasional table within grasping distance of his right hand. "But Andy Drury, the care worker, asked if I would swap duties with him because next weekend, he needs to visit his wife's parents in Romania. Hence, thou hast me all to thyself this…"

The insistent, strident bell of the phone interrupted his flow, causing them to cast furtive, ignorant glances at each other.

Jack sat on the built-in corner bench next to the fireplace with a sigh as he lifted the receiver. "Yes?" he asked pleasantly, until he realised it was his ex-wife, Lee. "And *now* what do you want?"

Through the garbled mutterings from the phone, Jack's changing expression and almost gasped responses, Jenny realised he was becoming more and more exasperated and angry.

"More money, you say?" Jack's voice burst in. "Do you mean the 'more money' we don't have? And you should have realised by now that your emotional blackmail doesn't work with me, and—"

Lee butted in again, cutting him dead and not allowing him to finish what he wanted to say in response to her unreasonable demands.

All this time, Jenny had been drinking more red wine than she knew how to handle. The spinning room gathered momentum and speed, and, sinking to all fours, she crawled across to her husband. When her forehead butted his knee, she looked up to his face and blurted out, "Tell her to bugger off!" Then, still on hands and knees, she wove towards the downstairs toilet under the stairs.

"Got to pee," he heard Jenny mutter and then – silence.

"Well then, you can whistle!" he retorted angrily, slamming down the receiver. He sat for a moment to compose himself. Realising he hadn't seen his wife for a little while, and that she seemed to have been in the loo for some time, he drifted into the hallway through the door in the decorative glass screen at the end of the lounge.

The door to the toilet was still closed but he could detect a sliver of artificial light squeezing out down the hinge side. "You still in there, Jenny?" he asked quietly, concerned that she might be ill. The only response was a faint moaning groan. "Jenny? Are you all right?"

Further, more audible moans told him she wasn't. Not wishing to alarm her, he opened the door slowly – to see her body wedged on its side between the toilet bowl and the wall.

"I can't move," she whimpered pitifully. "I don't feel well. Can you…?"

Very carefully he extricated her from the restraining

toilet wall and bowl, realising she would be better off in bed. Carrying her gently upstairs, it didn't take an Einstein to realise that her slurred speech meant she'd had more than enough red wine with the three-quarters of a bottle she had already consumed.

"Feeling a bit sick," she muttered, as Jack reached the head of the stairs and the long corridor of a landing that led to the bathroom. The ever-so-slight gypping sound from her throat that warned him of something more urgent gave pace to his legs. Bursting through the bathroom door, he clamped his hand over her mouth in an attempt to hold back the waves of nausea that were threatening.

Didn't work.

A serious wave of vomit erupted from her mouth, brushing aside his finger to splatter the pale-grey bathroom carpet with a purple starburst. His valiant attempt to direct the deluge into the bath had failed.

-o-

"You realise, of course," Jack advised her, once he had cleaned up and settled her into bed, "that for the next day or two it will be pobs on the menu for your meals."

"Can't do with that, Our Jack," she replied in a delicate whisper, a look of fear growing. "I never did like the lumps of white bread floating in a bath of hot milk. Yuk! I'll be all right tomorrow."

"You don't want a red-wine nightcap then?" he grinned, kissing her forehead goodnight.

"Do you want another bucketful of sick to clean up?" she gasped, a horrified grimace playing around her mouth.

"I've a bit of schoolwork to finish," he replied, "and then it's bed."

"Schoolwork?" she puzzled. "But it's Saturday tomorrow

and you said you weren't on duty this weekend."

"Correct," he agreed. "But I want my weekend totally free so I can minister to your every need."

He looked at his wife to find her head had lolled back onto her pile of pillows, her mouth had dropped open and the sound of a soft circular saw without teeth was rattling around her tongue. He smiled, making his way to the bedroom next door that he had set up as a temporary workspace.

He had one or two reports to write about the perceived success of his new French course and his thoughts about a couple of newcomers in his group. Adam Rayban, in particular, puzzled him. As an experienced teacher of boys with social, emotional and behavioural difficulties, Jack could find no reason at all why Adam should be at this school. Deferential, polite and above all well-presented, *this* eleven-year-old should have been developing career-building skills in some supportive comprehensive close to home. Was there something fundamental to his performance that Jack had missed?

Suddenly the sharp click of the bathroom door jolted him back to consciousness. A quick look at his watch warned him that he had dropped off to sleep over his work.

Half past one.

He undressed hurriedly and sidled round the bedroom door to see Jenny fast asleep once again. Her warm hand took hold of his as he slid into his side of the bed.

Two weeks to Easter, and the air was already warming up.

-o-

"Jack?" a male care worker built like the proverbial brick outside toilet asked at Tuesday morning break.

"Yes, Bozzy?" Jack answered, a steaming mug of Yorkshire Tea to hand. "What can I do for you?"

"May—" Bozzy started.

"Yes, you may," Jack replied, interrupting Bozzy's flow.

"Daft bugger!" Bozzy growled, a good-humoured guffaw erupting from his huge barrel of a chest. "No, smart arse, I'm about to tek 'arf a dozen or so older lads camping to Gordale Scar near Malham. Does tha fancy a few days away on camp next May time?"

"Am I first, second or third choice?" Jack chortled, sipping his favourite beverage and nibbling on a cheap digestive-type of biscuit. He didn't nibble for long. Not to his taste. Wouldn't be doing *that* again. Probably – definitely – bring his own when he'd had the chance to shop. "What facilities won't there be when we're at this camp site? Will we 'ave to pee in t'river or—?"

"This is t'1990s, Jack," Bozzy went on with a smile, "not t'bluddy Stone Age, tha noz. We'll be 'avin' proper sanitation and washing facilities in a little block close by."

"And sleeping?" Jack asked. "Four star? Four poster? And for breakfast?"

"Bring yer own tent," Bozzy went on, "along wi' a blow-up."

"Doll? Cushion?" Jack interrupted with a guffaw.

"I'm beginning to wonder if I picked the right companion here," Bozzy sighed. "Does tha know owt abaht camping, Jacky-boy? 'As tha iver bin camping afore? Does thy *'ave* a tent o' thi own?"

"The onny tent I iver spent time in was when I wor nine," Jack replied in all seriousness, "and that wor in 'Arry Bowles's back garden. There wor fower on us – 'Arry Bowles an' 'is brother John, Trevor Durant an' me, and we 'ad a blanket each. We wor supposed to stay owerneet but we packed up and went back 'om at abaht ten o'clock. I think after an hour or so we'd done that theeyer camping lark. Don't 'ave a lilo. Don't 'ave a tent. Don't even 'ave walking boots or any o' that sort of country-living paraphernalia."

"Point teken, Jack," Bozzy said, grimacing through a sage sort of a nod. "Tha can share mi one-man tent wi' me, and mi lilo. Might be a bit on a nip an' tuck affair, though."

"Be rayt, Our Boz," Jack said, once he had finished his mug of Yorkshire Tea and grimaced through his last mouthful of 'plastic' digestive. "Never again!" he muttered, judgement on his 'artificial' biscuit delivered with tongue-clacking distaste as he wandered out of the staffroom door into a fresh bright morning, out of the cloying humidity and throat-rasping sharpness of a smoke-filled near-windowless room he had promised himself he would never enter again.

After all, he was the only civilised Yorkshireman in the area to drink proper tea. None o' yon LP Tips rubbish for him, or whatever it wor called, and that was his *only* reason. When all's said and done, he had only ten minutes break in the morning and that wasn't enough time to rush back to the cottage to share it with Jenny. By now she was also working in the school as … a classroom assistant.

"Bloody 'ell!" Chris, one of the male care workers, gasped as they poured out of the back kitchen door into the sunlight. "Did you see *that* big bugger?"

"See what, Chris?" Jack replied nonchalantly, used as he was to Chris's statements of gross hyperbole.

"Tha blind or what, Jack?" Chris went on. "It wor a rat as long as mi arm, nibbling on yon side of waste food outside of yon second kitchen door."

"Yeh, right!" Jack scoffed. "My arse!"

"Chuffin' 'ell! There it is agen!" Chris went on aghast. "Behind that second sack! At least as long as mi lower leg! When will you ever start to believe what I say?"

"I think it all stems back to the time you likened the

size of that tasty pork pie you had at the Drovers Arms to a dustbin," Jack replied with a grin.

They all laughed as the zebra-sized rat scuttled off into the undergrowth behind the old building. No doubt it would be back when there was another batch of wasted good food that these picky lads wouldn't eat.

'Sarajevo food' one Scouse fifteen-year-old called it; although that was an over-reaction, it reflected the times. Although nowhere near Jenny's standard, the food was passable for an educational establishment.

-o-

Jack's classroom was quiet and cool – the perfect environment for him to work in. This, his one and only free one-hour lesson in a busy week, was brought about because his group of pre-leavers was out on a visit to the gym at the school's sister establishment a mile or two away.

"Jacky-man," a deep adolescent voice made Jack prise up his face from the work before him.

"Steve?" Jack replied, with a puzzled look as a large fifteen-year-old strode towards him. "No gym?"

"Nar," the youth answered. "Mi asthma tells me I can't do what the gym says I *should* do."

"Very poetic," Jack said with a smile, knowing his comments would resonate with the lad's lack of literary confidence. "What can I do you for?"

"Well," Steve went on slowly, "as you know, when I leave this place mi mam won't have me back at 'ome – her reasons, not mine."

"So, have you thought about what you might do?" Jack said, a concerned frown puckering his brow. "Any other close-ish relations prepared to take you on?"

"None – short of coming to live wi' you and your missis,"

Steve replied with a shrug.

"*Love* to, Old Chap," Jack offered. "But you know as well as I do that it's not allowed."

"It's just that since you came, my life got better," the lad said, "in all ways, save one – and that's mi mam's attitude."

"This is what I thought," Jack explained. "Over the next few months, we'll get you a billet to go with that job you're trying to secure, so that your move from school digs to an adult situation will be as seamless as we can make it. It might not be ideal—"

"But nothing's completely ideal in real life, is it, Jacky-boy?" Steve added, a reassuring glimmer of reality peeking through.

"Well said – and well-taught, eh, Our Steve?" Jack replied as they both laughed, comfortable in each other's company.

"Do you remember the occasional pork pie and Mars Bar you brought for me and Nathan and Danny," Steve said, drawing back fond memories, "when our evening meal was something we couldn't eat?"

"Like liver and onions, and kidneys?" Jack added with a grimace.

"Yuk!" they both added with a heartfelt retching sound and a laugh.

Lunchtime was fast approaching, threatening a meal that *all* the lads anticipated with lip-smacking relish – cod and chips. Everyone's favourite, every Friday.

-o-

"Is there any chance we might invite a couple of my lads round for an evening meal before they leave next Easter?" Jack asked his Jenny one evening after school after his all-time favourite meal of meat and taty pie. She knew that this was his favourite – along with everything else she had ever cooked for him – because he said so at the end of every meal.

"Of course there is," she replied enthusiastically. "Just find out their preferences and we'll do it. Three or two courses?"

"I'll find out ower the next week or two and come up with a plan," he said.

"You really care about those lads, don't you, my man?" Jenny said softly, once their backsides had rediscovered their places on the settee and their usual drinks of Yorkshire Tea had found their way onto occasional tables at either side – his in a giant mug and hers in the delicate bone-china cup and saucer that Jack's mother had preferred.

"They weren't born bad," he answered. "Just born with the wrong parents. Damage was done long before they came to us, and we have the task of unpicking all the nastiness laid on them by thoughtless and uncaring adults."

"Am I right in thinking it will be Steve, Nathan and Danny?" Jenny asked with an understanding giggle. "The three biggest lads you could find? That's ma Jack. Could you tell me, please, why you allow them to call you Jacky-boy?"

"The long or short version?" he laughed. "Onny, there's no difference. It's all in the way I tell 'em."

"Enigmatic as ever," she replied with an understanding chortle.

"Big words will only … earn you my admiration," he said chuckling at *her* use of the vocabulary she'd heard falling out of *his* mouth at some time. "Well," he started to explain, "it's all to do with the bureaucracy and strict regulation I don't like."

"You? Never!" she replied, a sarcastic smile adorning her mouth corners.

"One day early on, where we were indulging in a little

physical horse play – you know the sort, shoulder punching and ear flicking – that sort of harmless fun," he went on. "Well, they were all calling out each other's nicknames and Steve Harris called me Jacky-boy, and it stuck. Powers-that-be in the school tried to stop it, but they couldn't – adolescent lads like ours can tend to dig in their heels at times – and *I* wasn't going to stop them. Call me old fashioned."

"Anti-authority and anti-bullshit, more like," she laughed. "Just like you, Our Jack."

Carry on, Our Jack!

-o-

"Do we 'ave to do this 'ere camping crap?" Steven White, one of the group of six asked as the school minibus pulled into the layby just outside Gargrave on the way to their week's joyous countryside experience. He was originally from a village just shy of Spurn Point at the very south end of the 'face' of the East Riding's coast. Jack appreciated his outspoken attitude but occasionally the boy's views fell out of his mouth a little too … forcefully.

"Tell me, Steven," Jack asked, ostensibly seriously, "what does the word 'camping' actually mean?"

"Acting like a lass when you are a lad," Paul piped in sharply to everyone's mirth, including Jack.

"Nice one, Paul Matson," was Jack's rejoinder, once the laughter had subsided. The lads all knew that with these two adults there would be a good deal of banter and give and take. That's what they were all here for. "You couldn't get less like camp than camping."

Laughter again broke the ice and allowed them to leave the layby and head for the road that led them across country to their goal at Gordale Scar.

Forty-five minutes later, tents were pitched, toilets

visited and the primus stove was roaring merrily, taking the chill out of a kettle laden with cold water. Now for the first lesson for the lads – how to mash a rayt good cup o' Yorkshire Tea, even for the non-Yorkies in their midst: Paul, Andrew and Nathan.

"Owt to ayt wi' mi cup o' tea?" Steven White burst into the quiet.

"In the back of the van," Bozzy advised, "you'll find a large square tin. Ease the lid off, if you're man enough, and let us all know what you see. Do you know what a tin is?"

"Cheeky bugger," Steven muttered, shuffling to the van to find the tin, which he did in double-quick time. "Bugger me! That's not a tin! It's a metal coffin!"

They all burst into peals of laughter as he managed, finally, to loosen the lid and gaze inside. Heaven of all heavens! Talk about striking gold! What had he found? Manna from the Gods! Buttered and jammed scones – only his favourites of all time. You could almost *hear* him drooling over them.

"'Ere, Whitey," Paul warned, "don't thee dare slaver on *my* scones, or else tha'll find thissen flushed darn t'toilet, an' we'll ayt all *thy* scones as well."

"What's next, Bozzy?" Andrew asked, once a couple of scones each had been seen off.

"Well, mi boyos," he replied, "Jack's about to tek you all for a walk across the prehistoric limestone causeway and round Malham Tarn to work up an appetite while I cook tea."

"A walk?" Steve Harris said, joined by Nathan McLean. "But an't we done enough of that wi'out doing some more?"

"You've only managed to walk to and from the van today," Jack replied with a snort. "A matter of twenty yards. You need to have a bit of exercise to work up an appetite for tea."

"But I've already got an appetite," Nathan insisted.

"Stop being such a mard arse," Paul butted in. "We did a march every day twice as far when I was in the army cadets. Do you good. You could do with losing a deal of fat anyway, McLean."

The lads quite enjoyed what turned out to be a stroll, particularly when they had a competition skimming flat pebbles across the Tarn to see who would get second helpings of pie and dessert for tea. Happy days.

-o-

"Last full day, chaps," David Bosworth said on a damp but clear morning, once they'd breakfasted after a bit of a rainy night. Half past seven and they were *en route* for the White Scar cavern for a trip underground to gawp in awe at the formation of stalactites and stalagmites.

"I'm not goin' down thiyer!" Steven White harrumphed, having left the van and headed for the cave's entrance.

"You'll have to," Bozzy insisted. "We are required by law to take both members of staff underground. So, we can't leave anyone up here unsupervised."

"Don't give a bugger," Steve growled, insistence sitting on his face. "I'll walk back to Doncaster if I have to."

"Let me have a word with him, David," Jack said. "We'll find a common ground, I've no doubt."

-o-

"And what did you say to him to have him stay here and wait for our return?" Bozzy asked, astounded that Jack had been able to talk the youngster round.

"I persuaded him that he would be spoiling his friends' day that they were looking forward to," Jack replied, "and if they asked why, I would tell them honestly. I also gave him the responsibility of looking after the belongings they weren't allowed to take underground. That, of course, had a cost implication so I gave him a fiver to spend on Coke, chocolate or whatever, to keep him grounded. I asked for his agreement, which he gave, and we shook on it."

"And you trust—" Bozzy butted in, unsure of the wisdom of the agreement.

"Implicitly," Jack assured him. "Steven and I have an understanding here, and I *know* he won't let me down. I also know that it's not a sham because it's on record that he suffers from serious claustrophobia in enclosed spaces, and you don't get more enclosed than underground."

-o-

"Stevie!" the other lads shrieked, once they had re-entered the foyer close to the gift shop.

"'Ow *you* doin'?" the other Steve asked. "I bet you've been bored out of your skull. We've had a fantastic time. What have you been up to?"

"None of your kiss-arse business," he replied sharply. "But I have got one of these for each of you."

Out of a bag with a gift-shop logo, he produced a large Mars bar for each of them, including the two adults, the larger of whom cast a surprised eyebrow-raised glance at the other. *He* simply smiled and raised his shoulder non-committally.

"And now," Andrew asked, as they piled into their seats ready for the next stage of their excited journey, "*we* have a favour we'd like to ask."

"OK," Bozzy said, turning to Jack, a serious face betraying his puzzlement. "And what does that entail? Bank robbery?"

"You *can* be hurtful at times, Mr Bosworth," Andrew said, a look of mock sadness trying unsuccessfully to persuade them of his upset. "No. We know of a stream close by that flows under a bridge and cascades into a pool. We'd like to go there – to play Pooh Sticks."

"Pooh—?" Bozzy puzzled, looking again to Jack for explanation and support.

"Winnie the Pooh?" Jack explained, with a smile. "Pooh, Christopher Robin, Tigger and Eeyore throwing sticks into the stream and having a competition to see which stick emerges from under the bridge first?"

"OK," Bozzy agreed. "Directions to the stream, please."

Once there, the lads piled out of the van and proceeded to strip off to their shorts.

"'Ang on a bit!" the care worker shouted. "Don't you need to gather some sticks? And what's with the stripping off?"

"Haven't you guessed?" Jack said with a grin. "*They* are the sticks. They will enter the water two at a time and let the stream carry them down under the bridge to the waterfall. The first over the cascade into the pool wins. They then let the other groups of two do the same. The winner of the final is the overall winner. Sharp, eh?"

"And so are those bloody rocks surrounding the cascade!" warned the care worker, panic almost setting in.

"They're not stupid, David," Jack assured him. "They won't allow each other to get hurt. Last day. Let them do their thing."

A goodly amount of yelling and shrieking told the adults the boys were having the time of their lives and wouldn't have missed it for the world. The overall winner? Paul Matson – who else?

-o-

Tea around the campfire was an amazingly enjoyable affair. Marinated chicken breasts cooked over the flames in a large hanging pan, and jacket potatoes cooked *in* the fire while the lads' clothes dried around it, proved to be very popular.

"I'm off up to Malham to phone my wife," Jack announced, "to check that all's well at the *hacienda*. Anybody want to come along to walk off all that fab tea?"

The two Steves volunteered, happy to tag along even in the pitch dark.

"How's it going so far then, lads?" Jack asked as they rounded the last garden before the red telephone box swung into view.

"Great," they both assured him. "Had an excellent time. Telephone box, Jacky-boy? Ower thiyer."

"Hello? Jenny?" Jack said once he had made sure his money would deliver. "You all right?"

"No, Jack," she replied, a note of panic ringing in her voice, "I'm not!"

"Now what's happened?" he asked again, fear of the unknown chasing around his mind. "Are you *physically* all right?"

"Physically, I'm fine," she answered, "but mentally not so good."

"Come on," he insisted, "give."

"Well," she started, hesitantly, "I sat down to watch the news and the most awful thing happened. An enormous spider as big as a bird dropped down the chimney and started towards me. It was dreadful. I jumped onto the settee and pulled my trousers up to my knees, shouting at the creature to get away from me all the time. Then—"

"Steady! Slow down!" Jack urged, trying his best not to laugh, knowing how she loathed large spiders, or even spiders of any size. "It won't hurt you, unless it's five feet between the eyes!"

"You may laugh," she gasped, "but you can't see it staring at you!"

"Start to be afraid when it eyes your big toe for its tea," Jack laughed. "If you leave it alone, it will go away. Anyway, I'll be back tomorrow around lunchtime. So, we'll have a complete weekend when I can build a protective wall around you."

She had calmed down a little by the time he hung up, but the conversation lingered in his mind, causing him to smile from time to time.

"Come on then, lads," Jack urged. "Time for bed. Steve? Where's Steven White?"

"He nipped off ower there for a pee," the lad replied, nonchalantly.

"Come on then," Jack urged. "Let's go."

As they approached Steve in the dark in front of the picture window of a seemingly deserted pub, his trousers unzipped, relieving himself in the gutter, a blinding wall of artificial light cascaded over the peeing boy as an occupant of the hostelry opened the curtains to peer out.

Once he had overcome the inertia generated by the momentary shock, Steven White rezipped and hot-footed it down the lane to Gordale Scar, Steven Harris and Jack in pursuit, guffawing so much they could barely walk.

Hence the origin of Steven White's new name – The Flash.

Chapter 22

"And today, ladies and gentlemen," Peter Giles, the deputy head, informed the teachers gathering at morning briefing, "we, as an efficient educational unit, are being inspected by the powers that be in the Hesley Group of Schools, which, as we know, is the parent organisation based at Hesley just down the road from Wilsic School."

If you were to rearrange 'arse', 'wordy', 'boring', 'mind-numbingly' and 'hole' into a well-known phrase or saying, you would have had a reasonable description of the man.

"Inspection?" John's educated but undeniably Lancastrian voice cut in. "What's that all about? And why weren't we told before?"

"It's a spot inspection," the deputy replied, a minimally sardonic smile on his face.

"And did *you* know about it?" Pam, the science and RE teacher, asked pointedly.

"As a matter of fact," Peter replied, becoming more than a little hot under his open collar at this, "I did."

"Then why weren't *we*, your colleagues, informed, er, sooner?" Geoff Turner the senior teacher in this recalcitrant gathering emphasised in his bluff Yorkshire way.

"Er," Peter said, trying to soften the blow that would inevitably follow, "I was told not to by Mr Linsley, the head."

"Is that the head *teacher* who isn't confronted by children on a day-to-day basis, then?" Jack added in his usual pragmatic, questioning way.

Following Jack's pointedly direct question, silence seemed to ooze out of the walls, deadening all in its path, rendering their powers of speech useless until Jack re-opened *his* line.

"Wouldn't it have been prudent to have dropped the tiniest of hints to Geoff, so that we wouldn't have been caught short in a tight corner?" Jack suggested. "When all's said and done, Peter, without our co-operation you would have been – stuffed, big style! If I were you, I'd—"

"There you go again, Jack Ingles," Peter butted in brusquely, "offering me advice when—"

"Then for goodness' sake, man," Jack interrupted, equally sharply, a silencing smile stopping the deputy in his tracks, "act upon it!"

They didn't call Jack 'The Smiling Assassin' for nothing.

Carry on, Jack! Just what the doctor ordered.

"Timetable for this fiasco?" John asked, becoming bored by this tedious charade.

"There isn't one," the deputy replied quietly after something of an embarrassed pause.

"Bloody Mickey Mouse organisation," John added bluntly. "If Blackburn Rovers' management were to carry on their daily business like this, they'd *all* be sacked. Don't apply for a football manager's job any time soon, Old Chap!"

The gathering burst into peals of derisory laughter as he delivered his last line with an upper-crust plum in his mouth, leaving the deputy sniggering nervously having been well and truly stamped on.

-o-

"What's the problem?" Jack asked, as a line of teachers came to a halt at the kitchen's back door – main thoroughfare to the education block from the staffroom – after morning break. "Why aren't we moving? I have a class of lads and a group of dignitaries to entertain."

"It's Big Danny," John Wallbank replied with a grin. "He's jammed himself behind the huge oil tank and the wall, outside the back door. Refusing to move despite the group principal – Terry Hoskins – trying to persuade him. He won't move, even for Steve Lloyd, the owner. He's telling them all in no uncertain terms to f*** off."

Everyone in the queue started to titter at the ridiculously inept senior manager of the group – and *these* people were inspecting and judging the folks who were in daily line of fire.

"This is Danny in my personal tutor group we're talking about?" Jack asked.

"It is, Old Man," John shrugged. "What another fiasco!"

"'Scuse me," Jack said, as he shouldered his way through the queue to the door.

Squeezing though the doorway into the cloudy but bright morning, he was confronted by a bunch of very senior managers huddled – not too closely – around a large, old and very rusty domestic oil tank that was probably eighteen inches from an outside wall by the kitchen door. Jammed firmly between metal and brick was the huge frame of one of Jack's personal students, fifteen-year-old Danny 'Mr Fix-it' Broom.

Jack noticed the head teacher, deputy head teacher, owner of the group of schools, and group head principal all trying to coax Danny out, and all being told to f*** off by the boy. Shouldering his way to the head of the group, he could no longer stand by and watch the lad taken for a fool and being made a spectacle of. He knew how clever Danny was and how much work *he* had already done with him to bolster the boy's self-worth and self-confidence. Jack knew also that mechanically and electronically, there wasn't a machine that had been invented that Danny couldn't fix when it stopped working.

"Excuse me, please, gentlemen," he ordered as he reached the 'trapped' boy, forcing himself into the gap to speak to him. "Let's not give them any more of a spectacle, eh, Dan mate?" he whispered. "I'm sure we two have better things to do than entertain these buggers, don't you think? Shall we nip off and do something more productive? What do you say, eh?"

"Lead the way, Jacky-boy," Danny whispered back. "Made mi point."

Jack shuffled out, followed by his lad, and they made their way through astounded, gob-gaping looks from the powers towards their haven of peace in the classroom block.

"Nice one, Jacky-boy," John Wallbank and Geoff Turner chorused as all the other lads trooped back to sanity.

"Perhaps now they'll understand the sort of a job we have to do with these lads," John went on, "and the support *they* need to be able to fit into society when they reach sixteen."

"You all right, Dan?" Jack said when the door of the classroom had finally snecked behind his six fifteen-year-olds.

"Just had to mek a point about our lack of facilities in this 'ere shit 'ole," the lad replied, "wi' all t'traipsin' abaht we 'ave to do to gi' us summat productive to do ahtside these fower walls. That's all."

"I'm sure they took note," Jack replied with a smile of understanding. "And now back to our application-letter writing. You remember…"

-o-

"Has anybody seen Mr Giles?" Jack asked a group of lads on the field behind the school's older building during dinnertime break.

Half a dozen of them were playing football in a walled and netted five-a-side court under the canopy of a large group of immature oaks. Various others were playing chase or catch, or simply lying down in the warm afternoon sun.

"He's sitting up in yonder tree," answered Dougie Haig, a large flaming redhead from Tyneside, "like the dick that he is, playin' wi' his bloody bongos."

"By that, you mean dicky *bird*, I presume, Dougie?" Jack corrected with a knowing smile.

"Why aye, man" Dougie agreed with a grin. "That's wor ah *meant* to say, layk."

Jack turned away and trudged towards the head's unlikely perch in the crook between two huge branches, where he was rattling away tunelessly on the miniature drums between his crossed legs.

"Mr Giles?" Jack shouted up to him. "Can you come down, please? I have something important to tell you."

"Hang on ten minutes while I finish this piece?" the new head offered.

"Not really," Jack insisted. "I'm due back in class in five."

"Can't it wait until later on today?" the head replied, reluctant to relinquish his new perch.

"I'll tell you from here then," Jack sighed, "and then you can judge how important it is. I have an interview for the headship of Greystone Hall School next Wednesday and Thursday, so I won't be in school on those two days. You remember? The residential school near Penrith in Cumbria? I told you about the application a while ago."

"Oh yes," the head said, carrying on with his drumming. "OK."

With that, Jack turned on his heels and headed for class,

muttering the word 'tosser' as he went.

-o-

"And you'll never believe where Peter Giles was when I told him about my interview," Jack said to Jenny over dinner that evening.

"I've heard already," she replied as she served his favourite Yorkshire puddings – just as his grandma Marion used to make, he would have said. "Geoff Turner had told us by the end of school. Shows you how important we all are to him. Can you tell me again why you want to leave?" she went on after a mouthful of *her* favourite roasties.

"This school is changing from an organisation catering for social, emotional and behavioural problems," he stated, "to one that offers support for youngsters with all sorts of severe difficulties. That's not my expertise, I'm afraid. More money in it for the company, I believe, but not my cup of tea at all – nor yours, I would imagine. This post was the only one on offer within our time scale."

"So, uprooting and off again, then," she added with a sigh. "Another adventure, eh?"

"It's the onny thing I can do," he replied with a shrug. "You know I'd do anything to make you happy but it's either this new school, or stay here, or … no job at all. I know what you're thinking – we should have stayed in Leeds. Yet hindsight is a wonderful luxury none of us can afford."

This was the only time in his life Jack had felt he was caught in a cleft stick. Usually there had been a sense of adventure, a feeling that it would all work out to their benefit. But now...

-o-

The South Lakes Hotel was an amazing place to hold an

interview for a job in education. The only place to hold a candle to it was Great George Street Education Office in Leeds, but nothing Jack had ever experienced came close to this.

Set on the outskirts of Penrith, a town in South Cumbria, it boasted a leisure centre with gym and swimming pool for the hotel's residents as well as the facility to cater for non-staying guests. The owner of the school, a Mr Brian McDonna, had hired a small suite of rooms in which to conduct the interviews.

Jack had been a little disconcerted and concerned that the tour of the school had been a swift whistle-stop affair that gave them only one idea – that it was exceedingly small. Catering for nineteen boys from eleven to fifteen, when full it housed them in a dormitory for eleven, with four twin rooms equipped with bunk beds. Immediately, it smacked of parochialism and claustrophobia.

In at the front door, and fifteen minutes after that they were at the hotel. Alarm bells should have pealed in Jack's ears, but he wanted it to be right. The other glaring omission was seeing the residential accommodation for the head teacher. That was neither mentioned nor seen.

A minor detail that all the candidates overlooked.

-o-

"Well?" Jenny asked as Jack walked through the door at the end of Thursday of that week. Straight away she expected the worst by the gloomy grimace on his face. "Ah well, I suppose—"

"That I got it!" he interrupted, lifting his face to betray his qualified joy.

"You—!" she exploded, grabbing his non-protesting body, pulling him to her and covering his face in congratulatory kisses. "So obviously it went well? Salary?"

"It was no sweat at all," he replied, when they were sitting down with a decent cup of tea. "The other five candidates were convinced to a man that the job was mine. I'm allus sceptical when it seems to be a foregone conclusion because there's quite often a catch. But everything was above board and the questions seemed to have been tailor made for me. Boom, boom. Job's a good 'un. Salary half as much again as I was getting at Wilsic."

"When do we start?" Jenny asked, quite excited at last, rubbing her hands at the thought of being able to afford to live again, at last.

"Monday, 9th January 1995," he replied, a little bit of a frown spoiling an otherwise perfect outcome.

"Where's the catch?" Jenny asked, noticing his almost imperceptible hesitation.

"Catch?" he replied, realising she had seen what he hadn't wanted her to notice. "What catch?"

"Come on, Buster," she insisted. "How long have we been together? You can't hide your reservations from me."

"Slight difficulty in that we are to live on site," he explained.

"I know that," she said, casting her eyes up to the gods. "I knew that from before you applied. So that's the real reason you're hesitating?"

"The accommodation we are supposed to have is still occupied by the owner and his family," Jack explained, "and will continue to be so until they have secured the house they are buying."

"And that is how long?" she asked, her joyful smile having now evaporated.

"We have to find somewhere else to live until at least early February, I'm afraid," he sighed. "I'm sorry."

"Well, as it turns out very fortunately, mi mam has gone

to stay with her sister," Jenny added, "to look after her until her new hips have settled in, and—"

"And how's that off to help us, Our Jen?" Jack puzzled.

"I *was* going to say that her sister lives in Lancashire," Jenny replied, a triumphant smile on her face. "Auntie Effie has a big house near Carnforth – you know, *Brief Encounter* country? She's always lived alone. Had many offers, no doubt, but she's never wanted – or needed – to get married, and now she's had both hips replaced she needs special care and attention. So, Mum's looking after her for the next few months."

"Jim's looking after the *hacienda* in Methley, then?" Jack said. "No doubt he will have no problems there because—"

"Not, really," she replied. "He's in Carnforth with her. It's a big, big house, you know."

"This will affect us how?" he asked, although he could probably hazard a reasonable guess.

"I'll phone Mum and ask her if we might stay with them," Jenny explained, "at least until the flat in the school is ready. It is travelable from there, I hope?"

"M6 is a cock stride from Carnforth," Jack replied, punching the air in relief. "Half an hour or so from Shap, which is the nearest junction to the 'A' road we'll need. So, we'll have to travel both ways every day for a month or two…"

"From January next," she added. "I know, but you and me can mek anything work, Our Jack."

Carry on some more, Jack … and Jenny!

Chapter 23

"You've got to be joking me!" Jack gasped, once he had settled down to his morning Yorkshire Tea break. "That sounds like one of the daftest, most hare-brained schemes as iver struck ground. Is tha sure, John, or is thy 'avin me on?"

"Straight up, Jacky-boy," John replied, a half-smile also registering his mild disbelief. "From the horse's mouth on Sunday's duty day, which was – yesterday."

"So, run it past me again, then," Jack urged, hutching up to the edge of his more-than-uncomfortable wooden chair, "and I'll see if'n I can pick a few holes in its concept."

Once John had explained what he had been told, Jack sat back quietly contemplating his steaming mug.

"Day trip – from Doncaster, mind – to Calais and return," Jack muttered slowly, "wi' ten lads, starting about half one on a Friday morning and getting back – to Doncaster – around twenty-four hours later, in a super-charged jet-propelled minibus we don't possess that 'asn't bin invented yet. Mmm. Interesting."

"Is tha being sarcastic, Our Jack?" Chris the care worker broke in. "Or do I detect an ever-so-slightly frightening glimmer of insanity creeping in?"

"You could just be right, Chris," Jack replied with a disturbing smile. "But it may well be … interesting. Or here's a thought," he went on, looking over both shoulders as if to check nobody else was eavesdropping. "It may well be a well-conceived but illegal undercover – dare I suggest it – booze run."

Several wide-eyed, mouth-covered gasps betrayed their well-founded cynicism at such a thought. They would never be allowed to do that with vulnerable children on board. Would they?

-o-

"Are you insane?" Jenny gasped. "How can you possibly contemplate taking a party of young ne'er-do-wells on a day trip to another country that's at least twenty-two miles outside the UK? In a day?"

"Not my idea, my lovely, and I have neither hatched, nor am in charge of, this hare-brained scheme," Jack replied calmly. "For once I am only a passenger in this adventure. You're not in, then?"

"You're darned tootin' I *am*!" Jenny replied with a grin. "Day trip to France? Wouldn't miss it for the world. How could you turn a chance like *that* down?"

"You do realise, of course, that each of the adults will have to take turns at driving the minibus?" he warned her. "Even through the night?"

"No sweat," she replied cockily. "Don't forget that I passed my minibus test with distinction. Did you? When do we go?"

"Won't get to know until the meeting next week," Jack said. "I've no doubt that at least *some* of the details will be available by then."

"Only *some* of the details?" Jenny puzzled.

"Come on, Jenny," he urged. "How many schools do you know where planning for an event has been done meticulously down to the last detail? Teachers – other than me, of course – are not renowned for being brilliantly organised planners."

They sat for a while, glorying in each other's company they had always enjoyed. He thanked God earnestly every day that she had chosen to spend the rest of her life with him when perhaps she could have done better, although she would have called him a silly beggar for thinking that way.

A pounding on the door startled them both. "Not expecting anyone, are we?" Jack asked, casting a puzzled frown at his wife.

"Nobody knows we're here," she replied. "Do they?"

"Val?" he said. "Although *I* didn't tell her."

"Door then, Jack?" Jenny urged, realising she might have been the one to give the game away.

"Look who we've got here, Jenny," Jack shouted, shouldering his way through the lounge door.

"Val!" Jenny gasped, hugging her sister until her eyes almost popped out of their sockets. "What are you doing here?"

"I love you too, Sister dear!" Val replied with mock sarcasm. "Not seen you for a while and I just wanted to share some good news with you."

"You're on your own?" Jenny asked, more than a little puzzled. By this time Jack had sloped off into the kitchen to make a pot of tea. It was good to see his sister-in-law, but the fact that Val's soon-to-be husband wasn't with her raised tiny doubts in his mind.

"Mike not with you?" Jack asked as he put down a tray of coffee, tea and cake.

"Well," Val replied hesitantly, "that's one of my pieces of news."

"You're not going to marry him, are you?" Jack added, sitting back with his tea and cake.

"Jack!" Jenny gasped.

"You know he's right, Jen," Val agreed, a dithering smile plaguing her mouth corners. "He's *always* right – damn him. I'm sorry Jack … I didn't mean it to sound so harsh, but—"

"No harm taken, lovely lady," he replied, his usual winning smile overlaying the concern he felt.

A pregnant silence drifted in, forcing them all into an uncomfortable claustrophobic corner as they finished their drinks and cake. What could have happened? Val and Mike had seemed *so* wrapped up in each other.

"Mike's decided he can't cope with being married again so soon after his wife died," Val began tentatively. "He wanted us to carry on as before – no strings and no permanent commitment."

"You weren't going for that one, I assume, because in your head *you* have already committed," Jack added, getting about as close as it was possible to get without being inside her head.

"And I wasn't going back to the previous status quo," she agreed, "because I was ready to chase what you two have always had. I don't need to revisit the sort of claptrap I've always been subject to with your brother." She paused for a moment to gather herself, a tear glistening and her voice about to break.

"So—?" Jenny butted in quietly.

"So, I decided to end the relationship," Val added bravely. "I don't want to wait any longer and I told him so. I've not seen him since the day after you left."

"Why haven't you been in touch?" Jenny asked, hugging her sister.

"To what end, Jenny?" Val said, shrugging her shoulders and shaking her head slightly. "To be reminded what you've always had with your Jack, and that I am likely to remain on my own for the rest of my life on this earth? I needed time to come to terms with it all."

Another rattle at the door stopped her in her tracks, a frightened look betraying her feelings.

"I'll get it," Jack said on his way to the front door. "There's probably a problem in school."

The sisters were silent, straining to hear what was being said and trying to make out who might be saying it.

"Come on through, Old Chap," Jack offered, opening the lounge door to usher in an older man. Before he had time to introduce him, Val sat down unexpectedly with a bump, her face covered by both hands.

-o-

"Why did you decide to come here, of all places?" Val asked, not understanding the rationale driving his action.

"I wanted to sort out our differences," Mike explained, "so we might perhaps get back together … again?"

"Couldn't you have made that decision before we parted company?" she asked sharply. "I can't do with all this indecision. After what's happened, I don't know whether I *can* forgive and forget. What's to prevent it from happening again?"

"My word?" he replied simply, a pleading look on his face and sorrow in his eyes.

Jack and Jenny had retreated to the kitchen to give them space and time to try to sort out what had gone wrong and if there was a way it might be possible to put it right. Jack had his doubts.

"Half an hour, Our Jen? Should we ask if they would like a cup of Yorkshire?" he asked, impatiently. "I'm ready for one. You?"

"Come on then," she replied eagerly. "Let's ask."

"Like a cup of tea, you two?" Jack asked cheerily,

shouldering his way into the lounge.

The room was empty.

No sign of either person or any indication anyone had ever been in the room – except for a piece of folded white notepaper bearing Jenny and Jack's names. Jenny unfolded it and read its contents.

"What does it say, Jenny?" Jack urged. "Any explanation?"

"It says simply *Will ring you later – Val and Mike,*" Jenny said. "No indication as to where they've gone, by your leave, or—"

"Kiss mi hairy arse?" he added for good luck. "Is she getting desperate in her quest to find that elusive bit of happiness, do you think?"

"No idea," Jenny replied. "Why can't folk just get on with their lives and leave us alone?"

"Because she's your sister, perhaps?" he pointed out with a shrug. "I've no doubt they'll include us when they've sorted stuff out. Meantime, I wonder if you might like a cup of tea, Our Jack?" he asked himself. "Do you know, Old Chap," he replied, "I do believe I would.

"Good man," he said again. "Then we should nip back into the kitchen and mash one, don't you think?"

"Agreed, Our Jack," he told himself again, trying to pat himself on the back. "Excellent idea."

"What on earth are you doing?" Jenny said, a smile splitting her face. "Trying to persuade yourself to have a cup of tea? Now, that's a first!"

"I had to get somebody to answer me," he explained. "You wouldn't. In another world, I think you were."

They both laughed as they usually did at his pathetic attempts at trying to sound like Yoda, and at the simplest of things, before wandering arm in arm into the kitchen to mek a rayt good cup of Yorkshire Tea.

"Week on Friday, Jack," John Wallbank said as they passed on the education block corridor.

"Week on Friday what, John?" Jack replied, after a moment or two of puzzling.

"Is the 14th of October," his friend replied.

"And I'm supposed to whoop and jump for joy because it's soon to be Friday 14th of October?" Jack scoffed. "Yay! Friday the—!"

"Forgotten already that it's our lazy day out to … France, Old Chap?" John said, not really knowing whether Jack was serious or not. It had always been difficult to read this dour Yorkshireman, being himself from across the border in Lancashire's glorious Blackburn. Different as limestone and Wensleydale.

"Lazy day?" Jack scoffed. "I don't consider a sleepless twenty-four-hour plus, crammed in a tiny minibus wi' five other adults and ten recalcitrant kids, a lazy day out. I'd rather be in Bridlington in January in a tent! At least it'd be healthy and bracing thiyer, wi' no recycled belching and farting in a warm, cloying, enclosed tin can."

They both laughed heartily as they took their leave, John to a football kick-about with a group of eleven and thirteen year olds that neither liked the 'beautiful game' nor had any skill in it – smart lads – and Jack back to the cottage to write up his report on the success of Steven Harris's placement so far.

About as exciting and appetising as running into Doncaster and back in bare feet through six feet of snow!

Steven was a grand lad who was smart and eager to succeed at work he considered relevant to *him*. Historically he'd had problems with education folk who were overly bureaucratic and inflexible in their approach to his work ethic that seemed right for him but not to them. He tended to make good progress in a relaxed environment, working at his own pace where urgency was managed and manageable. Unfortunately, mainstream day schools did not encourage that sort of ethos, which resulted in their dropping young men like him by the wayside. It had to be the goal of special schools like Wilsic to reconnect the Stevens of this world with a feeling of excitement and worth in learning in general, which had been driven out of mainstream schools by over-exuberant bureaucracy.

The likes of Steven and Danny and Paul were doers, not deep thinkers concerned with solving abstract, intellectual conundrums. Given the opportunity, and with the appropriate support, they could become useful members of their own society – factors that Jack had always built into his work with strugglers in school.

"What are you doing in my house, Jack Ingles?" a very familiar voice cut through the silence, bringing a welcoming smile to his face. "Lunchtime and not a piece of bread buttered, or a kettle boiled."

"Have a look in the fridge, oh ye of little faith," he shouted, as he scuttled downstairs to greet Jenny. "And take one of your index fingers and wave it over the kettle's switch to warm up t'watter. Then you'll see that two mugs – matching, mind you – have had milk added ready for a strange concoction to be added that is called … tea from Yorkshire."

"Sarcastic bugger," she muttered as she sat down with the sandwich he had made, leaving him to mash the tea as only he knew how.

"Is that the postman's dulcet rattle of the letterbox?" Jack said, already on his way to the front door. "I can always tell when it's her. The rattle of the letterbox is almost *pizzicato*."

"Her?" Jenny asked, puzzled at the reference.

"Indeed," he replied. "Didn't you know they've started employing post*women* nowadays? So Violet and Hannah's sacrifices were *not* in vain."

"That's a bit obscure, even for you, Our Jack," Jenny said scratching her head. "Violet and Hannah?"

"Violet Key-Jones was a prominent female emancipation activist in the Doncaster area before the First War," he replied, matter of fact. "Hannah Clark was the same but, as a Quaker, she was more prone to *peaceful* protest. *She* was the first female councillor in Doncaster in 1920 and very successful she was, too. Not a lot of people know that." Unfortunately, his Michael Caine impersonation didn't even warrant a mention from Jenny.

"But," Jenny said, aghast at his obscure knowledge, "how do you know all this … this … stuff? I've never heard of all this and I did history at university."

"Just part of the jumble of disparate facts in my strange mind that pop out now and again," he replied, quite amused by her reaction. "Letter? Addressed to you. Are you going to open in and relieve the mystery and misery of it remaining unopened on your lap? Are your fingers useful only for tickling these days?"

"Would you like me to demonstrate, buster?" she warned him, deftly slitting open the envelope.

"It's from Val," she continued. "She's talking about going away with … Mike, for goodness' sake, for a few days to 'sort things out'. She, of course, is on half-term break next week. So, it seems like Benidorm here they come!"

"And what's wrong with that?" Jack replied, tongue in cheek. "*We're* doing the same thing at the end of next week. There's no satisfying some people. I don't know."

"The difference being, my man, that our 'holiday' will last all of twenty-four hours," Jenny pointed out. "And we get to spend it with ten children, and we get to do some of the driving. Goody."

"Sarcasm doesn't become you, Our Jenny," he replied with a smirk. "We get paid, and what more could you ask? Seems like things are back on, then?"

Go for it, Val!

Jack had always known she had it in her, now that her useless husband was no longer on the scene. He still had to be sure that this *Mike* was bona fide, though. He wouldn't allow *anyone* to play fast and loose with his favourite – his only – sister-in-law.

Chapter 24

"Wow! What a fantastic smell of frying bacon!" John Wallbank said as he walked through the doorway into the school's dining hall. "Who's cooking at just after midnight? Early breakfast?"

Joan and Jenny's pinny-clad bodies sidled through the kitchen hatch doorway bearing trays of bacon sandwiches and baps ready for the lads to eat, some of whom were barely awake and some of whom were not even borderline.

The staff members, on the other hand, stifling the occasional give-away yawn, set to demolishing those delicious sarnies with a vengeance, discussing the merits of ketchup versus brown sauce as they did so. The result? Four to one in favour of … brown sauce.

"What time are we setting off, Geoff?" John asked the senior teacher on the trip.

"Half past one at the very latest," Geoff replied firmly. "No shilly-shallying on this one. We've a timetable to stick to, particularly when there's catching a boat to consider.

"Jack's first driver," he went on. "A1 to Doncaster, south on to the M25 and clockwise round to Dartford Crossing and on to the M2 exit towards Dover. Joan will then get us onto and off the ferry into Calais. We'll decide the other orders when we're on our way over to Calais."

Once the last crumb had been smothered in brown sauce

and consigned to a memory, ten lads and five adults were ushered into the school's minibus. Jack settled in behind the wheel and started to rev the engine as it juddered up the drive to the open road.

"What on earth's up wi' this bloomin' thing?" he growled as the minibus chugged and shuddered.

"Be rayt, Jack," Joan piped up, "once it's warmed up. Be patient wi' it."

Jack showed impatient restraint with a machine that needed to take them safely for several hundred miles but might, by the sound of it, last only two. However, once they hit the A1 South, the engine magically began to purr as if rolling up its sleeves ready for a good run to the distant Kent coast.

Jack was the only person on board to witness the smooth but swift acceleration on to this fast southbound and almost deserted road. Snoring and grunting and farting were the only sounds to be heard – after all, it *was* two o'clock in the morning of Friday 14th October 1994.

-o-

"And that's how I remember it," Jack sighed as the story slowly unfurled, a captive and captivated audience metaphorically glued on the edges of their seats. "It was an almost uneventful day—"

"Almost?" Val said, unsure as to what he meant. After all, he *was* prone to minimise and understate at times. "Why was it *nearly* uneventful?"

"Once we had disembarked but were still in the van, a whole city opened up before our eyes without leaving the port," Jack went on, still quite mesmerised with what he had seen. "We parked the van and set off in different directions with our groups on the hunt for two important things – food and drink. There were cafés and eateries galore that needed only … someone who could understand the lingo. But that was only one person spread thinly between four other adults and ten children. Everything seemed miraculously to have been covered until I heard raised voices in a nearby cafeteria. Steven Harris thought he'd been done over a glass of orange and a salad sandwich – which he hadn't. Fortunately, just a brief word in the Frenchman's ear soon restored the *entente cordiale*."

"That must have been interesting seeing a French waiter trying to make himself understood by a Yorkshire sixteen-year-old intent on not being done out of his food," Mike added with a snort.

"It was almost pistols at dawn, I can tell you," Jenny gasped. "Until this peacemaker intervened to put things right."

"Now that can't have been all there was to upset the apple cart," Val observed. "Can it?"

"Well," Jack drawled slowly, "now you come to mention it, the journey back to English *terra firma* – very late evening, after a stop for food and to stretch our legs – was interesting, to say the least."

"You have to bear in mind, of course," Jenny butted in, "that we had almost all taken a share of the driving to this point, some of us without sleep, I have to add."

"On his stint, John Wallbank missed the turn-off for the A1M Northbound from the M25," Jack went on with a wry grin, "and took us for a heady jaunt through Hertfordshire's country lanes past St Albans – bearing in mind it was now getting on for eleven o'clock at night."

"At one stage, we thought we were going to have to spend the night with a herd of deer that had blocked the road," Jenny explained. "Lots of funny night animal noises kept Jack and me awake. We were the only ones not asleep because I had taken over from John who cracked on he was tired. Weren't we all!"

"We managed to regain the A1 eventually," Jack went on, "and arrived back in Doncaster without further mishap at around half two on the morning of Saturday the 15th."

"The end of a very busy and eventful day then?" Val said, with a heartfelt sigh.

"Not quite," Jack added

"There's more?" Mike asked, with a surprised and nervous laugh.

"The other adults on the trip had to unload the boxes of bottles of wine and beer into their cars as surreptitiously as they could," Jack explained with a grin, "once the youngsters had been trooped off to bed – bringing us back to my original thoughts about the *real* reason for the trip."

–o–

"Cup of Yorkshire Tea?" Jack suggested. "And explanations' time, perhaps?"

"Jack!" Jenny gasped. "Not helping!"

"Just saying," he replied, an unapologetic grin lingering. "The last we heard from you two amounted to two lines on a scrap of paper just over a week ago, and then – here you are. Any news?"

"We are obviously 'together'," Val explained. "And—"

"Will be staying together," Mike added, "because we have set plans in place for our nuptials."

"Now that's what I'm talking about!" Jack chortled, standing up to hug his sister-in-law and to wring the hand of his new notional brother-in-law – or something like that. "Have you set a date yet?"

"One of the reasons I left in such a rush the last time we were here," Mike explained, "was that I needed to see my twin daughters – not to seek their approval but to talk things through. They told me not to be so stupid, and to get on with what I wanted and had to do. Very fortunately, this beautiful lady here has forgiven that immature stupidity and has agreed to marry me. Hence—"

"A week on Saturday at the Registry Office where you were married, and where Joyce gave birth to her Valerie – in the toilet, of course. After all, Mike *is* originally from Castleford," Val added happily. "Will you give me away, Our Jack? Please?"

"Of course I will," he replied hugging her. "It will be my pleasure. How much can I expect to get for you?"

They all laughed, knowing that finally Val was destined to spend the rest of her life with a good man who loved her and whom she loved in return. She had only two years to retirement at sixty and Mike had already reached that milestone. Their ultimate goal was to retire to the sun, thereby escaping the unpredictability of the English weather. Hopefully, that meant free holidays abroad for Jenny and Jack.

Way to go, Val!

–o–

Jack and Jenny started at Greystone House Residential School five days after his forty-ninth birthday in 1995. It should have been a gloriously exhilarating day and a foretaste of things to come. Unfortunately, although they were staying with Flo and Jim at Aunt Effie's on the outskirts of Carnforth, their first day had started at six in the morning (after breakfast) with a journey through driving sleet, and their arrival at the school to moderate drifts of snow and … no heating.

"This doesn't bode well," Jack growled, as they shouldered

their way into the office to be met by a thermometer boldly announcing a temperature of four degrees Celsius.

Although the wife of the owner, Brian McDonna, assured them the engineers in Carlisle had been called two days before, and had promised to attend to the central heating within twenty-four hours, it seemed like the weather had defeated them. Fortunately, none of the boys had returned from Christmas holiday – but neither had the owner.

"The post needs attending to first job," Jenny warned him, pointing to a large pile of envelopes of many different sizes and colours on the floor under wrap-around worktops near her desk.

"*I* think the first job has to be putting on yon kettle," Jack insisted, making his way out of the office to find water, his coat and scarf still tightly wrapped round his chilly body.

The small, windowless medical room boasted a bed, a toilet and a source of water but little else – no medical cupboard where medication might be stored, and no register where entries concerning illnesses might be logged. What he encountered didn't fill him with any feelings other than gloom and foreboding.

Plugging in the kettle after begging milk from the kitchen, which luckily was inhabited by humans, Jenny beckoned him to the pile of post. "You'd better read this," she warned, as she handed over an official-looking letter signed by the Chief Inspector from Her Majesty's Inspectorate of Schools.

"You've got to be kidding me!" he gasped. "A group of HMIs is to visit us ... on Friday? That's ridiculous. We've only just walked through the door and we're being inspected already?"

"I believe it's a follow-up to previous visits," Jenny said, looking through a five-page document from the same source. "It seems the school was inspected last October for the second time in as many months, and the owner was given a list of improvements to put in place before this coming inspection. The upshot? Closure, if he doesn't comply."

"Looks like we've fallen on our feet again!" Jack added sarcastically. "Does our bad luck never change?"

"That's not all," she went on, skimming through a letter from Social Services. "The day before *that* visit – next Thursday – we're having the pleasure of a visit from Social Services to assess the school's response to their concerns about health and safety among the children and their physical safety in and around the building."

"I'd better take these away wi' us," Jack replied with a sigh, "so I can look at 'em tonight. We're not staying here much longer in this cold, seeing as Brian McDonna is nowhere in evidence."

-o-

"This makes me feel like I don't want to be here, Our Jen, if we're confronted with this fiasco on our first day," Jack explained as they turned onto the M6 Southbound, and when they had left the A6 and Shap behind them, with the car's heater on full blast.

"That's not like you, Our Jack," Jenny replied, putting her hand on his thigh to reassure him. "Shouldn't we be giving it a go first, to see if we have any leeway?"

"That's what these letters are going to tell me tonight," he continued. "And if I can come up with a reasonably viable solution to both questions, I will telephone both parties and suggest a way forward. If it turns out there *is* no solution, we're out of here in double-quick time and I will instruct my union – the NAHT – to sue. But let's see where it takes us first, eh?"

"What about Mrs McDonna?" Jenny asked. "Does she

know anything of her husband's whereabouts?"

"I spoke to her before we left," Jack explained, "and she is under no illusion about our intentions. Unfortunately, she still has no idea where her husband is."

-o-

"So, how on earth did you manage to sort it out?" George William asked several weeks later, on one of his rare, fleeting visits to see his Mam and Dad.

"Still in the process, Old Chap," Jack replied with a shrug. "Got clearance from Social Services yesterday, after several unannounced visits at various times of the weeks we've been here. And HMI want to make their final visit next week."

"Did the owner ever return?" his son asked, still not really understanding how anyone could get away with what Mr McDonna had done.

"He came back two days ago," Jack explained, "following a threat by his wife that she was about to sell the school to me for a pound. Nobody knows where he was or what he'd been doing. He wasn't too enamoured by the amount of money I've had to spend on heating and safety features imposed by Social Services, either."

"Does that mean everything's all right, then?" his son asked again.

"Watching brief, Old Chap," Jack replied with a rueful smile. "We'll have to see what Her Majesty's Inspector of Schools has to say."

-o-

"It looks like they're in," Jack said, as they turned into the drive of *their* home in North Leeds.

"Jack? Jenny?" Val gasped, a knotty curl of her lip and

a puzzled frown betraying her surprise at discovering her sister and brother-in-law at the front door. "What are you doing here? Holiday from school?"

"Not really, in so many words," Jenny replied.

"For goodness' sake, come in," Mike insisted, interrupting his wife. "Don't stand around on *your* own doorstep."

"Wow!" Jack said, as they sat down to tea and scones. "That's a tan and a half. No mistaking where *you've* been for the last week or two."

"Try 'month or two'," Val said, a wicked glint betraying her mischievousness. "Anyway, it's good to see you. How's school these days? Long summer hols, eh, to boost your batteries for—?"

"What school?" Jenny answered curtly.

"Mid-August?" her sister queried. "Lazy school holidays in preparation for September's re-entry of the hordes? Don't forget, I used to be part of that scenario."

"Used to be—?" Jack said, a flashing bulb in his head suddenly lighting up his face. "You've decided to retire, haven't you?"

"Make that '*have retired*', Old Chap," Mike corrected. "But enough of that until you tell us the obvious news that is weighing on your shoulders."

"We are now homeless and jobless," Jenny said, her stark message rocking them back in their chairs.

"Homeless and—?" Val gasped. "What did you do? Steal the Crown Jewels?"

"Long story," Jack added with a sigh. "Following threats of closure from HMI and Social Services within a day of our arriving there in January, because of the owner's incompetence and not sticking to agreed rules, we put everything right and were awarded a clean bill of health by both HMI and local Social Services."

"Jack worked nigh on eighteen hours a day to put things

in order and fell asleep in his tea more than once," Jenny interrupted. "Seven days a week he toiled – you know him."

"We'd moved into a tiny flat in the school – unfortunately next to the dormitories, sometime after Mr McDonna reappeared from his 'absence' at the beginning of February," Jack went on. "Late one evening at the end of July, there was a banging on the door between the dorms and the flat. That had never happened before, so I *had* to investigate. Ginger-haired Ashley – a lovely lad who knows every song from *The Bodyguard* – informed me that one of the lads had absconded.

"I found it a bit odd that a window had been left open and the bed occupied by Robert was empty. Strange, because the open window was fitted with a restrictor that allows it to be opened only for air flow. Tim, the lad in the next bed said nothing but pointed his eyes upwards as if trying to indicate something.

"It turned out that Mr McDonna had a tiny flat upstairs that he used when he was on duty. The cat burglar instinct in me insisted I mount the stairs silently, which I did. I heard scuffling inside, so I knocked on the door and asked if Robert was there with him. No answer. I asked again. Still no answer.

"We were due to go away on holiday the following day, but I confronted him in the kitchen before we set off, warning him that I knew what he was up to. On our return, after a week away in Scotland, he confronted *me*, telling *me* he wanted us out."

"Can't believe you let him get away with that!" Val gasped.

"We didn't," Jack continued. "I refused and contacted my union rep straight away. He negotiated a term's salary in lieu of the statutory notice. So now we will be paid in full until the end of December while we look for other jobs."

"Will you do anything else about it?" Val continued. "I mean like letting the authorities know?"

"Already done so, Val," he replied. "I visited the local Education and Social Services divisions to alert them to his practices. He won't get away with it. It turns out that the ancillary kitchen staff were desperate to advise me not to take the job when we went around school on that initial visit pre-interview."

"We are well out of it," Jenny agreed.

"Funny you should say that," Mike explained, "but we are in the process of buying a house in Southern Spain in the Frigiliana area – permanent move. So, you can have your house back with our grateful thanks. You must come and stay with us – we'll work out reasonable rates, don't you fear."

They laughed easily, as this was something Jack would have offered. When all was said and done, Mike *was* from Castleford – Jack's neck of the woods.

Ee, Yorkshiremen, eh? *I* don't know.

Chapter 25

"I understand you weren't to know," Jenny's Aunt Effie said, one cold and snowy Friday morning mid-December. "But if you'd mentioned Brian McDonna's name to me, I'd have given you chapter and verse on his life as a teacher in the Manchester and Liverpool areas. What you have told me bears out what I know about him already."

"Did you know him personally, Aunt Effie?" Jenny asked, a glass of Croft's sherry to hand.

"Not really, my dear," her aunt replied with a smile, feet up on a corduroy-covered footstool, "but reputation always precedes. Anyway, is there a *real* reason for you being here? I mean, you've hardly visited before your recent escapades."

"Before this year, the last time I came here was when I was five and my sister was fourteen." Jenny replied. "We went to see where *Brief Encounter* was filmed, and then we had a steam train ride to Carlisle. We've usually lived so far away from you, but I've always regretted not visiting more often."

"The reason we're here, apart from visiting to say thank you for putting up with us at the beginning of the year," Jack explained, "is that we're selling up in Leeds and moving over here to live."

"Why on earth would you want to do that, pray?" Aunt Effie replied, surprised that the larger city of Leeds couldn't offer them more than much smaller Lancaster.

"We're beginning to appreciate the area," Jack went on with a rueful smile. "And there are more jobs here than where we live now, so—"

"Try Jerry Wilkins, education officer at White Cross Education Department in Lancaster," Aunt Effie offered. "I worked with him for a few years and he is one of the good guys. He'll at least give you a hearing. And what's more, like you he is from the West Riding."

"I had intended giving that education office a try," Jack replied, a grin of triumph gracing his face, "but now I know whom to target. Thank you, Aunt Effie. Forever in your debt."

"Now, *that's* for another day," she said. "Does anyone fancy a drive out to Arnside? We could watch the tidal bore, and I know a nice little pub where they do a particularly good rack of lamb."

-o-

"Please come in, Mr Ingles," said Lancashire's education officer at White Cross Education Department, "and thank you for writing to me. Now, please tell me how I can be of assistance to you today."

"My letter gave you my background," Jack began, "so I thought I would bring my CV to you in person to see what – if anything – you might be able to do with me."

"A fellow Yorkshireman, indeed," Mr Wilkins observed with unerring accuracy and a smile, as he flicked through Jack's CV. "And straight to the point, which I appreciate. Your details and experience look interesting and I *may* have something in your line that you could latch on to and develop. It won't be fully available until January, but I need to speak to the head of that particular service to let her sort things out for you. She's called Lee McKee. Give me a couple of days, and I'll telephone you with more details. OK?"

"Indeed yes, Mr Wilkins, "Jack replied. "I'll look forward to that."

-o-

He couldn't help skipping back to the car park with a smile on his face despite the chill growing round his thinly coated body. Perhaps he might now be able to afford a *real* winter garment to guard against searchingly cold northern winter days. His blue Rover 420 had seen better days, but its seats were still comfortable, especially with their fast-working, built-in warmers and the car's three-speed heater.

His journey from Lancaster through Bolton-le-Sands to Carnforth and beyond to Aunt Effie's house seemed to last but a short time because of the excited thoughts crowding his mind. At last, someone who was honestly prepared to take his experience and qualifications into serious consideration for a job with youngsters who would benefit from working with him.

"I'm back," he called, unlatching the door. "Anybody here? Anybody put the kettle on? I know it won't suit you all, but—"

"I see your weedy jokes haven't improved, Our Jack," a familiar voice greeted him as he disrobed and sauntered into the lounge.

"This is a surprise. I thought you'd be sunning yourselves in Nerja by now. What's up, too warm over there?" Jack answered with a chortle.

"We leave tomorrow," Val explained. "Taking over a three-bed villa with a huge amount of outside space in a couple of weeks. So, we need to lounge about a bit before the work starts."

"It's all right for some," Jenny laughed. "Chance would be a fine thing! Well?" she asked as conversation faded.

"Well what?" Jack replied.

"You know perfectly well what!" she said sharply.

"We've set the educational ball rolling," he said. "Mr Wilkins liked what he saw, but he's to involve the Head of Service – Lancaster's School Support Service – in anything to do with appointments and general stuff involving children. I should get to know within a couple of days. Is it all right that we stay for a while, Aunt Effie? At least until the house in Leeds is sold and we find another?"

"Please, Jack, yes," Effie replied with a smile. "For as long as you need. I'm rattling around in this place on my own. There's plenty of space, and we'll agree a reasonable rate for the stay, of course."

"Are you sure we're not distantly related?" Jack said with a hearty guffaw.

"We're all distantly related, Jack," Effie explained. "We're Yorkshire – underneath our amiable, accepting surfaces we're all chiselled from the same granite."

"Amiable? Accepting?" Val laughed. "Which Yorkshire folk are *you* talking about?"

"I bet you're relieved to be rid of that place in Cumbria," Mike observed.

"You don't know the half." Jack sighed. "We accepted employment in good faith, and he stamped on us all the way. Still, we did get our justice in the end."

"Justice?" Val said. "How do you reckon that? You did all that work, had unlimited aggravation, and ended up with no job."

"True," Jack agreed. "But we brought the school up to standard, costing him the best part of a hundred grand into the bargain, and we are being paid until Christmas.

How good is that? I've heard, by the way, that the lads have refused to co-operate since we left, and the staff that should have supported us have been paid with rubber cheques for the last four months. That's what I call Karma."

-o-

"Hello," the telephone line crackled. "Is that Jack Ingles?"

"Does he owe you money?" Jack replied, a smile lurking.

"Sorry?" the voice replied, sounding nonplussed. "Well, er, no. Why?"

"Then yes, this *is* Jack Ingles," he replied, trying not to laugh.

The voice on the other end giggled. "I like your sense of humour. I'm Lee McKee and I'm phoning to welcome you to our group, Lancaster's Pupil Support Service."

"Wow!" Jack gasped. "I wasn't expecting to hear so soon. Thank you for the offer. I'm really looking forward to becoming part of the group."

"Could you perhaps come around to see me tomorrow?" she suggested. "There are lots of things you need to know… Where? Do you know Central Lancaster High School, off Crag Road on the Ridge?"

"No," he replied quickly, "but me *A–Z* probably does. I don't know Lancaster yet because I've not been here before, but I'll find it. Why?"

"Because that's where we hang out," Lee replied with a chuckle. "Tomorrow at ten be all right for you?"

Jack hung up, having agreed the meeting time and place, and turned towards Jenny who by this time had mashed a pot of Yorkshire Tea and brought in some scones that Aunt Effie had baked a little earlier.

"Family trait, eh?" Jack said, as he tucked into proper scones and butter.

"How's that then, Our Jack?" Jenny replied, looking round at her aunt's beautiful lounge with its antimacassar-covered luxury suite, inlaid rosewood coffee table and genuine Persian rugs.

"You're a fabulous baker," he replied, replenishing his now-empty mouth quickly. "So is your mum, and now . . . Aunt Effie is as well. Such a talented family."

They both laughed, comfortable in the thought that although they wouldn't be drowning in cash, they would be able to manage and to look for a place of their own.

"I've seen a nice little house for sale just down the road in Bolton-le-Sands," Aunt Effie said, as she hobbled into the room on her walking frame – a contraption she had to use to exercise her new hips. "Semi-detached bungalow with a room upstairs. I think you'll enjoy the price."

"Come on then, Auntie Effie," Jack said eagerly. "Spill."

"As far as I gather," she went on slowly to build the suspense, "it's on at offers over £40,000."

"We'll have it!" Jack replied. "Who's the agent?"

"Farrar and Haywood, I believe," she said, a triumphant smile decorating her happy face.

"Phone them then, Jack," Jenny added, "and we'll get to see what they have on offer as soon as possible."

-o-

"That was a call from the estate agent," Jack said, when he had re-joined his wife and her aunt. "Our offer for the house has been topped by another couple. They've offered £41,950."

"I don't know," Jenny said. "What do *you* think Jack?"

"I've already made a counter-offer, though I don't agree with this 'ere gazumpin' lark," he replied, with an annoyed grimace.

"And that'll be their reply, no doubt," Jenny said, as the shrill sound of the telephone interrupted their peace.

Jack's somewhat elevated tone from the hall as he answered the phone concerned her slightly. She was wondering how high he might be prepared to go to secure their new home. He entered the lounge moments later, a grim yet defiant look growing.

"Well?" Jenny asked reluctantly.

"Another hike from our competitors." Jack said, with a resigned shrug. "So, I've told them which part of my nether regions to kiss. Not getting into that upward spiral so that the agents get to rake in their escalating fees. I've also researched new-builds in this area. Back to the drawing board, our Jen."

Chapter 26

"T'Ridge? Crag Road? Where the 'ummer are they?" Jack muttered to himself, driving his car around the streets of the council estate. "I might 'ave to … Ah! There it is!"

Jamming on his brakes, he did a sharp right turn into Crag Road and again trawled along slowly. Fortunately, there was no traffic except for dozens of cars parked along the street, mostly with at least two wheels on the pavement and sometimes three, with the fourth parked in thin air.

"Wow!" he gasped, catching sight of an enormous seven-feet-high boulder that seemed to be growing from a grassy knoll just inside what had to be a school's outer fence and gates. Why was it that all school fences and gates always seemed to be painted green? On the boulder was carved—

"Central Lancaster High School," Jack muttered. "This has to be the place. How many schools in the same area would be likely to bear the same name? Here goes."

He parked in the Visitor Car Park and sauntered toward an official building that screamed Admin Centre. "Excuse me," he said, poking his head around the office door, "but I'm looking for Lee McKee."

"Mrs McKee?" the lady behind a large black typewriter said. "You must be Mr Ingles. Come in and I'll let her know you're here."

"Jack!" a wispy voice floated by him from the office door. "I may call you Jack?"

"It would be my pleasure, Lee," Jack replied easily as he turned to see a petite brunette, eye-catchingly dressed, of around fifty years of age.

"Come over and meet the rest of the team," she said, beckoning him to follow.

The building was typical of most schools that had appeared in the 1960s – dour grey concrete and so many windows that looked out at the identical council houses surrounding it, like rectangular, blind, lidless eyes.

The room they entered, off a bland featureless corridor leading to … nowhere, was equally bland but boasted enough tables, chairs and cupboards to accommodate enough workers to staff a reasonably sized organisation. There were three other people in the room – two females and one male – all busy with either report writing or planning of some sort.

So, this was the team that provided support for most of the children with special educational behavioural and emotional needs in Lancaster's secondary schools. Jack couldn't help remarking to himself that none of them seemed to have superhuman powers.

What made this bunch of unprepossessing teachers so overwhelmingly special that they could stem the rising tide of misfits in the normal school system? Or is that what they were *supposed* do? Sprinkle the magic dust to make all problems evaporate like dew in the morning sun? Is that why Jack had been drafted in, to add gravitas to an almost impossible task? He wondered when he would be issued with *his* wand and *his* bag of magical sparkly powder.

Pragmatic and cynical? Jack? Never!

"Jack," Lee said, once the door on reality had been closed, "I should like you to meet Jacki, Madeleine and Barry. The

Three Musketeers—"

"Or the Three Stooges," Barry added quickly, "depending on your perspective. Call me old fashioned."

"But I thought you were called Barry," Jack shot back equally quickly, causing a polite titter to bubble out from Lee but no reaction from the other three. Not amazing senses of humour, then, it seemed.

"This is our base?" Jack asked, wondering if this was what he *really* wanted.

"For now," Lee replied. "We will be moving to our own base in Caton in the very near future. Do you know where Caton is, Jack?"

"Somewhere down the Lune Valley?" he ventured. He didn't know but he was an avid map reader. He liked to plan out his own itinerary whenever they decided to travel by car and he was meticulous in his planning of detail, as with everything else he did.

"Can I assume that this isn't all we will be doing?" Jack asked, an innocent look on his face. "Or is this just a one-off?"

"I can see we're going to get along fine," Lee replied with a laugh. "Is your sense of humour always like this?"

"More or less," Jack agreed with a mock-apologetic grin. "Folks either love it or … hate it, I'm afraid."

"Tomorrow," Lee advised him, "I should like to you visit Stuart Vernon, head of Special Needs at Heysham High School. Just to introduce yourself, you understand, and to put in the groundwork ready for taking up post there. Do you know where that is?"

"In Heysham, I assume?" Jack replied, a slight frown showing her that he had no idea what she was talking about. "Your face tells me that it's *not* in Heysham."

"It's not," she warned, "but your *A–Z* should show you. It's only a preliminary meeting and not essential, but it would be good if you could make it for eleven. Just in time for a cup of tea at break."

"Will it be Yorkshire Tea?" he asked, his seemingly serious question stopping her in her tracks.

"Why?" she asked slowly. "Is that important?"

"If you were a Yorkshire Tea drinker, Lee," he went on, with one eyebrow raised and his head tipped slightly to one side in surprise, "you wouldn't be asking that question. Just saying."

Not sure whether he was being serious, she giggled nervously and turned the kettle on. Lifting the lidless tea caddy to her face, she sniffed the contents suspiciously.

Jack smiled when he had taken the first mouthful in his new workplace after sniffing the brew. "It's not Yorkshire," he declared deliberately, moving his lips as if he were testing the bouquet, like a wine taster ready to spit out the tasting mouthful, "but it'll do."

-o-

"What on earth is … that?" Jack asked, nonplussed at what seemed like a huge model of Postman Pat sitting on the floor in the corner of the hall, leaning its back against a wall as if it were resting.

He closed the front door behind him and wandered over to the object. He poked its shoulder tentatively and took a swift step backwards as if he expected it to poke him back.

"It's my new uniform," Jenny replied as she finished off her cup of tea. "For work tomorrow."

"Where are you working, for goodness' sake?" he asked, casting a wary eye at the object again.

"Mothercare," she replied quickly. "It was the only job I could get. It's temporary, but I do get six pounds an hour. Have to wear it outside the shop in Market Square in

Lancaster, to advertise."

"But it's huge!" he gasped. "And you're not tall enough by a long shot to see out of its eyes!"

"Have a look closely at the middle of his chest," Jenny instructed. "Where his topcoat button is. See? Two holes."

"How on earth are you going to move about in that … thing without falling over?" he scoffed. "His boots are three times the size of mine! And … where did it come from and how did you get it … here?"

"One of the staff dropped him off and will pick us up tomorrow," she replied, shrugging, matter of fact, "in a works van."

"And what's all this *his* business?" he scoffed. "Anybody would think it was alive."

"It is," she laughed, "when *I'm* in it."

A heartfelt sigh escaped from Jack's body as he settled with his Yorkshire Tea mug in front of Aunt Effie's roaring log fire that puthered out enough heat to warm the entire ground floor. Very much ahead of her time, Effie had created a huge open-plan space that she loved – kitchen, dining and living space to die for. Couldn't do with enclosed, claustrophobic, poky little rooms when she was quite a gregarious animal that loved to entertain. She'd had underfloor heating installed that rarely needed stoking up because of the wood burner; there was just the odd occasion when the chill needed to be taken off the magnificent Italian porcelain tiles that covered the entire ground floor.

Although Aunt Effie still had many male friends, she had never entertained an urge to share her living space or life with any one of 'em. "All right for a Saturday and Sunday social, but definitely not for Monday breakfast," she would say, a triumphant smile overpowering her expressive face. She was a one-off was Aunt Effie, and nothing like her sister Flora Mae.

"How's this new job going to pan out, do you think, Our Jack?" Jenny asked as they drank their tea together.

"Not sure yet, Our Jen," he answered tentatively. "It seems to be a bit of a Mickey Mouse affair, but then I've been there onny a bit on a day and can't really judge until I've experienced a much bigger picture.

"Got to go into a secondary school tomorrow called Hayshum High to meet a chap called Stuart who's in charge of special needs," he went on. He could be a bit sharp about stuff he didn't rate immediately, could Our Jack.

"Don't you mean Heysham?" she corrected. "Pronounced Heesham, I believe."

"Whatever," he added. "I thought it would be in He..e.. sham, but apparently not. I'll need to consult my *A–Z* and maybe have a sniff around first."

"Now then, Jenny and Jack," Effie's gentle voice greeted them as she hobbled into the room. "Somebody here to see you."

"Hello Uncle Jack and Auntie Jen," a softly spoken male voice accosted them as they turned.

"I'd recognise that voice in any crowd," Jack replied, jumping to his feet to greet… "Young Joey! Good to si thi, lad. Or should I say 'not-so-young' Joey. And who are these three delightful people?" he went on, hugging his nephew.

"I should like you to meet my wife, Izzy, and my twins, Jack and Jenny."

"Twins?" Jack gasped, almost not believing what he was hearing. "I didn't even know you were married. Not seen you for an age. Thought you'd either emigrated or died. We weren't even invited to your wedding," he went on, in a low-key, admonitory tone.

"It was a spur of the moment thing," Joey explained, "and we had no idea where you were. Mum was otherwise occupied, and Nana Flo and Grandpa Jim were out of the country on a month's cruise. So, we just … did it."

"Good for you, Our Joey and Izzy," Jenny butted in. "You have to do what you have to do. But now you're here, and glad we are to see you."

"Excellent," Jack enthused, wringing Joey's hand again. "Izzy? That's an unusual name. You are from…?"

"Normanton," she said quietly, her soft, gentle voice caressing their ears. "Where else would I be from?"

"Jack and Jenny?" Jack asked, not sure whether he had heard right. "You're not having us on?"

"Why would I?" Joey replied with a grin. "And yes, I will stop calling you 'Wood Eye'!"

Jack burst into an astounded guffaw as Jenny giggled in a more controlled way. "He's got *you* sussed, Our Jack. Comes of knowing you so well."

Izzy remained unmoved and unamused, probably because she had no idea about the history and sense of humour Jack shared with his favourite nephew.

"We're moved and very honoured that you've named your children after us," Jack said quietly.

"How do you know it was after you, Uncle Jack?" Joey butted in, eyebrows raised, and head tipped quizzically to one side. "It might have been our neighbours, Mr and Mrs Egon-Smythe, just up from us on Haw Hill View."

"Oh," Jenny replied, "I'm sorry. We thought—"

"It's OK," Joey explained. "We don't have any neighbours bearing that name, and we certainly wouldn't name our children after them even if we did talk to them."

"You bugger!" Jenny chided good-humouredly. "You had me going there. You, Jack?"

"Not a cat in hell's chance," he guffawed.

"You know me too well, Uncle Jack," Joey laughed, slapping him on the back.

"Cup of Yorkshire, both?" Jack asked finally.

"At last!" Joey joked again. "That has to be some kind of record for the length of time it took you to get around to offering a 'cup of Yorkshire'!"

Throughout this give and take, Izzy had remained mesmerised by their repartee. She had never observed, let alone shared, such fun interaction with any of *her* family. She had a lot to learn about Joey's uncle and why he was held in such high esteem.

"How come you're here, anyway?" Jack asked. "Normanton this isn't."

"I've got a very distant relation who lives in Lancaster – Halton, I believe – and we're spending a day or two with her," Izzy replied. "It'll be our teatime soon and I need to change and feed the twins, Joey?"

"OK, Uncle Jack," Joey said. "I just wanted to let you know, seeing as we were in roughly the same neighbourhood. Will you be a visiting Normy any time soon?"

"Up to this point, we hadn't planned to," Jack answered honestly. "But now we've seen you, we'll make it top of our agenda. Another cup of tea and I'll explain where we are in this world and then we'll arrange to see you soon. OK?"

"Izzy?" Joey asked his wife. She nodded and settled to another cup of Yorkshire Tea.

"Fifteen minutes, mind," Izzy warned.

"Well," Jack started, "we…"

Chapter 27

"Lee?" Jack said, telephoning her from Effie's place after his abortive attempt to find Heysham High School. "Would you please pass on my apologies to Stuart and let him know I couldn't find the school. The nearest I got was a country lane with houses on one side and farmers' fields on the other. Would it be Oxbow Road?"

"Oxcliffe Road, perhaps?" she replied with a giggle.

"Whatever. Anyway, I could see what I think must have been the school over some fields – a big building that could have been a sports hall or something," Jack explained. "Only I didn't know how to get to it. I explored the beginnings of Heysham just off the bypass, but the industrial-looking buildings there turned out to be just that."

Lee laughed as she told him not to worry. They would have a chat the next day about his next stage. "I'm going to Heysham High tomorrow afternoon," she advised him, "so I could pick you up at the County Hotel in the centre of Carnforth at about noon. If that's all right with you?"

"I'll be there," he assured here, "without fail."

She laughed and hung up, leaving Jack to spend the rest of the morning on his own until Jenny returned from her morning stint at Mothercare. He wondered how Postman Pat had got on in Lancaster's Greendale, and whether Jenny had managed not to trip over those size eighteen boots.

"How's Jess today then?" Jack asked as they sat down to their ham-salad lunch. Effie's conservatory was warm and inviting. Although south facing, the sun rarely warmed its interior at this time of year. That's when underfloor heating came into its own – not cheap to run but very effective.

"Do I know a 'Jess'?" Jenny replied, a smile of relief on her face for the half-day break just ahead and for the lunch Jack had prepared for her.

Strictly speaking they didn't need to earn on the run-up to Christmas because they were being paid by Greystone until the end of December. However, it was the daunting reality of being without income from January 1st that drove them on.

"Jess, your black-and-white companion?" Jack explained, a grin developing as a precursor to bursting into the song about Postman Pat and his black-and-white cat.

"Beautiful rending, my man," Jenny said though a mouthful of ham and lettuce, a wicked smile forming.

"Don't you mean rendering or rendition, my lovely?" he corrected.

"No, I mean rending, as in tearing to bits, Our Jack," she laughed and was joined heartily by her husband.

"So, you'll be sitting, feet up, while I'm toiling with my nose to the grindstone, I assume," Jack observed once they had finished dining and were having ten minutes in the lounge.

"Planning, my dear man," she replied. "Planning."

"What? To overthrow the world?" he guffawed. "Up the workers!"

"What celebration will be approaching us very soon?" she asked, with a warning raising of her eyebrows.

"And what will you be planning – Christmas in the

Canaries?" he asked flippantly.

"Deciding on where we are to spend the very short break I will be getting, no doubt," she replied seriously.

"How short?" he asked tentatively.

"Try three days for size," she answered with a sigh.

"You're joking me!" he exclaimed. "Is that all? Then give your notice in and we'll manage until I get you into school to do what you are good at."

"You serious?" she asked.

"Never more so," he replied. "I've a paid teaching job from January 1st."

"Still got the problem of where we go," she ventured. "Family in Normanton? We can't go to Val because she's still lazing in the sun. Jessie and Florence May and Mary are all abroad with their families and intendeds. Where's our George, apart from Normanton or … elsewhere? The only logical one would be to our Eric, because he's the only person we can guarantee will be at home. Always loved Christmas with the family, he did."

"What about staying here with me?" Aunt Effie's voice broke into their conversation as she hobbled into the room. "Hips are almost ready for a full test drive and I have all the space you might need to entertain."

"Wow!" Jack replied, looking across at Jenny, who was nodding enthusiastically with a big smile. "What can I say other than, yes? Thank you for the offer. We didn't ask because of your infirmity and because we thought you didn't do… Entertaining, you say?"

"The infirmity is a passing annoyance, Our Jack," Effie went on, "and one which is almost a memory. This house is big and needs to ring to voices again, as it used to. There's plenty of room for over-stayers, so invite whomever you wish. Your mum should be back in a couple of days, Jenny, so she'll be the first – hopefully."

"Aye," Jack said. "They'll be wanting a rest after their holiday, no doubt. It's busy stuff, this cruising lark, so I'm told."

-o-

The centre of Carnforth was busy in the middle of the day at the crossroads where the A6 acknowledged the existence of the B6254 Kirkby Lonsdale road. The County Hotel stood almost at the meeting point of the two busy thoroughfares – perfect for folks on the A6 needing access to the hostelry, but not so for the opposite side - a no less busy road to the station. *Brief Encounter* days were long gone, living on only in the cafeteria on Platform 1.

The single bleep of a car horn drew Jack's attention to the hotel's car park, where a lone female stood waving beside a small Citroën car. "Lee," he said, as he approached. "Didn't know where to look. Not spent any time much here."

"Don't worry, Jack," she replied as she started the engine.

Jack remembered one of the car's precursors very well. The 2CV, or 'Deux Chevaux' to give it its full name, was a popular, very economical motor boasting canvas seats and a draw-down, press-stud fastened canvas roof that was easy to open – when stationary – but difficult to re-engage and re-secure as a roof.

His one memory of riding in a 2CV was during the time he and ten fellow male college students spent three weeks at a French teaching college in Arras on exchange in 1966. Because they had spent a lot of time during those three weeks drinking at a local café, on their last night the café proprietor – Jean – closed the establishment very early and invited them all into the back room for a few drinks. Those 'few drinks' became a lot of drinks – wines, beers, cognacs – and many more. Jean closed his café at midnight and his friend loaded all ten students into his 2CV to drop them off at their individual lodgings to have a few hours sleeping before setting off back to Leeds. Heads out of windows and feet hanging out of the open roof made it a very interesting journey.

Jack and his pal Tony Martin were the only ones on the next day's return to the UK who had either the head or the stomach for the bacon sandwiches provided for their journey. *They* had a wonderful journey back, but the others did not.

"This is Heysham High?" Jack observed as they drew into a tight little car park at the front of the school.

Most schools of the 60s' era must have been built to a common blueprint where designers were allowed a little bit of individual leeway. Seeming to be shy of the outside world, this school passed almost unnoticed at the end of a cul-de-sac of imposing semi-detached houses built at around the same time. The only hint of some important building was the impressive regulation-green metal gate that persuaded casual passers-by that here was not a public right of way.

"Small front entrance," Jack observed. "I rather thought the school might have boasted a more impressive façade."

"It matters more what happens inside, don't you think?" Lee replied. "Our job is to make sure the children on our list have the support they need to ensure trouble-free access to a reasonable education across the curriculum."

"Couldn't have said it better myself," he agreed as they entered the building. "But here's the rub. How do mainstream schools respond to youngsters with emotional and behavioural difficulties? Would they not prefer for those children not to darken their classroom doors?"

"That's one of the reasons why we are here, my friend," Lee replied, touching his hand gently to reinforce her words.

Lee had the reputation of being a great judge of people

and in Jack she recognised strength of character, intellect and the ability to carry folk using argument and actions. She recognised also that he wasn't afraid to say his piece, no matter the status of his audience. He was a Yorkshireman, after all.

"The foyer looks like it's been newly painted," he observed as they passed through the second set of glass double doors. "But not the rest of the ground floor, it seems. First impressions are more important, eh, Lee?"

She simply smiled as they signed the visitors' book and waited for the deputy head, Mrs Riddell, to emerge from her den to welcome these new insurgents to her beleaguered fort.

"What you have to remember, Jack," Lee replied, as they walked towards the staff room to meet the head of Special Needs, "is that these people know next to nothing about behaviour disorders. As far as they are concerned, children should *know* how to behave properly when they are in school. According to their teachers, if they don't, they should have no place in school. In this respect, and probably many others too, you have a far greater knowledge and expertise than they do. They need you as much as you need them, although they don't know it yet."

"Then it's a good job we came here today, Lee," Jack said, as they clicked the staff-room door latch.

"Hello, Lee," the deeply resonant voice from a smallish man greeted Jack's companion. "And this giant among Lilliputians must be Jack."

–o–

"So, what did you think about Our Stuart?" Lee asked on the way back to Carnforth.

"I liked him," Jack replied. "He seems to know what

he's about. I wasn't too sure about certain others in his department, though. The large lady, for example? No idea what she's called, but 'bees' and 'knees' don't seem to fit as a description of her abilities – although you could be closer to the mark if you rearranged the words of a well-known phrase or saying: *side, back, own, up, her.*"

Lee burst out laughing as she drew up outside Aunt Effie's house.

"Come in for a cuppa, Lee?" he offered. "Our Yorkshire Tea is the best cuppa in the known universe."

"Another time perhaps, Jack," she replied. "Several more calls to make before I will be able to sniff that hot liquid. A good day today – but please keep on saying stuff as you see it. Absolutely priceless."

Jack kissed her on the cheek in thanks for her company and kind words just before he opened the car door. Nobody had done that to her before, but enjoyment swamped any surprise or embarrassment she might have felt. What a shame he was already married!

"Hello!" Jack called as he snecked the front door behind him. "Anybody home? Any tea mashing?"

"Yes indeed, Our Daddy Jack," a very familiar voice jumped at him from the kitchen doorway.

"Jessie?" he said swinging around, as a look of shock accosted his face. "What are you doing here and—?"

"Daddy Jack," Jessie began," I'd like you to meet your granddaughter, Alice. She's two."

"You were a baby in arms the last time I saw you, Little Lady," he said quietly, as he picked up Alice and kissed her on the forehead.

"Dow peas, dada dack," the little girl said, trying to shuffle out of his grasp.

"You're lucky she stayed *that* long," Jessie said with a giggle. "She doesn't like being held."

"She obviously prefers freedom," Jack replied, "like her mamma at that age. Brian at work?"

"Something we need to talk about later," Jessie explained quietly, trying to evade the direct question.

"I remember the last time you had a secret that you didn't want your mother to find out, when you were in junior school," he reminded her. "Something you wanted to sort out yourself. And then the business of changing schools, that I—"

"We are separated," she blurted out. "Isn't working out. Shouldn't have married in haste. Don't know where he is, just that it's not … here ... with us."

Tears welled up into her eyes as Jack drew her to him to comfort her, just like he had always done throughout her life. He was still her Daddy Jack and she was his beautiful daughter Jessie, and that would never change.

-o-

"Well, if it isn't my favourite daughter and her lovely hubby," another well-known voice overtook the gathering.

Jenny spun around quickly, surprised to hear that voice here. "Mum!" she exclaimed as she drew Flo to her bosom. "I thought you were still cruising."

"I think four weeks is enough for anyone to be living on water," Flo replied. "Problem is, I think we'd run out of places to visit. People *do* say that the world is getting smaller. We got back to Normanton day before yesterday and found this couple of refugees virtually on our doorstep. Val had left a note saying you were here, so we decided to come over. There's plenty of space so Effie has asked us to stay over Christmas, and then we need to find somewhere for Jessie and Alice to stay."

"That's quite an easy one, really," Jenny said. "We were

going to sell our house in Leeds, once Val and Mike had no further need for it, but now Jessie can use it for as long as she needs, eh, Jack?"

"'Course she can," Jack agreed with a smile, "and we will arrive at—"

"A fair price for rent?" Jessie said, with the usual raised right eyebrow and slight tilt of the head. "Now, how did I know you were about to say that?"

"Probably psychic, like your mother," Jack guffawed. "You know me so well."

"Bit o' bad luck about your jobs, eh, Jack?" Jim ventured over a cup of Yorkshire Tea and a piece of lemon-drizzle cake – Effie's speciality.

"Not so much bad luck, I'm afraid, Jim," Jack replied. "More like poor judgement on my part. Given the choice of two separate paths, I followed the wrong instinct. That was compounded by a chain of events over which I had no control. I now have to start again at the beginning and salvage some sort of career ready for retirement in ten years. I owe my Jenny that much. But it *will* happen."

Jenny smiled, knowing that her Jack would make it his goal for the rest of his working life to hoist their standard of living back at least towards where it was before he'd left Leeds.

Carry on, Jack. We know you'll do it.

Chapter 28

"Could you tell me again, Lee why I'm being moved from Heysham after only a couple of years?" Jack asked his boss pointedly. "What about the classroom assistants, Jenny, Anne, Mary and Kath, that I've been working with? Don't they deserve some choice in the matter?"

"It's because of those two years and the excellent work you've done in the school that I've chosen you to go to Fleetwood High," Lee explained quietly in the meeting at the service's new base in Caton. "Your team has learned such a lot from you that they can manage without you. They do know, because I've told them. I'm sending my best to fire-fight the considerable problems there – and it's not just the children causing the problems."

"OK, I accept that," he replied. "But won't there be a cost implication – travelling, petrol, etc…? I'm not med o' brass, tha knows, Lee."

"Spoken like a true Yorkshireman," Lee laughed. "All expenses paid, Jack. Put a chit in at the end of each month and you are paid all you spend at the end of the next one. Tax free!"

"Wow!" Jack replied, rubbing his hands together gleefully. "I'll 'ave sum er that! When do I start this malarkey?"

"September," Lee said, "until the following July, in the first instance. I'm arranging for you to spend the rest of this summer term – that's only two weeks – over there to identify areas of difficulty and to get used to the school's working practices – and the travelling, of course."

"So that would be … next Monday," Jack replied, somewhat surprised at the speed at which events were unfurling. He had never had decisions made for him before in his professional life, making this feel a little uncomfortable.

As a significant compensation, travelling seventy miles a day at 42.7 pence per mile would give him at least an extra five and a half grand for the year. Those magic words 'tax free' made all the difference. But would the extra cash compensate for losing the friends and acquaintances he had made in the last couple of years?

Too right it would! Why wouldn't it? No brainer.

-o-

"It's not right to have me on like that, Our Jack," Jenny said, over a cup of tea and a home-made mince pie in the back garden of their new three-bedroomed detached box on the new Grosvenor Park estate between Lancaster and Morecambe.

Why was it that mincemeat in jars could only ever be bought, it seemed, around Christmas time? As mince pies were his favourite nibble with a cup of Yorkshire, he had taken to stocking up with jars of the stuff when they appeared on the supermarket shelves so that Jenny could bake the occasional batch throughout the rest of the year.

Clever thinking, Jack. Anyhow, *he* thought so.

"Not having you on, sweet pea," he replied. "Got it in black and white. It appears that the powers-that-be are desperate to force an extra few grand into my hands for driving a few extra miles to work. I like that sort of benevolence. We will need to buy you a little run-around of a motor to compensate for not having me as your loyal chauffeur. Summat like a Metro or Fiesta, perhaps."

"Are you sure?" she gasped, not quite able to believe their

luck, especially, after what had happened with his recent school postings.

"As eggs is eggs," he said, with a grin. "We'll nip down to John's Metro Centre second-hand garage during the summer break to see what he has on offer."

"Excited!" she whooped, clapping her hands together in front of her face. "It's a bit of a while since we had a run of good luck. I hope it lasts."

"I hesitate to say 'trust me', Our Jen," he said, a grimace hovering, "because my occasional decision has proved to be not as prudent as it might have been. Yet I've got a bit of a feeling…"

"Only a *bit* of a feeling, Jack?" she laughed. "Losing your touch?"

"I'll show you what a 'bit of a feeling' looks like, young lady," he warned, drawing her to him, his exaggerated mock-heavy breathing making her giggle.

The jangle of the telephone, with its insistently annoying mood destruction, interrupted Jack's 'bit of a feeling'.

"Who on earth—?" he mused, reaching for the new wireless handset and trying to put on his shorts at the same time.

His hopping about crazily around the bedroom with both feet locked in one leg hole forced Jenny to bury her face in her pillow to avoid her hearty guffaws from being heard at the other end of the telephone line. His collapse on the floor plunged her into uncontrollable fits of shoulder-shaking laughter, while he tried to hold a rational and normal conversation with his brother Eric.

"Oh my God, no!" Jack said quietly. "When?"

Jenny sat up slowly, able to hear the chatter from the other end of the line but unable to make out what Eric was saying.

"OK," Jack's voice faded back in. "We'll be there."

Click. Gone.

"Jack?" Jenny urged, forcing her way into his introspection.

"Elizabeth, my Uncle Jack's wife," Jack replied quietly, "passed away yesterday."

Jack was not usually given to much of a public display of emotion and Jenny could see how *that* news had affected him.

"Funeral next Friday, at Normy graveyard," Jack went on. "Need to organise a wreath or flowers or summat."

"Leave that to me, Our Jack. You've no idea about that sort of stuff. Woman's work," Jenny added.

"Apparently she went to bed early the other night," he carried on, "and didn't wake up. Seemingly nothing amiss with her."

"Had enough, I should imagine," she said. "Went to be with him."

-o-

"'Ello Our Jack and Jenny," a deep, rasping voice greeted Jack and his wife. "We'll 'atter stop meetin' like this."

"Eric! Me old mate!" Jack gushed as he spun round to greet his brother. "It's been a ridiculously long while since we've spent any time together. Unfortunately, a lot of muddy water has washed the bridge away over recent times. We must get together soon to refresh."

"Aye, we will that," Eric replied quietly.

Very few people had turned up to this sad affair and they didn't include Jack … Elizabeth's son.

"I don't see many mourners," Jack whispered to Jenny. "Come to think of it, the main one I don't see is her son Jack! Where the hell's *he* got to?"

"Decided he worn't comin'," Eric whispered behind his hand. "Said 'e 'ad to be somewhere else, and it worn't any on 'is business. She'd med a will – not much in it apparently except for a 'ouse and *that* she left to 'er sister as lives somewhere dahn Foxholes Lane in Altofts, and 'er brother, Joe, as lives dahn Cas Road in Normanton. She also left enuff money to bury her, he said."

"'E refused to meet me," Jack added. "Preferred to sup ale in t'Swan when I visited 'is mam. So, I didn't reckon much on him at all. Still, I'm sorry *she's* gone. We met several times. A very interesting but unfortunate woman, as lost the love of her life in the war and 'ad *'im* as a son."

Burial over, Elizabeth had arranged for a 'decent spread' at the Majestic Café; she must have known few people would attend because she always kept herself to herself. Eric and Ellen and Jack and Jenny stayed back out of respect but ate little.

"How's your brood these days, Ellen?" Jack asked his sister-in-law. "All flown the nest?"

"One almost there," she replied, "and t'other two in t'wings awaiting. He gets his A-level results mid-August, and Victoria gets her GCSEs a week or two later."

"T'lad wants to be a arkitek," Eric explained, "which is all rayt bi me."

"Victoria doesn't know what she wants to do," Ellen chipped in. "She's set for good grades, particularly in sciences – takes after her dad there. Julie wants to be a fashion model, and that would be *my* influence."

"And the million-dollar question?" Jack asked tentatively. "Your business, Eric?"

"Gone from strength to strength sin yon young uns joined me," Eric eulogised. "Clever stuff in different ways from them two. I certainly couldn't a managed wi'out 'em. Different ideas in many ways – meks mi eyes water at what they can do. I let 'em ger on wi' it mostly and I just … manage the business. Tha's got to come and stay wi' us for a few days in August to see 'ow they're both getting on."

"'Ow about when your James gets his results?" Jack suggested. "And then we can celebrate?"

"Sounds like a rayt good idea, Our Jack," Eric replied. "Good to si thi back agen."

"Thee too, our Eric," Jack threw back at 'im, wi' a yuge grin. "Si thi in August."

-o-

Swings and roundabouts, Jack would often say when there were compromises to be made in some situations. That described the fortnight's journey back and forth to Fleetwood from their new house in Morecambe.

He had chosen the route that he deemed to be the easiest, quickest and that bore the least volume of traffic to delay him. He had, of course, not taken into account the country lanes swanning through farm land that presented him with herds of cows crossing slowly from one empty field to another stacked out with new luscious grass, cows that stopped periodically to brush up against and blink at this shiny contraption with its two unblinking eyes. He also had to contend with tractors hauling heavy, wide trailers that couldn't be overtaken, and other unexpected and unsought eventualities.

Nonetheless, chance had presented him with an opportunity to haul back on the misfortunes the last three or four years had placed in his path. The extra cash for his travelling expenses would help to redress the imbalance in salary caused by having to take lesser-paid jobs.

Eric and Ellen's home was a warm, welcoming place to escape to at the end of a busy day. One or two significant alterations had been made since Jack and Jenny were last there. A glorious conservatory had been built across the entire back of the house, allowing them to enjoy the garden even in bad weather. Ellen's flower beds were still in full bloom, with a myriad of colours cascading onto the lawn throughout.

"Taken to gardening in a serious way, then, Ellen?" Jack asked, pointing to the large greenhouse in the lee of the back fence.

"She's allus been serious abaht 'er flowers, plants and stuff," Eric explained. "And I'm glad she does, because I know nowt about abaht 'em."

"How's the job, now you've been at it t'best part of ten years?" Jack asked Ellen, pretty sure what her response would be. "I knew your deputy in passing at college – Jane Alison Bradley."

"She's no longer our deputy, Jack," Ellen replied, putting a replenished afternoon tea tray on the conservatory's wicker coffee table.

"How come?" he asked, more than a little surprised. "She's not been in post long, has she?"

"She was deputy for only a short time," she replied, "and a good one she was, too. Not as good as you would have been though, Our Jack. We *did* hear about the trick your brother William played as a parting shot. Nasty."

"Water under the bridge now, I'm afraid," Jack sighed, shrugging and grimacing. "Has she gone anywhere local? Back to Sheffield?"

"None of those," Ellen explained. "She's become our head."

That bit of news dropped like a lead balloon, leaving Jack completely at a loss for what to say – a most unusual occurrence.

"Mrs Silvester retired because of ill-health," Ellen went on, "and Jane's application and interview were successful."

Strange world that would reward inexperience and basic

qualifications over greater aptitude in all necessary areas.
   Still, got to carry on, eh, Jack?

Chapter 29

"Why din't tha tell 'im thi news, Ar Lass?" Eric asked his wife pointedly when their guests had departed.

"Not really appropriate, don't you think, Husband?" Ellen replied, on the defensive for once in her life.

"How does tha mek that aht?" he carried on, pushing her to explain herself. He'd never seen her like this before. Usually his wife was as straight as him – straight to t'point and said it as she saw it.

"His job, and all that has gone with it," she huffed, trying to wriggle out of his onslaught.

Surely, she should have known by now that, although her husband was usually a kind and soft man, at times he had a toughened steel core that wouldn't give up when he was convinced he was right.

"That's a bloody load o' baloney, and thy knows it!" he insisted. "Our Jack's one on t'nicest chaps in t'world when it comes to supporting 'is family. 'E would a bin overjoyed for thee, had thy 'ad t'sense to tell 'im. Telephone 'im now, Ellen, 'cos if'n tha dun't, I will."

"Can't," she insisted, "because he ain't got a phone. They'll still be on the road."

"They'll be 'ome in an hour," he said. "So tha'll be able to phone 'im when they get back to Morecambe, wayn't tha! All rayt?"

She muttered and harrumphed almost under her breath, shuffling into her favourite chair with a cup of lemon tea in her hands. Eric couldn't stand the thoughts of that 'plastic' tea, as he called it, but 'er tastes were 'er business.

"Come on now, Ellen," he finished his argument. "'Oo got thee to realise this dream in t'first place, eh? Wi'out 'im, tha'd still be working nine to five somewhere. Rayt's rayt."

"All right!" she agreed finally. "I'll phone in an hour. Never heard so much hot air fly out o' thy gob as long as I've known thee! Tha's like a tramp's overcoat – allus on!"

Eric started to guffaw loudly at his wife's assessment until the telephone interrupted him. "That'll be our James wanting me to pick him up from yon cinema," he said, leaping to his feet.

"Hello, Our Jack," Eric said, as soon as the line opened. "I thought it might be our James… No need to thank me … we've 'ad a rayt grand time in your company… Just a mo, Ellen wants a word."

As soon as he had handed the handset to Ellen, he sloped off into the kitchen to put the kettle on. Best leave her to her unwanted conversation wi'out 'avin' an audience, he thought. He knew how her mind worked – or, at least, he *thought* he knew.

"For once in your life, Eric Ingles, you were right," Ellen muttered, once she'd joined him in the kitchen to rustle up some of her home-baked sticky black gingerbread that he hadn't known existed.

"Bloomin' 'ummer!" he gasped. "I feel a little faint. You admitting I'm right? How did that come about, then? I telled thee so!" he exclaimed, a note of triumph in his voice.

"He said that he thought it was a sensible idea to apply for the deputy headship of the school," she went on calmly, ignoring Eric's excitable interruption. "And that they would have regretted it had they had not appointed me. Happy now?”

“I am that!” he agreed, a grin underlining his words. “Jack strolling into our lives were one of the best things to happen to us.”

Nice one, Jack.

Family is everything, eh?

-o-

The six weeks’ school summer holiday in 1998 was a wonderful affair, with family and close friend get-togethers regular occurrences. Most people were very wary about arranging outdoor events because of the thunderstorm and nineteen millimetres of rain that fell on the first day in August, but that was soon cast out of their minds by warmer days culminating in temperatures of thirty degrees or so for a couple of days closer to mid-month.

Although Jim Arkwright’s health was generally stable, bearing in mind his time spent down the mines, his heart blips caused Flora Mae several sleepless nights. They were both aware of what *could* happen whenever one of those episodes kicked in but, he had to live his life and cope with whatever came his way.

Flora Mae looked after him to the best of her ability, but *she* wasn’t getting any younger and she found it increasingly difficult to give him the help he desperately needed.

“You *do* realise, Flo,” he would start, “that I’m likely to snuff it before you, given the state of my health?”

“Nay, lad,” she protested, “I could die tomorrow, and you could live another twenty years.”

“And cockroaches might rule the world,” he added. “We’re talking reality, here, Flora Mae.”

“I thought cockroaches did! So, what are you proposing?” she asked, not sure where this line was heading.

"Neither of us is getting any younger," he replied slowly, choosing his words carefully. "So, I thowt that as I'd made quite a bit of money from t'sale o' mi engineering company, I'd use some of the proceeds to set up a private care plan, for both of us, like. I know we've paid us dues into t'pot from us national insurance contributions ower t'years, but I don't trust the NHS these days. There's a lot of money been wasted that could have gone towards people in greater need than us. What does tha think, Flo?"

"It's up to you, Jim," she hummed and hawed a bit. "It's your money. And all that will happen if it's saved in t'bank is it'll go to somebody else as what'll spend it. Better to do stuff with it as'll benefit you *now*. That's what I think."

"I'll tek that as a yes, then," he said, with a smile and a nod. "I've sorted it all out, and all it needs now is our signatures and a stamp."

"*Our* signatures?" she queried with a frown.

"Aye," he replied. "It'll be in joint names. No argument. No huffing and puffing. Joint decision. Joint benefits."

-o-

"A bit concerned about Jim's outlook on his health," Flora Mae said, as she talked to Jenny on the phone the day after.

"In what way, Mam?" Jenny asked, not really understanding what her mum meant. "Is he poorly?"

Their voices faded gradually into background shush as clouds darkened and started to unleash their wet loads onto the unsuspecting earth. People usually say with an indulgent sigh that the earth and its plants needed the rain, once it has passed, but the opposite is usually the truth. Can't have too much water? That, of course, depends very largely on where that water is falling.

Although their street was slightly elevated, Jenny's

garden was sodden from this over-watering that had lasted a little too long. It didn't, however, seem to affect the younger children from the four-bedroomed houses that surrounded *their* little box. They whooped and splashed in the abundant surface water that rushed down the gutterings in hasty rivulets to the drains, seeming to want to make their hurried escape from these children's attention.

Fleeting flashes of summer sun seemed to promise much but delivered little, except for disappointment for the older children in the cul-de-sac.

"Well, I think it might be prudent to let him get on with his plans but keep an eye on him," Jenny advised as their conversation drifted back. "You know what men are like. Won't be told. I assume Jim's not there at the moment?"

"He's out with a long-term pal at a local working men's club," Flo went on. "Playing snooker – something non-tiring for him and unworrying for me."

"Got to go," Jenny said quickly. "Jack's back in and needs to talk to me. Speak later."

"Your mum?" Jack asked, once she had replaced the received. "Is Jim all right?"

"Concerns is all she'd say," Jenny replied. "But it's more than that. He's making preparations."

"In case…?" Jack replied with a knowing shrug.

"He has to have greater physical care than she can provide," she said, as they sat down with a cup of tea. "I also had a reasonably lengthy telephone conversation with our Florence May while you were out."

"And?" he said, eager to hear of anything about his distant daughter.

"They've decided to stay in Australia and … to get married," Jenny explained.

"Hmm," Jack mumbled, a creased brow betraying his concern – which was as usual for him as snow in the Sahara.

"Not unhappy, Jack?" Jenny asked, more than a little surprised at his reaction. "They've both got good jobs – and a house."

"Not so much that, Our Jen," he said, "but cash flow to go ower might be an issue. Not cheap them big jets, tha knows. Don't forget out biggest asset in North Leeds has our daughter living in it. Also, they'd have to remember that we only have enough time in t'summer holidays. So, it would have to be next year, and—"

"Don't overthink things Jack," Jenny advised. "I'm sure plans haven't been made yet. Florence May – and Billy, for that matter – are well aware of our collective situations as far as jobs are concerned."

"Hang on a bit," Jack gasped, having only just latched on to his wife's earlier statements. "Lengthy conversation? From Australia? Telephone?"

"Don't get apoplexy, dear heart," she laughed. "*She* phoned *me*, and she said at the start of the conversation that the call was costing her only about two Australian dollars. International calls from there are a lot cheaper than from here."

"I'll get it," Jack offered as the telephone burrowed into their conversation. "Bound to be a wrong— Hello? Joyce!" he gushed. "How wonderful to hear from you . . . yes, we're healthy and well, if a little impecunious . . . How? Well—"

His voice tailed away into the whys and wherefores of life on the bread line – including everything they'd missed since the last time they'd spent time together, well over a year before. Jenny decided to make a cup of tea and a sandwich, realising they might be gossiping for quite some time.

The new kitchen-diner could be closed off from the lounge by a single door but offered them the facility to open onto an as-yet non-existent patio through sliding doors. Jenny didn't know yet, but Jack had already planned to have a small conservatory built and to lay, by himself, a patio and paths to the back of the garden. He never let the grass grow under his feet, didn't Jack, because they didn't have any. Not enough garden space for Jenny to grow both plants *and* grass.

"They've not set a date yet," Joyce's voice wandered back in, "but obviously it can't be before next summer, unless … they decide to do a spur of the moment thing."

"They wouldn't do that … would they?" Jack replied, taken aback by the suggestion.

"Anyway," Joyce said, "why don't you both come to ours and we can have a catch up."

"Excellent idea," he enthused. "We can stay with Jessie overnight Saturday and come to yours Sunday morning. We're only a couple of hours away."

"If you're a couple of hours away, where does Jessie live?" Joyce asked a little perplexed. Everything used to be simple before Jack and Jenny … moved away.

"She lives in our old house," he laughed. "Just around the corner from you. I'll tell you all about it when we see you."

"What did Florence May say?" Jack asked, when he'd replaced his backside on his favourite seat next to his wife and noticed a steaming mug of his favourite Jenny had placed on his side table.

"You know as much as I do, Jack," she replied, teasing him with a shrug and non-committal smile.

"Come on," he insisted, "she must have said *something* more than 'hello – we're getting married – bye'?"

"They've both got temporary jobs, found a house to rent," she went on, "and have applied for a permanent residency visa which would allow them to reside and travel freely in and out of the country. Unlike this country, where you apply to central government, apparently, out there the visa has to refer to the individual state. And that's about it."

"I suppose you never know with youngsters how they will react in a given situation," Jack added, after a moment's further thought.

"How do you mean?" she replied

"Well," he explained, "they can make a decision about anything on the spur of the moment, if they want it enough. We can't blame them if they want to be married badly enough that they simply nip out and do the deed."

"Don't you *want* to walk your beautiful daughter down the aisle?" she harrumphed.

"Course I do," he agreed, "but we have to be realistic. They'll make up their own minds. Goodness knows, they'll have long enough to make their decision."

Pragmatic – and realist – as usual, eh Jack?

Chapter 30

"Not had too fantastic a time, professionally and personally then, Jack?" Stick observed, over a glass of Guinness.

"The odd decision or two should have never been taken," Jack replied. "And once one of 'em goes awry, it becomes a downward spiral, and everything seems to go wrong."

"How are things now?" Stick asked. "Still on that primrose path of dalliance to perdition?"

"Not quite," Jack said with a reassuring smile. "Things are just about ready to crawl to the light, as long as some other self-important despot doesn't put in his oar and knock us sideways again. Headship soon then, Stick?" he went on as he munched on a piece of Joyce's forest gâteau that she did so well, and *he* so loved.

"Nar," Stick insisted. "Not my scene. I've seen too many good teachers become poor heads, largely due to man-management failings and pressure of what to do to maintain a good school. I'm happy as I am to bide my time to retirement. We've got Billy off our hands and Our Valerie is doing very nicely in a flat of her own and working with Joyce at yon library."

"Is Valerie all right then?" Jenny asked. "Only…"

"She was assessed many years ago as having Asperger Syndrome, as you know," Stick went on. "Top end of t'autistic spectrum. Turned out to be not as bad as we thought. She's tunnel-visioned and quite pedantic in some of her views – aren't we all? – but she's a good worker and knows that library inside out. In fact, she knows as much as Joyce, and certainly more than the supervisor."

"You must be very proud," Jenny went on.

"She has her moments," Joyce joined in, "but we are. She has her own living space and we go in to help when she asks, but she has all the support she needs from her carer, who has been with her long enough to become her best friend. *She* helps with all the stuff Valerie has trouble with. Comes in three or four times a week, and that's all Valerie needs. Anything more would become an intrusion."

"And the next thing for you two?" Stick asked, pouring Jack another glass of Guinness into a Guinness glass.

The conversation changed to the gentle hum of back and forth while Jack explained where they were and what they hoped to achieve over the next year or two. Jack had his PhD presentation in a month or two that Jenny was exceedingly proud of and she couldn't wait for him to be called 'Doctor'. Jack didn't want any fuss, but Jenny had her mind set on joining the celebrations. He could have been firm and put his foot down, but he knew she loved all that sort of stuff and he didn't mind having to put up with it for a short while.

An urgent rattling of the letterbox flap paused the conversation and they all pricked up their ears as they frowned at each other.

"Come in, love," Joyce said as she ushered Jessie into the hall. "Your mam and dad are in the lounge. Go on through."

"Jessie?" Jenny said, puzzled to see her daughter here, her baby in tow. "What—?"

"Bad news, I'm afraid," Jessie urged. "Had a telephone call from Nana Flo to say that Grandpa Jim has been rushed

into hospital, and could you go round to hers in Methley
– now."

Jack looked at Jenny, grimaced and shrugged, resigned to
a late evening in Methley, raising her eyebrows in apology.

"Thanks for a lovely day, Our Joyce." Jack said. "Sorry
we can't stay into the evening. You coming with us, Jessie?
To see your nana and grandpa?"

"I was hoping you'd ask," she replied. "Not seen them
for some time and they've not seen Alice for a bit. I'd like to
come along. Besides, I am concerned about Grandpa Jim's
well-being. He *is* in his late eighties, after all."

"Is that a good idea, do you think?" Jenny's concerned
voice cut in. "If we're going to the hospital, there may be
a lot of sitting around for a few hours and that mightn't
be good for little Alice. Perhaps better, maybe, to see them
after we know the score?"

Jessie saw the sense in her mother's reasoning and
agreed reluctantly. They dropped her off at home and moved
rapidly on to Flora Mae's bungalow on Pinfold Lane, a
tedious journey from North Leeds at best.

Flora Mae didn't like hospitals at all, and so would spend
only appointment time in them, or visiting time – rarely.

"Mam!" Jenny called out as they clicked the lock to the
front door. "It's Jenny and Jack. You in? You all right?"

"No, I'm not," Flora Mae answered as she came into the
hallway, tears streaming down her cheeks. "My husband's
about to die and I can't do anything to stop it."

Jenny drew her mother's ageing and convulsing body to
her to try and comfort the gasping sobs now rocking her
frail frame.

"Have you been to see him, Flo?" Jack asked quietly.

"No point," Flo replied. "He'll be dead by tomorrow, I
know it."

"I'll phone the hospital now," he insisted, "just to satisfy our peace of mind. If you haven't been to see him, you don't know. He may be on his way home as we speak. Anyhow…"

Jack made his way into the hall to phone, as Jenny led her mother into the kitchen to put the kettle on.

"OK. Thank you very much for your help," Jack said as Jenny came back into the hall, her body language questioning what he had found out.

"He's serious, but stable," Jack said, as they sought the lounge again. "Your mum?"

"We're having a cup of tea and then I'm going to put her to bed," Jenny said, a look of serious concern etching her face. "We can't leave her on her own, Jack."

"I've no intention of leaving her, Our Jenny," he replied. "My mam had nobody in her hour of greatest need. That's not about to happen with yours. You'll probably have to sleep in Jim's bed, and I'll sleep on the couch in here. We'll see what needs to be done in the morning."

"Cup of tea and then bed?" Jenny suggested.

-o-

Jack wasn't used to being in bed by ten o'clock and, because his mind was still whirling with the day's events, he found difficulty in slipping into unconsciousness. He had never been a sound sleeper, finding early nights anathema.

Finally drifting slowly into a shallow doze, he was startled into stark reality by Jenny's shrill stentorian voice.

"Jack!" she gasped. "Come quick! Mum was making a gurgling sound a few moments ago, and now she's not breathing. Help, please?"

Frank English

Born in 1946 in the West Riding of Yorkshire's coal fields around Wakefield, he attended grammar school, where he enjoyed sport rather more than academic work. After three years at teacher training college in Leeds, he became a teacher in 1967. He spent a lot of time during his teaching career entertaining children of all ages, a large part of which was through telling stories, and encouraging them to escape into a world of imagination and wonder. Some of his most disturbed youngsters he found to be very talented poets, for example. He has always had a wicked sense of humour, which has blossomed only during the time he has spent with his wife, Denise. This sense of humour also allowed many youngsters to survive often difficult and brutalising home environments.

In 2006, he retired after forty years working in schools with young people who had significantly disrupted lives because of behaviour disorders and poor social adjustment, generally brought about through circumstances beyond their control. At the same time as moving from leafy lane suburban middle-class school teaching in Leeds to residential schooling for emotional and behavioural disturbance in the early 1990s, changed family circumstance provided the spur to achieve ambitions. Supported by his wife, Denise, he achieved a Master of Education degree in his mid-forties and a PhD at the age of fifty-six, because he had always wanted to do so.

Now enjoying glorious retirement, he spends as much time as life will allow writing, reading and travelling.

Adult books he has written in his semi autobiography series:

Volume 1   Jack the Lad (2016)
Volume 2   Jack (2016)
Volume 3   Hit the Road Jack (2017)
Volume 4   Welcome Back Jack (2017)
Volume 5   All Right Jack? (2018)

Children's books he has written to date:

Magic Parcel: The Awakening (2010)
Magic Parcel: The Gathering Storm (2011)
Magic Parcel: A New Dawn (2012)

18 Mulberry Road (2011)
25 Primrose Walk (2013)
Autumn Adventures (2013)
Winter Tales (2014)
Towards Spring (2016)
Juniper's Tale (2018)
Honey (2019)
The Story of Lemuel Pecker (2019)
Josephine's Journey (2019)